D0727282

Hannah Tovey is from South Wales, but grew up in Hong Kong. She graduated from Faber Academy in 2018, after completing the Writing a Novel course under tutor Richard Skinner, where she finished *The Education of Ivy Edwards*.

Hannah lives in Bow, East London.

NEWHAM LIBRARIES

90800101112467

THE EDUCATION OF IVY EDWARDS

HANNAH TOVEY

PIATKUS

PIATKUS

First published in Great Britain in 2020 by Piatkus

1 3 5 7 9 10 8 6 4 2

Copyright © Hannah Tovey 2020

The moral right of the author has been asserted.

*All characters and events in this publication, other than those
clearly in the public domain, are fictitious and any resemblance
to real persons, living or dead, is purely coincidental.*

All rights reserved.
No part of this publication may be reproduced, stored in a
retrieval system, or transmitted, in any form or by any means, without
the prior permission in writing of the publisher, nor be otherwise circulated
in any form of binding or cover other than that in which it is published
and without a similar condition including this condition being
imposed on the subsequent purchaser.

A CIP catalogue record for this book
is available from the British Library.

ISBN 978-0-349-42470-5

Typeset in Bembo by M Rules
Printed and bound in Great Britain by Clays Ltd, Elcograf S.p.A.

Papers used by Piatkus are from well-managed forests
and other responsible sources.

Piatkus
An imprint of
Little, Brown Book Group
Carmelite House
50 Victoria Embankment
London EC4Y 0DZ

An Hachette UK Company
www.hachette.co.uk

www.littlebrown.co.uk

For Ivy Jones and Ivy Bloomfield,
the originals.

Chapter 1

Working from home

I am trying to teach my mother that saying sorry is different to being sorry. The sort of lesson you might give to a three-year-old, only this three-year-old is sixty-seven.

'Ivy, do you want a little gin?' she asked, opening the door to the study and giving me her classic pout.

'No, Mam. I am meant to be working.'

'Ivy, I'm bored. Your father's alphabetising his maps again and you're not speaking to me.'

She was right; I wasn't speaking to her.

'Can we be friends now, please? I've said sorry.'

'Mam, come off it. Anna's not even pregnant yet and where is all my stuff?'

Despite having quite a sizeable family home, my mother had decided that my room was the most appropriate to turn into a nursery for my sister's not-yet-fertilised egg.

'Ivy, darling, don't be like that. I needed something to do. You won't let me plan anything.'

I ignored this comment and got on with my work. She sighed and walked out the door.

There was no way I was letting her get involved in planning

1

my wedding. If you knew her you'd understand; she'd want a lavish affair befitting the Royal Family – not quite tiaras and thrones, but almost. When I told her she was only allowed six friends to the wedding she went ballistic and said I was ruining her life. This is exactly why I wanted Jamie and I to pay for it; I thought it would stop her meddling. I can't imagine what it would have been like if she'd had a financial stake in it.

I tried to carry on working but I could hear her pottering in the kitchen. When Mam is restless, she potters like nobody's business. She's got to be busy all the time, or, as I would call it, busy doing nothing, a phrase she loathes because she knows it's true.

'But Ivy, darling, what about golf?'

She can't play.

'But Ivy, darling, what about all my charity work?'

Getting drunk with Linda in the name of a rare disease doesn't count.

We got her the *Game of Thrones* box set for her birthday to get her to sit still for once, but it backfired. She ended up using her iPad to make notes, messaging the family WhatsApp group after each episode to see if she'd got the plot right, asking our opinion on every single detail and going on and on about how attractive Kit Harington is. We had no choice but to block her from the group.

I found her in the kitchen, reorganising some Tupperware. She looked up at me and frowned.

'What's wrong with your hair, darling?' she asked.

'I don't know, what's wrong with it?'

'It's a bit flat,' she mused.

'OK . . .'

'I wish you'd wear it down more.'

'Well, it's easier up.'

'But is easy always the better option, darling?'

I ignored this as I focused on her outfit. She was dressed in a bright-green polo shirt, with matching capri trousers and a stripy visor. I asked her where she was going.

'To the club, darling, of course.'

'Mam, you don't play golf.'

She turned around and looked at me with utter contempt.

'Ivy, you are so negative. You know I have weak wrists.'

I decided that 3pm was the cut-off time for working from home on a Friday – especially when it's Mam's home in Wales – so I put my trainers on and went for a run. I couldn't get Anna out of my head. Once you say you're trying for a baby, that's it, it becomes public domain. Everyone starts asking questions and all you want to do is tell them to piss off and mind their own business. Mam wasn't a great help. Her way of solving any problem is to get the gin out, and I don't think you should be drinking that much gin when you're trying to get pregnant. If ever at all.

I ran four miles before I landed on Gramps' doorstep. The door was always open, and I don't mean that in a neighbourly sense; he was just getting a bit forgetful. I found him, as I always did, on the sofa with a black coffee in hand, watching the Welsh-language TV channel, S4C.

I passed him the paper I'd picked up on route and kissed his forehead as I propped myself down beside him. He took one look at it and grunted, 'But I wanted the *Sun*, babes.'

'Well, tough. This is actual journalism.'

'Why can't I read what *I* want to read?'

'You'll like this – there's a feature about Woody Allen's son and how everyone thinks he's Frank Sinatra's. They've included loads of photos of Sinatra too.'

'He doesn't look Jewish.'

'What are you on about?'

'The son. I saw a photo of him, *mun*.'

'That isn't a real word, and you're being annoying.'

'I'm only winding you up, babes.'

'Can I change the channel?'

'No, you bloody well can't.'

'You don't even speak Welsh.'

'So? God's language, this is.'

I ignored him and opened *Brides* magazine.

'What's that shit you're reading?'

'Anna said there's a dress I'd like in here.'

'Your sister's *twp*.'

'Oh good, another made-up Welsh word.'

'What?'

'Nothing.'

Gramps' language had got a bit more colourful recently. Last time I came down to Wales, I found him on the porch effing and blinding at the kids in the street, calling them little shitting cunts. They were only about five. He called out Mam's friend Linda in Tesco the other week when he saw her pick up a packet of Digestives. Now, one might argue that Linda doesn't need those Digestives, but that's beside the point.

I flipped through the bridal pages, failing to hide my frustration over the extortionate cost of everything. How can flowers – which are essentially perishable goods – cost an average of £2000?

'You're all out of sorts today, babes,' Gramps said.

I put the magazine down and let out a big sigh.

'Did you know Mam threw away all my stuff?'

Gramps started to laugh so hard that he almost choked on his coffee.

I started to laugh too.

'It's not funny!' I cried.

'Your mother is—' He took a long pause as he struggled to find the right word.

'Totally mad?' I chimed in.

'Restless. That's the word, babes. She's restless.'

'But it's my room.'

'Don't you think you're a bit old for this?'

'What, to want to keep my stuff?'

'Ivy, you have your own place in London, *mun*. So what if she moves you to the smaller room to make room for Anna's little one.'

'Yes, but, said little one isn't even here yet.'

'If preparing for the baby helps your mother cope with it all, it can only be a good thing.'

He was right. It wasn't just me who was worried about Anna.

'I really hate it when you get all old and wise on me,' I said.

'Be nice to her, she's the only mother you've got.'

I squeezed his hand tight and gave it a kiss.

'Show me the photo of Gran again, on the beach when she's pregnant,' I said.

'I thought you'd never ask.'

Whenever we're together, we talk about my grandmother. He's got a framed photo of her next to the sofa; she's wearing a red swimsuit, her hair all done up and bright-red lipstick. She looks sensational. I miss her so much and I didn't even really know her. There's a box under the sofa that he gets out every time I come around: more swimsuit shots, their wedding day, Gran and Mam on the swings in the park. This routine goes on for about fifteen minutes; he says how much he misses her, how hard she fought to beat her cancer and how, despite her tumour being inoperable, they never lost hope. Then, without fail, we watch *Sleepless in Seattle*. We must have watched it about a hundred times together. When it gets to the part where Sam says, 'I knew it the first time I touched her. It was like coming home, only to no home I'd ever known,' he always gives my hand a squeeze, and I'll look over and there'll be a tear rolling down his cheek. People just want to be loved, don't they?

As I walked back home later that night, I rang Anna.

'I wish you could've come home this weekend,' I said.

'I know, I'm sorry. But I'm in court all of next week and I've got to clear some of this mounting paperwork.'

'Yeah, I know. Hey, what do you think about my hair?'

'What?'

'My hair, Anna.'

'I understand the question, Ives. It's just a bit random.'

'Jamie once told me I had hair like Penelope Cruz, but Mam says it's flat.'

'Penelope Cruz? Come off it.'

'Not every day! On a good day!'

Anna laughed.

'You know Mam lives for comments like that, Ivy. At least it means she buys you fancy shampoo.'

'That is true, she's the only person who can get me away from Herbal Essence.'

'Which nobody has used since 2005.'

'Piss off, Anna. Anyway, have you heard from Mark? I can't get hold of Jamie.'

'Why are you so worried about my husband leading your fiancé astray this weekend?' Anna mocked.

'I'm not worried; I want a text message, that's all.'

'Lower your expectations, Ives.'

'It's nice that Mark invited Jamie along.'

'Yeah, it's good for them to have some proper bonding time, before he's officially part of the Edwards gang. Speaking of which, did you like any of the dresses in *Brides*?'

'No, I hated them all.'

'Ha, I knew it. Look, you don't have to buy an expensive dress, you don't even have to buy a wedding dress for that matter, but I'd like you to open your mind to considering buying a *nice* dress.'

'Why did you stress the word "nice" like that?'

'Because you live in old ripped jeans and shabby T-shirts and all your socks have holes in them.'

'They do not!'

'They do. Listen, I've got to go; *Grey's Anatomy* is back on and I can't find the remote to pause it.'

'I thought you had loads of work to do?'

'I do!'

'Yeah, whatever. Speak to you later.'

'Bye! Love you.'

Chapter 2

What not to do on a Monday

I got back to London late Sunday night and found Jamie in bed. When I woke the next morning, he was facing me, half asleep. I moved closer towards him and pressed my lips against his, moving my hand down to his crotch. He opened his mouth and I ran my tongue over his lips to wake him up a bit more. I put my hand into his boxers and he moved his hands onto my bum and grabbed me tight, his kisses deepening as he did so. As I went to pull off his boxers, he flipped me over so that I was on my front and took off my underwear, before taking his off too. I was glad of this: it was far too early for a blow job. When we first started going out, there were a lot of blow jobs. I tried hard to make it look like I was enjoying them because in my head I thought more blow jobs meant more chance of him saying, 'I love you,' a theory which now seems a little off. Now, they were bi-monthly, which is still too much in my opinion, but I was learning that, in adult relationships, compromise is key.

He bit my ear and pushed my head against the pillow as he entered me. His hands moved to my chest and I could feel his hot breath on my back as he thrust hard against me. My hands moved to the headboard to steady myself, and then, just like that, it was over. When he was finished, he kissed my cheek and walked out of the room.

When I came out of the shower a little later, he was sitting on the edge of the bed, fully clothed, staring out the window. I went over to the drawers to take out a bra, finding one of those annoying ones that looks sexy but is in fact totally impractical – no clips, just get it over your head and hope for the best type thing. I caught his eye in the mirror; he was still staring, unmoving.

'Are you OK, Jamie?'

I turned around to face him and his eyes met mine. His face was expressionless.

'Ivy, I don't want to go to Thailand.'

'Jamie, I've spent ages sorting out an itinerary; it's not like we can just rock up. We have to book places.'

I rambled on about how much time we had off, how I knew he wanted to go to the Maldives, but Thailand was much more adventurous.

He shouted my name to interrupt me. I was still trying to pull the bra over my head.

'It's not just Thailand, Ivy. I don't . . .'

'What is it?'

'I don't think I want to get married.'

'Don't be a dick, Jamie.'

'I don't want to get married, Ivy.'

'What?'

'I don't think I can see a future with you anymore.'

'You were literally just inside me.'

'I know how you like it in the mornings.'

'What?'

'I thought it would relax you.'

'What?'

9

'Ivy, I'm trying to be honest—'

'Hang on, is that why you wouldn't look at my face?'

'I'm sorry, Ivy. Maybe I should go.'

'What? No. What?'

I looked down at the unmade bed; there was a stain of semen from earlier, still a little wet. He went on, but I kept staring at the stain.

'It's a fucking Monday!' I shouted.

I've never understood people who choose to come back from holiday on a Sunday. Why not come back on Wednesday or Thursday? That way, you can minimise time in the office and have the weekend to get over the inevitable post-holiday blues. The same principle applied here – why would he do this on a Monday?

He said he'd been feeling like this for a while. He was under a lot of pressure. He didn't feel excited about the wedding. He said lots of things that I couldn't register. There could have been a riot outside the front door and I wouldn't have known any better. I couldn't speak. I have no idea how much time passed before he walked out the door.

I stood with my bra hanging around my neck. There was a framed photo of us on the wall; we were in Florence, he's kissing my neck and I'm laughing. It was only taken three months ago. What happened?

Jamie has always experienced low periods where he goes to a place of darkness, somewhere I can't reach him. He jokes that I'm his defibrillator, the only one who can spark joy out of him when the black clouds loom over. I've tried my best to be supportive, to listen, to cajole him into talking about his feelings, but he always assures me he's fine. We exchange a few tense words but, inevitably, the conversation moves on.

The last time it happened was shortly after our trip to Florence. As soon as we got back home, he began obsessing over work. He would go over every minor detail of his day with me, picking at everything, trying to analyse what people said to him, and why. I always blamed his father, for never telling him that he was doing a good job, or that he was proud of him. But deep down I knew it was more than that. Jamie needed professional help, but it was hopeless telling him that.

That day, he'd come home from work irritable and argumentative again. After kicking off at me for not having had time to pick up the Nespresso refills he'd asked for, I went into the bedroom to give him space to cool off. After a short while, he came in holding a beer and sat down beside me on the bed.

'I'm sorry,' he said.

'It's OK.'

'I just need the weekend to clear my head. Dad's been on at me for weeks now about this client . . . '

I moved closer to him and took his hand in mine.

'I'm worried that the job — being with your dad — is too much for you.'

He couldn't look me in the eye. He looked exhausted . . . defeated even.

'I know you haven't been sleeping — you're up and down to the bathroom about fifteen times a night. You're drinking more and more . . . '

'I'm sorry, Ivy.'

'Don't be sorry. There is no need to be sorry. Talk to me, that's all.'

'I'll talk to Dad about spreading out some of the key accounts.'

'OK,' I said.

I knew that, if I pushed it, he'd end up feeling worse than he already did, so I chose to say nothing. I put my arms around him and nuzzled my head into his neck. I loved the smell of him after a long day at work. His hair was a mess and his shirt was buttoned down a little lower than his chest, revealing the tiniest bit of dark curly hair.

'I know I've been difficult, Ives, and I know you're only trying to do what's best for me.'

'That's all I ever try to do,' I said, kissing him.

'That's why I love you. You're always looking out for everyone, aren't you?'

He pressed his lips hard against mine and I felt my whole body melt into his.

I didn't feel like I was losing him then. Maybe I should've been paying more attention.

I couldn't go into work. I rang Anna, but she didn't answer, and I couldn't face ringing Mam − not yet. I went to call Gramps but stopped myself; I didn't want to worry him. A day ago, I was in his house showing him photos of wedding dresses in *Brides* magazine. What happened? Jamie's words whirled around my head. He said he hadn't been happy for a while, but none of that was to do with me, surely? And why didn't he say something earlier; give us a chance to work on it? I was stressed, apparently. I don't think I was. I was concerned about Anna, but I wasn't stressed. And anyway, what does it matter if I was stressed? I had to listen to him go on and on about work and the pressure from his father. Why wasn't I allowed to have problems? Where was my shoulder to cry on?

I grabbed my coat and headed for the park. I had my pyjama bottoms on, muddy running trainers, a jumper ridden with holes and a silk bomber jacket. In Hackney, this passes as acceptable attire, but I had the look of someone on the verge of a complete breakdown. A man got in the lift as I headed downstairs, took one glance at me and started shifting his feet anxiously as we made our way to the ground floor, petrified of making eye contact. I didn't realise until later that morning, but I'd picked all the skin around my ring finger, and my left hand was stained with spots of blood.

I stopped at a corner shop and bought a pack of cigarettes and a lighter before lying down on the grass. I couldn't process a single thought; I just had to lie down. I smoked cigarette after cigarette until I felt sick with dizziness. I don't know how long I was there for, but, before I knew it, it was lunchtime, and Broadway Market was filling up with people on their break. My stomach growled, and I was reminded that I'd not eaten since the train journey back to London on Sunday night. I couldn't face food. I couldn't face anything. I picked myself up and walked towards the canal.

I kept checking my phone to see if Jamie had messaged. I kept going into my settings and making sure the volume was on loud, when I knew full well it was. I remember him messaging me the day before, when I was in Wales; seeing that banner appear on my screen and smiling at the thought of hearing from him. He was hungover after going out with Mark to watch the greyhounds race. Mark had made a point of saying how ridiculous it was that, despite us having lived in Hackney for over a year, they still hadn't had a proper East End booze-up. Jamie had said the level of organisation for the weekend was like a stag do. He'd seemed so excited. What sort of psychopath goes out on the piss with their fiancée's brother-in-law the day before he splits up with her?

I opened Instagram – there we were last week, at brunch. He had ketchup all over his mouth and I was trying to lick it off, laughing as I did so. I took a photo of us; his cheeks were stained red and he was pretending to be annoyed with me. He'd commented: 'You're lucky I love you'. He looked so cute. I looked so smug. What the fuck happened?

My phone rang; it was Mam. She always likes to check in at lunchtimes, usually out of boredom. I braced myself and took a deep breath but before I could speak she was already off on one.

'I think we need lobster as a transitional dish,' she said.

'Mam, please—'

'I know you don't want me to get involved but I think it would send the right message.'

'Mam—'

'Lobster and champagne. Very classy, very us.'

'Mam, can you just—'

'I'm not interfering, but we could get oysters for the canapés and wouldn't lobster be such a fabulous accompaniment?'

'Just stop for one second, Mam.'

'Darling, what is it?'

'He's gone . . . Jamie . . . he left.'

With those words, my knees buckled beneath me and I sank to the ground. The tears came so fast that it was hard to breathe. I hadn't cried yet, and when it rains, it pours.

Chapter 3

Pancakes with Prince Philip

'They'll hate me,' I said.

'Would you stop this, Ivy?' Jamie replied.

We were walking through Clissold Park, near to where Mia and I were living at the time, and Jamie was saying how keen he was to get his parents down to London to meet me.

'I don't like horses and I don't own any pearls,' I protested.

'Ivy, this isn't *Downton Abbey*. We're not having five-course dinners in black tie every night.'

'I bet you have done, though,' I joked.

'We're normal.'

'Define normal?'

'Stop it!' he cried. 'They will love you.'

'I'm nervous, that's all.'

'You've got nothing to worry about; you've got loads in common.'

'Have we?'

'Of course. You love the outdoors, you like to travel—'

'I've never been proper travelling.'

'Don't make out like you've been stuck in South Wales your whole life.'

'No, I made it all the way to Bristol University, after all,' I joked.

'Exactly. And you're interested in art—'

'Posh people love art, don't they?'

'And you don't care about money ... which – and I know you don't want me bringing her up – is a nice contrast to Andrea.'

'We're allowed to discuss your ex-girlfriend if it's solely for the purpose of slagging her off.'

He laughed.

'And Dad will fancy the pants off you.'

'I'd be OK with that,' I said.

'He'll take one look at that beautiful smile, and your big green eyes.'

He leant into me, squeezed my bum and put his lips on my neck. They lingered there for a few seconds as he moved in closer to me. I went all hot.

'Mr Langdon, are you trying to get into my pants?'

'Always, Ivy.'

'I think we should skip brunch and go back to mine,' I said.

'It was a waste of time leaving the bedroom in the first place.'

Unfortunately, the first meeting didn't go quite as we'd planned.

We were at Jamie's old flat, in Bermondsey. We'd been together for a few months and I was trying really, really hard to be sexy all the time. Being sexy all the time requires a certain level of commitment that does not come naturally to me, and I was exhausted by all the effort. Every weekend we'd languish in bed for hours on end, having sex and asking each other personal questions we'd never remember the answers to. Afterwards, I'd saunter into the kitchen in some revealing and entirely impractical outfit, which of course he was made to believe I had thrown on, casually. I'd make him bacon and eggs just the way he liked it, which I'd then serve to him in bed with a smile and a snog. No normal person can sustain that level of effort.

That particular morning, I was pulling out all the stops because I was desperate for him to tell me that he loved me. I bought new lingerie from Rosie Huntington-Whiteley's Marks and Spencer's range, which I felt set the right tone for such an occasion – not too slutty, but eyes very much on the prize. I'd also been to four spin classes that week, which was a big deal for me because only people who hate themselves go to spin. Truth be told, I was looking fantastic and I was mystified as to why he hadn't said it. I'd even given him my best blow job and made all the right noises to make it sound like I was enjoying myself. After my performance, I made my way through to the kitchen in my beautiful but uncomfortable lingerie and started to make blueberry pancakes, his favourite. In hindsight, cooking hot liquid when you're naked wasn't the brightest of ideas, but I was too preoccupied with the 'I love you' to think of such practicalities.

Despite my best efforts, I didn't have quite enough hands to manage the pancakes, bacon, fruit and coffee. As I went in search of some instructions for the new espresso machine, the tea towel I had under my arm fell onto the stove and caught fire. I grabbed it and threw it into the sink and in doing so clipped the frying pan, which sent the pancake mix hurling across the room at full pelt. I had it in my eyes, on my bra . . . it went everywhere. I could hear noises coming from outside the kitchen and so I ran to close the door, desperate to conceal the mess I'd created. I'd also managed to burn my hand in the process, which was getting quite painful. I was mortified when I saw him come in.

'I am so sorry!' I cried. 'I was trying to make you pancakes and I've cocked it all up. There's mix everywhere and I've burnt my fucking hand.'

He stood there staring at me. I couldn't work out what his face was doing, part frown, part smirk. He mouthed, 'I'm sorry,' as he opened the door a little wider to reveal his father, William Langdon.

'Ivy ... my dad's here.'

I stood motionless as his father walked towards me with his hand out.

'My darling girl, it is an absolute pleasure to meet you.'

At this point I mouthed various expletives before running behind the kitchen unit in a bid to conceal any shred of dignity I might have had left.

It's hard to come across as an independent, together young woman when you've got pancake mix stuck in your hair and you're standing there with your arse out. His father was a total gem about it and didn't make me feel at all like the complete idiot I was, which only consolidated my belief that posh people have impeccable manners. Jamie described his father as a difficult, cold man, but, standing there with that big handsome grin on his face, he looked like an older version of Jamie, and that was fine with me.

After failing to hide my assets, Jamie suggested I go take a shower while he made tea and tried to clear up. I had to grab the half-burnt tea towel to hide my backside as I walked back into his room, all the while with his father there, looking like Prince bloody Philip as he stood with his hands behind his back, surveying the mess.

I tried to string out the shower as long as possible, in the hope that by the time I'd finished, his father would have left, and I could pretend he hadn't just seen my erect nipples (it was a chilly morning). I also kept thinking that, from that angle, I must have looked a bit bloated. All in all, not an ideal first meet.

I came out of the bathroom and Jamie was sitting on the bed, looking very pleased with himself.

'Jamie, I'm so sorry,' I said.

He handed me a cup of tea and smiled.

'Don't be so hard on yourself. It's the most action he's had in years.'

He laughed and I whacked him across the arm. He took my face in his hands and kissed me hard on the lips.

'Hurry up and get ready,' he said.

I walked back into the bathroom, head low, feeling like a total tit, when he called my name.

'I really love you,' he said, and turned to walk back into the kitchen.

Chapter 4

It's going to be fine

I forgot that Mia had an audition on Monday, so we didn't speak until later that day.

'On a scale of one to Chris Brown, how angry are you?' she asked.

'I don't think you can do that anymore.'

'Do what?'

'Make cultural references to Chris Brown.'

'Says who?'

'Well, for a start, it's been about ten years.'

'Domestic violence is always relevant, Ivy.'

'Right. Can you focus?'

'Sorry. Fucking hell.'

'Yeah, I know. What time will you be home?'

'I'll try to be back for six. I have vodka and two hundred cigarettes.'

'That's quite a lot of cigarettes.'

'You know I always stock up in duty free.'

'Course you do.'

'What will you do in-between?'

'I don't know. I don't want to go home. Why did he do this on a Monday, of all the days?'

'Ivy, he's a psychopath. Give me four hours and I'll be pouring neat spirits down your throat.'

'OK.'

'We can have a big old cry. Whatever happens, we'll get through it together.'

I convinced myself that he'd be home by Saturday, because well, why wouldn't he? I would implement some new rules around communication. He wouldn't be allowed to retreat anymore. I would insist he spoke to a counsellor. We'd set a time limit on how much we could complain about work. All these things were achievable and realistic and it would all be fine.

I walked all the way along the canal up to Camden, where I got off and picked up some ready-made cans of gin and tonic, before heading over to Mia's in Highgate. I was early and decided to walk through the cemetery. I have always found solace in cemeteries. When Jamie and I went to Paris I made him take me to the Père Lachaise Cemetery; he complained that it was a waste of an afternoon, but I assured him it would be worth it, and it turned out to be the most memorable thing we did that weekend. It is an odd attraction for a weekend in the world's most romantic city, but there is something so beautiful about a cemetery. I play a little game where I go right up to the gravestones to see the names of the deceased before making up elaborate stories about their departure.

'This is Juliette, who lost her lover at sea,' I said to Jamie, as I skipped along the path. I was making wild, dramatic gestures with my hands to convey the true passion in my story.

'They were on his father's sailing boat; young and in love, they danced the night away on deck, listening to jazz and smoking hand-rolled cigarettes.'

At this point, Jamie was standing in front of me, shaking his head and laughing.

'They had too much champagne, the music pulsed through their veins and the stars glistened on the ocean. But then, going below deck to get another bottle, her lover, Claude, tripped and tragically fell overboard. She tried to save him, but alas, she failed. They say she never loved again. She died of a broken heart.'

'Ivy, you do know that you talk utter nonsense, right?' Jamie said.

'It's a love story, Jamie,' I said, whirling around the graves.

'You're so weird and . . . morbid.'

'I'm not morbid! It's romantic.'

'The restaurant last night was romantic, this morning's walk along the Seine was romantic, that rose I picked up for you was—'

'A bit cheesy, *non*?'

'Piss off, Ivy. I thought I did really well there,' he said, pretending to sulk.

'You did, you really did.'

I skipped up to him and pulled the collar of his coat towards me before snogging his face off.

Back in Highgate, I rang Mia's doorbell. She greeted me with a litre of Waitrose-branded vodka and a litre of Belvedere.

'I thought we'd start with the good stuff and then move on to the cheap shit.'

'It's still Waitrose,' I said.

'Bloody nightmare having that place down the road. I go in for a few limes and five minutes later I've spent eighty-five quid.'

She put the bottles down on the floor and gave me a hug. As soon as her arms enveloped me, I burst into tears. We stood there for a while, me sobbing onto her shoulder, bottles of neat liquor beside us. When my breathing finally calmed, she slowly peeled me off her, took me by the hand, and led me inside.

Mia moved in with her boyfriend Noah at the same time as I moved in with Jamie. Before that we'd been living in a tiny two-bedroom flat in Stoke Newington, with mould running up the walls and skirting boards peeling away from excess damp. We'd spent most of our living together eating Frosties in bed and falling asleep on each other after *Sex and the City* marathons. She had been an excellent housemate, despite her inability to cook, clean or buy anything for the flat, ever.

Mia's boyfriend Noah had inherited the house from his aunt when she passed away. It was an absolute dream of a home; huge garden, four bedrooms, and not even box-sized London bedrooms, but four proper-sized rooms. The house had tonnes of light and a massive fireplace in the living room that we were all permanently fixed to – we could smoke up the chimney and it wouldn't make the house smell. His aunt collected furniture from everywhere she'd travelled to as a photographer, and every piece had a story behind it. There was an antelope skull from Kenya mounted to the living room wall, a huge antique teal door from Mumbai, a calfskin rug from an ex-lover in Colorado – it was all so beautifully eccentric and completely up Mia's street. Noah's aunt had moved in various social circles, and the house had been notorious for parties, a tradition Noah and Mia fought hard to continue, even before she moved in. That night was the first time I'd been over where it was just Mia at home; usually they'd have one of Noah's struggling actor friends staying for the week, month, sometimes longer. It was a drop-in centre for the broken-hearted and the working poor. I hadn't ever thought that I'd run the risk of falling into either camp.

We were four drinks down and Mia was getting changed

into something more comfortable, which for her means a semi-sheer cream vintage silk nightgown and floral kimono. She was sitting on her dressing table, combing her long, wavy-blonde hair, one of her many night-time rituals (these include, but aren't exclusive to, excessive flossing, pretending to mediate and Instagramming Sarah Jessica Parker).

'Why don't you stay with me for the week?' she said.

'But I don't have any clothes. I need clothes for work, Mia.'

'Who cares about work.'

'I care; I've got rent to pay. We can't all have dead aunties.'

'God rest her soul. Shame she was a such a bitch.'

We finished our drinks and went downstairs to the kitchen for refills. We were way past double measures and I was starting to feel a bit woozy, but, in the deceptive way that makes you feel warm inside, just before your brain registers how drunk you are, and suddenly, you're unable to stand.

'What am I going to do, Mia? Tell me?' I asked, as I poured us another double.

'Don't think about that now. It's too much. For now, we have vodka, and I think there's a pizza in the freezer.'

'Why don't you ever have any proper food?'

'What's the point? I've got Noah.'

'What happens when he's away and you're left on your own, like now? You can't just eat frozen pizza.'

'That's why God invented ... ' and she went over to the fridge, opened the door and pointed to the only edible thing in there: a jar of green pesto. Beside it was a bottle of champagne, three bottles of wine and a multi pack of Diet Coke. Her insides might be dying, but the girl knows how to have a good time.

Later that evening, Anna called. She'd come out of court to find seventeen missed calls from me, as well as my deranged stream of consciousness on WhatsApp. She was shouting at

Mark in the next room, desperate for him to shed some light on Jamie's behaviour. Surely Mark picked up on something over the weekend? Had Jamie been acting strange; had he said anything out of character; had he given any hint whatsoever as to what he was going to do thirty-six hours later? Apparently, he had not.

'I'm so sorry I couldn't get to my phone. I should have been there for you.'

'It's OK. I spoke to Mam.'

'Oh god, what did she say?'

'Well, she's convinced he's seeing someone.'

'Christ. What do you think?'

'I don't know. If I let myself think about the possibility of that I . . . I can't do it.'

'Darling, try to breathe. Whatever you need, we're here.'

'I know.'

'I could kill him. I think Mark is actually going to kill him.'

'I want to speak to him.'

'He will ring; of course he will.'

'What if he doesn't?'

'He will. Why don't you come here tonight?'

'I'll stay at Mia's. I'm here now anyway.'

'Is the cast of *Wicked* there again?'

'It was *Les Mis*, not *Wicked*. Remember that middle-aged bloke with the cravat? He spent the night doing cocaine on his own in the corner of the room and shouting, "Do you hear the people sing?"'

'Yeah, Noah has some odd friends.'

'Actors are odd.'

'Promise me if you wake up in the middle of the night, you'll call me? Or just come over? You've got the key.'

'Thanks. I don't know what I'd do without you.'

'I love you, Ivy.'

Since I can remember, Anna has always had my back. When in comprehensive and a group of girls started picking on me, for no reason other than my current obsession with fashioning my dad's ties as belts – something I thought made me look like Britney Spears – she went up to them and told them that if they were ever to pick on me again, she would tell everyone about the time she found them in the park screaming over a Ouija board, when in reality it was a bunch of eight-year-olds hiding in the bushes making wailing noises at them. Or when the rain nearly ruined my final piece of A-level art work, and she cancelled a weekend away with her friends to help me finish it. Or when in netball, I missed a key goal and the team wouldn't speak to me, she took me to the cinema to watch *Requiem for a Dream*, which, in hindsight, hadn't cheered me up one bit, but it had made me feel really cool.

I told her I loved her too.

'We've got this, Ivy,' she said.

I really hoped she was right.

Chapter 5

Hungover on work time

I woke up the next day with Mia spooning me. My mouth tasted like an ashtray and my vision was blurry. It felt like I'd grown a forest on my teeth. I reached over to the pint glass next to the bed, took a big gulp and spat it straight back into the glass.

'Mia, this is vodka!' I cried, trying to revive her.

She pulled the duvet over her head and groaned.

I found my jeans on the floor. They were stained a dark-green colour.

'Why do my jeans look like this?'

I held them close to her face and made her smell them.

'Ivy, go away,' she said, crawling further under the duvet.

I grabbed my phone – Jamie must have called. There was nothing. I put my head into my hands and took a few deep breaths.

'I need to borrow some clothes.'

'Can't you work from home?' Mia asked, popping her head out from under the duvet.

'No, Jane is already going to be on the warpath.'

'Why do you think she hates you so much?'

'I don't know. It's not like I haven't tried to make her like me.'

'Maybe we should take her out? We can—'

'Mia, no. There is no way you are ever meeting my boss.'

'I'm workshopping, Ivy! All you're bringing me is problems.'

I gave her the finger and asked what she was doing with her day.

'It's a bit of a nightmare, to be honest. I've got to do an audition tape this morning, but I really need to re-watch last season's finale of *Teen Mom*.'

I shook my head in bemusement.

'Ivy, you know it starts up again next month! I need to make sure I'm fully up to speed.'

Mia's greatest passions in life are reality TV shows, the Spice Girls and being dramatic. She likes to tell people that she watches *University Challenge* and *Fake or Fortune*, but the truth is, if it isn't in an unscripted format, she's not interested.

'Why is everything so stained?' I asked, as I tried to find something clean to put on.

'We were in the garden.'

'The garden? When?'

'Last night. I rolled a joint, we lay on the grass, and then it started raining.'

'What time was this?'

'Maybe four, maybe later.'

'Oh, for fuck's sake.'

I caught the tube into Holborn and walked down Kingsway, onto the Strand and towards the office. I picked up a box of Rennie, a bottle of Lucozade, three packs of chewing gum and a ham and cheese sandwich. If that wasn't going to see me through the morning, nothing would.

Jane cornered me as I walked to my desk.

'Are you feeling better, Ivy?' she said, her holier-than-thou face out in all its glory.

'Yes, I am much better, thanks.'

'Busy weekend, I take it?'

'Not really.'

'You haven't been taking those supplements, have you? I've started taking cayenne powder twice a day – it's got so many benefits – and I've also started—'

'Yes, Jane,' I interrupted. 'I will bear that in mind.'

I sat down at my desk and closed my eyes. I can do this, I thought. I am an adult, I have a degree and I frequently make my own packed lunches. But then I remembered that I didn't have my laptop with me; I'd left the house the day before with nothing on me. I sank deeper into my chair and let out an audible groan.

Jane's office was at the opposite end of the room. As office manager and executive assistant to the chief executive, she had a separate space for her and John, our CEO. Despite it being a large office, I always felt her beady little eyes on me, judging, assessing, waiting for me to slip up.

I walked over to her office, passing Ethan and the sales team, a young bunch of lads who only drank protein shakes, wore shirts two sizes too small for them and had very obscure musical preferences. They wished me luck as I knocked on her door. She was sitting at her desk, cutting the world's smallest avocado into even smaller pieces.

'As you can see, I am having my breakfast. Is this urgent, Ivy?'

'I'm sorry, but I left my laptop at home.'

She put her knife and fork down and looked at me with great intensity.

'You haven't lost it, have you?'

'No, Jane. It's at home.'

'Well, good job one of us always has a Plan B.'

She went into the cupboard and pulled out a spare laptop, handing it over with her classic sanctimonious smile. I was going to kill her.

It took me about an hour to compose two lines of an email that morning. I stared at the ham and cheese sandwich on my desk, unable to bring myself to eat it. Mam kept sending me photos of Kit Harington in a bid to cheer me up, but every time a message popped up I thought it was Jamie, so I told her to stop. I must have checked my phone a thousand times. How could he not have called by now? I went on Instagram and saw that he'd commented on a friend's post earlier that morning. I had to remove myself from the office, go downstairs, smoke two cigarettes in quick succession, run to the loo, cry, then go back to my desk and pretend nothing had happened.

Walking back from the bathroom, I spotted Lisa on the prowl for mindless chat.

'Babe, I missed you yesterday. We got the guitar out, you'd have loved it.'

I tried to look busy, an art I have perfected since working with Lisa. She turned the radio up and 'Galway Girl' was playing, which is no surprise to anyone because Ed Sheeran is always playing at any given time of day. She only knew one line of the song and kept singing it over and over again. I asked her to turn the volume down, but she carried on singing, doing air guitar with her eyes closed. I looked over at Ethan, who was pretending to hang himself. I don't have a particularly stressful job; I'm an office PA, and, day-to-day, things are all right. It's the people that make it hard work.

I can do this, I thought. If I can get through yesterday, I can get through Lisa's crap rendition of a mediocre Ed Sheeran song.

The email arrived later that morning.

Hi Ivy,
 I'm sorry for not getting in touch sooner. I don't want
to be in a relationship where I feel like this. I'm not in
the right place to continue seeing you and I'm not in a
position to plan a future with you.
 I'm sorry. I really am.
 Jamie x

I read it again, and again. Then I grabbed my stuff, ran downstairs and vomited all over the pavement.

Going back into the office was not an option, so I walked. I walked all the way through the City into Shoreditch, passing florists, lawyers, media moguls and construction workers. Why is it, when there's just shy of nine million people living here, that London can often feel like the loneliest place in the world?

By the time I got to Shoreditch, it was lunchtime and the pub was busy with trendy fashion types and aggressive networkers. At the Quiet Lady, I ordered a double gin and tonic and sat outside in the cold, chain-smoking. Smoking gave me something to do. If my hands were free I'd have ripped the skin around my nails even more, and they were already bloody and raw.

It was the 'seeing you' part of his email that got to me most. We weren't seeing each other; we were engaged. You don't do the weekly shop with someone you're 'seeing'. You don't speak on the phone to each other's parents and you certainly don't discuss children's names. No, we weren't seeing each other. And what was all this 'position' lark? What did that mean?

I rang Anna and read out the email to her.

'He's unable to plan a future with you?'

'Yeah.'

'But, he's already planned your future together. That's what you do when you get engaged.'

'Yeah.'

'Why does it read like an HR email?'

'I don't know, Anna, do I?'

'How much have you had to drink?'

'I'm on my second gin.'

'Single or double?'

'What do you think?'

'Right. Have you eaten?'

'No, I can't face it.'

'Stay where you are. I'll be there in half an hour.'

Anna arrived at 2pm and by that time I'd sunk another gin and my hands were beginning to shake. I'd run out of cigarettes but remained sitting outside. My silk bomber jacket wasn't all that appropriate for a cold March day, and I was freezing. Anna wrapped her arms around me and handed me a sandwich.

'We're going inside,' she barked.

'OK.'

'Eat these, and then we can start again.'

'OK.'

'You've got to eat, Ives.'

She eyed me up as I got up from the table.

'Interesting jacket,' she said.

'I know.'

'It makes you look like you're—'

'Auditioning for a nineties hip-hop tribute act?'

'Well, yeah.'

'Mia made me buy it.'

'Say no more.'

We went inside, and I ate. Then, we drank.

Later that afternoon, we decided I needed to go back home

and pack some of my things. I knew Jamie wouldn't be back for another few hours, so it was safe. I hadn't brushed my teeth since the previous morning – hence the three packs of gum – and I needed to wash the smell of gin and resentment off me.

I vomited again as soon as I got into the flat. I'd eaten the sandwich too quickly and it came back up in big chunks. I grabbed the nearest towel and wiped the saliva off my face. I looked at my reflection in the mirror and starting sobbing. I didn't recognise myself.

What do you pack when you don't know where you're going? How long you're going to be gone for? I went into the bathroom and started rummaging through the cupboards. For some reason, I was trying to find a charcoal face mask that Mam had bought me, as if that was going to help matters. I emptied a drawer in the bathroom and a candle smashed to the floor. I leant down to pick up the shattered glass and cut my finger. I heard my phone go off. It was a message from Jamie:

> Look, I know yesterday was a bit blurted out.
> The conversation just went that way naturally,
> and I wanted to be honest.
> I'm sorry.

I called Anna into the bathroom to show her the message. I sat on the toilet seat while she stood over me and stroked my back. Just like that, I moved into the next phase of break-ups: I was fucking furious.

It only took a couple of minutes before I knew exactly what I needed to say in reply:

> You need to be out of the flat by the weekend.

Chapter 6

This is a race issue

'I bid on a little holiday last night,' Mam said.

It was a couple of days later, and we were on the phone over my lunch break.

'It's for Linda's auction. For Sjögren's Syndrome.'

'I don't know what that is,' I said.

'Yes, you do. That tennis player has it.'

'Who?'

'The Jehovah's Witness who wins everything.'

'Do you mean one of the Williams sisters?'

'Yes! Mercury.'

'Venus?'

'That's it.'

'Sorry, she has what?'

'Sjögren's Syndrome.'

'How do you even know that?' I asked.

'I read, Ivy. Anyway, we won.'

'Mam, who is "we"?'

'Me, you, your father, Anna and Mark.'

'Where are we going?'

'To Loch Lomond. It's a walking holiday.'

'But you hate walking.'

'No, I don't.'

'Yes, you do. You get taxis everywhere.'

'You know I think driving is vulgar, Ivy.'

'Have you told Anna this?'

'It's exactly what we all need right now.'

'Is it?'

'Don't start with that tone, Ivy.'

'How much did it cost?'

'I don't think I need to share that, darling.'

'Mam?'

'It wasn't cheap, but it was very good value.'

'Mam?'

'OK, fine. It was upwards of three thousand pounds.'

'Mam!'

'Don't you dare tell your father.'

Dad's been retired for five years, and, having worked at the South Wales Housing Association most of his life, he has a good pension, but it's not going to last long if Mam continues to spend it all on charity auctions in the name of rare diseases. A few months ago, she successfully bid on sailing lessons, even though she gets terrible sea sickness and hates the water. Then there was the time she paid £500 for a signed copy of Phillip Schofield's book, citing the fact that she could never get such a personal message written to her otherwise. She hit the roof when Anna pointed out that she could've gone to his book signing in Cardiff – for free – and asked him to sign something for her there. How dare we ask her to stand in line and wait with everyone else.

I rang Anna as soon as I got off the phone to Mam and we agreed that under no circumstances would we be going on holiday with our parents anytime soon. However good Mam is in a crisis, she has no boundaries. Anna and Mark would be going off to their bedroom to try to procreate, and Mam would be standing by the doorway, gin in hand, shouting motivational quotes. I on the other hand would be out the back, chain-smoking, and, instead of giving me the headspace I so obviously needed, she'd follow me outside and ask for a 'cheeky puff'.

I went back to work the next day. Jane was off my back once she learnt that I'd vomited all over the street, so that was a bonus. Jane loves a stomach issue, so I told her that I had a bad bout of IBS, which of course isn't a real thing. When I got into the office, she came over to ask me how I was doing and left a box of peppermint tea on my desk to help ease the cramping. Apparently, people with IBS get bad cramps. What I really needed was a pack of wine gums and a full fat Coke, but Jane doesn't do sugar, and beggars can't be choosers.

Jamie assured me that he'd be out of the flat by Saturday night. He'd sent another email in which he'd reiterated how sorry he was, but what was he sorry for? The past three years? Proposing? Leaving me? On Sunday night, I had a fiancé, but come this Saturday, I'd be living alone, in the flat we once shared together. I was so confused and felt so utterly rejected. My anxiety dream was back; I'm on a boat and it's sinking. I'm crying out for help but nobody hears me. I am alone, and I drown. Clearly, I was doing just fine.

By late afternoon on Thursday, the shock of it all was starting to wear off and reality was sinking in. I didn't want anything to start sinking in; I wanted to remain in a state of numbness sponsored by hundreds of units of alcohol. My body was crying out for sleep, so I planned to leave work on time, head straight back to Anna's and get an early night. Or, I could forego my evening crying on the sofa with a kilo of budget crisps, and I could go out. 'Out out'.

I rang Dan, my go-to friend for when I want to get blind drunk. You can message Dan at 11pm on a Monday night and, even if he were about to get into bed, he'd come meet you in the pub as soon as he could and get the first round in. Whatever he's got going on in his own life, he'll always be available to cheer you up with tequila, back-handed compliments and inappropriate touching. At our engagement party, six months ago, he waltzed into the room with a bottle of champagne in hand and cried, 'Charlie's here!' My mother kept making remarks like, 'His skin is fabulous,' and, 'He smells fantastic.' She went around the room introducing him to her friends as, 'Ivy's gorgeous friend, Charlie.' I didn't have the heart to tell her that his name is Dan and Charlie refers to the gram of cocaine he always has on him.

Dan suggested we meet at a swanky hotel in Soho. He'd given a blow job to the maître d' the week before and this meant we'd be a shoo-in for the best table.

'Jesus, you look awful,' he said, as we greeted.

He went on to tell me that my face looked puffy and recommended I go see his friend Jason, who had inexpensive quick fix solutions to this sort of problem. I said a drink would be fine.

'Look, he's having a mare. You guys will be fine,' he said.

'You don't know that.'

'You're right, I don't.'

'I can't believe this is happening. Why is this happening?'

'I don't know, babe. Have you spoken to his mum?'

'God, no. I wouldn't know where to start.'

'Look, it'll be fine. Absolutely fine.'

'Don't say it like that.'

'OK, he's a fucking cunt and he needs to grow the fuck up.'

I moved my chair closer to his and rested my head on his shoulder.

'Maybe he's having a hard time and maybe he will come running back to you but—'

I interrupted him with a loud groan before downing the rest of my drink.

'What would you say if it were me in the same position?' Dan asked.

'I don't know,' I said, ushering the waiter to bring us more bar snacks.

Dan grabbed my hand and told the waiter to leave us alone.

'You might be heartbroken, Ivy, but you can't get fat.'

It was 1am when we got to the club. We were the only people there over thirty years old, by a long mile. I walked in and One Direction was playing. I ran to the dance floor screaming the only words to the song I knew, letting my limbs go soft and flailing my arms about like a madwoman. Dan left me to it and came back moments later with four tequila shots.

'I can't,' I shouted.

Turns out I could, and before I knew it I was two shots down and three sheets to the wind, as Gramps would say.

At one point, Kelly Clarkson came on with 'Since You've Been Gone', and I leapt onto a sofa. 'I can breathe for the first time,' I cried, which was ironic, because I'd smoked about ninety cigarettes that week and was quite short of breath.

Dan was dancing next to me, having the time of his life grinding up against some man's crotch. I made a friend in the bathroom; her name was Harriet. She told me she liked my top, I told her she had a lovely fringe and then we hugged and had a little cry. Bathrooms really do bring people together.

We stayed until they threw us out at 3am. Outside, Dan was glued to his phone, trying to cancel the next morning's meetings, while I tried to book an Uber home.

'Leave it a couple of hours then we'll get one together,' he said.

'OK,' I hiccupped.

'Great, then we're going.'

'Going where?'

'My favourite place on earth: Halo.'

We got in a taxi and I tried my utmost best not to be sick all over the back seat. I kept inhaling and exhaling, while Dan rubbed my thigh and whispered, 'You've got this, babe.'

We got out of the taxi and Dan stopped me before we turned around the corner and into the queue for Halo.

'We've got to look sober, Ivy.'

'I am,' I lied.

'Channel whatever it is you've got in you and pretend that you're a person who's got their shit together. Do you hear me?'

'Roger that.'

'Please don't say shit like that.'

We stumbled into the queue and I continued to take long inhalations and loud exhalations. I looked like I was on the verge of a panic attack. One of the bouncers clocked me and made his way over.

'Miss, how much have you had to drink tonight?'

'Very little indeed,' I said.

'Very little?'

'A couple of wines ... a few vodka limes ...'

He looked me up and down.

'Where have you been?'

'Good question.'

He pulled a face at me and shook his head.

'Please step outside the queue, miss.'

I did as I was told. Dan gave me a horrified look and followed behind.

'You need to breathe into this,' the bouncer said, as he pulled out a breathalyser.

'You're joking?' I said.

'It's club policy.'

'That's ridiculous. You're being ridiculous.'

'Please take the breathalyser test.'

'Don't tell me what to do,' I said, stumbling backwards.

'If you want to come in, you're going to have to take the test.'

'I don't have to do anything.'

'OK, then. I'm going to have to ask you to leave.'

'No. I want to see a manager.'

'You can't see a manager.'

'Yes, I bloody well can.'

'You need to leave.'

'I am not leaving.'

'Miss, you need to go home.'

'This is a total farce.'

'Please, miss. Don't make this any harder than it needs to be.'

'No, you listen to me. When I get home, I'm going to write your manager a strongly worded letter.'

'You go ahead and do that.'

'Is this because I'm Welsh?'

At this point, Dan dragged me away.

I woke up the next morning with Anna sitting on the edge of the bed, cup of tea in hand. I rubbed my eyes and tried to forget the image I had of Dan dragging me away from the bouncer as I mouthed off about modern-day xenophobia.

'Ivy, wake up,' she said.

I turned to face the wall, crunching my body into the foetal position.

'Ivy, please get up.'

'I can't. Go away.'

'Darling, please.'

She pulled at my body so that I was facing her.
'Ivy . . . it's Gramps.'
'What?'
'He had a stroke. He's in hospital.'

Chapter 7

Lumière

Gramps suffered a stroke in the early hours of Friday morning. He lost all feeling in his right leg and collapsed. I don't know how he managed to ring Mam, but Dad told me she found him lying on the bedroom floor, half-clothed and scared senseless.

Mam's not great at discussing her feelings, so I went to Dad to find out how she was doing. He said that she was calm, but very flirtatious with the doctor, which was all we could hope for.

I rang Jane and said that I needed to work from home. I told her about Gramps; she knew how close we were, and, in a bizarre turn of events, was quite supportive. This, however, turned out to be short-lived, as by 11.15 that morning, she'd sent me nine emails asking for detailed updates on tasks she knew full well I hadn't yet started. If I was ever feeling just a tiny bit low about my current circumstances, Jane would be there to make things that much worse.

I spoke to Gramps that afternoon.

'They've made a big song and dance out of nothing,' he said.

'I don't think that's true, Gramps,' I said, holding back the tears.

'It's bollocks, Ives. I tell you.'

'How are you feeling?'

'I'm fine, babes. Just can't feel my leg, can I?'

'Well, that's what physiotherapy is for.'

'Do you know they have male nurses now?'

'Yes, of course I know that.'

'And I don't have my shirts.'

'Do you need your shirts?'

'Yes! Come on, Ivy.'

'OK, OK. I'll tell Mam to bring your shirts.'

'Why didn't you tell me?'

'Tell you what?'

'About Jamie. Your mother said.'

'Oh.'

'You OK, babes?'

'I'll be fine.'

I heard him sigh down the phone.

'I wasn't going to say anything, but that's what you get for wanting to marry an Englishman.'

I laughed.

'That's not helpful, is it?'

'I'd marry you any day, babes.'

'Thanks, Gramps.'

'You can get through anything, Ives.'

'As long as I've got you.'

'You'll always have me, babes. But I really do need my shirts.'

'Fine, I'll ring Mam.'

I got off the phone, desperate to pick it back up again and call Jamie, but there was nothing to say. We used to be able to talk about everything; even the most mundane, trivial topics weren't off limits. Only a couple of weeks ago we'd idled away an hour discussing what household object we'd be if we were in *Beauty and the Beast*. But now that he'd said, 'It's over,' I couldn't think of a single thing to say to him. If this had happened a week ago, he'd have taken the day off work and we'd be at home, together. He'd make me his signature spaghetti Bolognese, my favourite, pour me a large glass of overpriced wine and bequeath me sympathy sexual favours. Now what did I have? A jar of Marmite and a £4 bottle of Echo Falls.

My brain felt like jelly, so I put on my trainers and headed out for a run. On the canal, I ran past a beautiful couple with their little French bulldog. The man had his arm across her shoulders and their hands were intertwined. They were laughing, proper belly laughs, as the dog circled them, craving their attention. My eyes went straight to her ring; a beautiful emerald stone with two diamonds on either side. I've never been fussed about diamonds or engagement rings of any sort for that matter, but since getting engaged I'd find myself seeking them out on random women on the street. This couple must have been newly engaged, because she kept holding her hand up to look at the stones. Her face glowed, and I couldn't stop staring. I'd tried not to think about my own wedding, but of course all I could do was think about my own wedding.

Jamie and I had taken a break from organising the big day. Our families were getting too involved and I was moments away from losing it with everyone – and by everyone, I mainly mean Jamie's mother, Cressida. Within a week of us getting engaged, she had gone into full Bridezilla mode. As the actual bride, I wasn't bothered about the wedding itself – the only thing that mattered to me was Jamie. Cressida wanted to put an announcement in *The Times*; I didn't. Cressida wanted an official engagement photo to mark the occasion; I didn't. Cressida wanted us to have a grand wedding at their family home in Hambleton; I didn't. I wanted something simple and small. I'd have been happy with a blessing from my dad in the back garden and some booze from Lidl.

I told Jamie that I was nervous about upsetting her.

'You're overreacting,' he said. 'It's not like Margaret stays out of things, does she?'

'Yeah, but I can tell Mam when to piss off; I can't do that with Cressida.'

'Yes, you can. Mum would appreciate the honesty.'

'I don't think I've ever even heard her swear.'

'I think she said "crap" once.'

'Can't we just elope?' I asked.

'Properly elope? As in, never to return?'

'Yes, why not?'

'Ives, I'm sorry. I want you to have the wedding you want,' he said, kissing me.

'Why is that so hard for everyone else to understand?'

'Because, Mum is bored and needs a project, and Margaret is . . .well, she's Mags.'

'Why do parents have to ruin everything?'

'I don't know, they just do.'

On top of the wedding stress, we were arguing over where to spend Christmas that year. Christmas is always contentious, but the expectations and meddling were getting too much for me to handle; I was being pulled in every direction, trying to please my family and not insult his. I didn't feel the need to spend Christmas together; surely you only do that when you have children? This had been an ongoing battle since our first Christmas together, back in 2014. I wanted to be at home in Wales with my family, but Jamie thought it would be a nice idea for us to spend the week up north.

'None of our friends spend Christmas together,' I said to him in protest.

This was true, and besides, we'd not even been together for a year at this point.

'Ivy, please, it would mean the world to me.'

'I could come up on Boxing Day?' I pleaded.

'But I want you to be there for Boxing Day. Dad and I will be on the shoot and Mum wants to spend quality time with you.'

'I can't get from Wales to Hambleton for Boxing Day morning.'

'You can if you come for Christmas.'

'I want to be at home. I want to be with Anna.'

'You're with Anna all the time.'

'No, I'm not.'

'This is about spending time with my family.'

'I'm only wanted there so your mum has someone to talk to when your dad's off doing whatever it is he's doing all the time.'

'Don't be like that. She loves you, Ivy.'

'Last time I was there she went riding all weekend and barely spoke to me.'

'You were in a mood. I knew you didn't want to come that weekend.'

'I missed Mia's annual end-of-summer party!'

'Come on, Ivy.'

'Look, it's not about me; it's about Anna. I want to be in Wales with Anna.'

'I think you're being selfish.'

'I think you're being a dick.'

I went to Hambleton that Christmas.

Chapter 8

Is it a banger?

When I woke on Saturday morning, Jamie's moving out day, my body was wet with sweat and the sheets were damp. What would our flat look like with 50 percent less stuff? Did I even own 50 percent of our stuff? What if all I owned were ill-fitting lingerie sets designed by supermodels?

Jamie and I had been living in Hackney for just over a year. He'd been living in this beautiful, spacious bachelor pad in Bermondsey, and it would've been easy for me to move in there, but I'd wanted somewhere that was on neutral ground for us. There had been women in the Bermondsey flat long before I'd turned up. Mark's uncle Aaron owned a one-bed in Hackney, near to Anna and Mark's flat, so you can imagine my joy when, after we went to see it, Jamie said he loved it. I thought that, given the proximity of our flats, Jamie and Mark would've disapproved – Anna and I were with each other enough as it was. But that was the thing about Jamie: he was a yes man, open to anything. Why wasn't he open to my advice about his dad then? Or about work? When had he stopped listening?

By the time I got out of bed, Anna had baked two cakes and

cleaned the whole house. I sat down on the sofa and put the television on as she placed a large portion of cake in my lap. She hadn't made my favourite, red velvet, and I didn't want to be difficult and bring up the fact that beetroot chocolate cake in no way constitutes as a real cake. After all, she'd put her life on hold to cater to my every need that week. I shut my mouth and pretended to be grateful.

'How are you feeling about today?' she asked.

'Oh yeah, great.' I let out a loud groan and she wrapped her arms around me.

'I need to speak to Aaron about the rent,' I said.

'So, you're set on staying there?'

'What's the alternative, flat-sharing with randoms?'

'Don't be like that, it could be fun.'

'Anna, I'm thirty-two this year, and you're a shit liar.'

'Fine. What about renting one of Mia's rooms?'

'God no, we've had our glory days. I think I'd end up killing her, and I can't lose Jamie and Mia.'

'Yeah, probably for the best. Look, I'll ask Mark to speak to Aaron. Don't worry about that now.'

'Can we go out tonight, please? "Out out"?'

'I would, but, well ... I'm going to take a little break from booze.'

'Well, that's rubbish timing,' I said, sulking.

'We're going to start trying again.'

'Oh, right ... I had no idea.'

'I don't want to unload this onto you, not after this week.'

'Please don't do that. Don't start treading on eggshells around me.'

'We've made an appointment with the fertility specialist.'

'When did you do that?'

'Yesterday, after speaking with Gramps. He's going to be around for my baby, Ivy. He has to be.'

Anna had her first round of IVF just over two years ago, and it was me who spent weeks treading on eggshells around her. Things with me and Jamie were perfect. We flew all around Europe for romantic getaways and spent lavish weekends in the country with his family. I wasn't there for Anna, and the harder it got, the more I pulled away. She and Mark were never in any rush to have children, but they weren't being cautious either. So, when two years had passed, and she still wasn't pregnant, they'd started to worry. Everyone had started to worry.

I told myself it would be different this time around. I would be there for her because I didn't have a clue how to be there for myself.

I don't know how I expected to feel, being back in the flat again, with all his stuff gone. For a moment, I questioned if I'd be able to stay there on my own, but the alternative – the logistics of finding a new home, starting again – seemed so much harder.

There wasn't a big reveal, tantrum, or meltdown; if anything, I was surprised at how much bigger everything looked. The bathroom felt the same, but the bedroom seemed stark and soulless. There was a picture hanging on one of the walls, of me and Anna at her wedding, but it didn't look right because there wasn't anything next to it anymore. The fridge was empty and the cupboards almost bare.

'How did I end up here?' I asked Anna, as I sat down on the kitchen floor.

'I don't know, Ives. It's the pits.'

'I'm in an empty flat and on Monday I go back to a job that I couldn't care less about.'

'That's not true.'

'I'm a personal assistant at a private bank.'

Anna was quiet.

'That nobody's even heard of,' I added.

49

'Yes, but it's a nice commute—'

'Wow, the only redeeming feature to my life right now is my commute.'

'Don't do this, now's not the time.'

'I wish I knew what I wanted to do with my life – like you.'

'OK, I might have always known I wanted to be a lawyer, and yes, it might be an easier path when you know what you want to do. But it's OK that you don't know, Ivy. You're only thirty-one. You're not meant to have everything worked out.'

'OK, but I thought I'd have at least have one thing worked out.'

'Ives, today's not the day to be having this conversation. Let's deal with one crisis at a time, OK?'

I leant back and slumped myself against the fridge. Anna came to sit down on the floor with me.

'Do you have any plans for tonight?' she asked.

'All I want is to get Dan over, drink myself into an oblivion and try to forget that any of this is happening.'

'Excellent plan. Though try to not be thrown out of Halo this time.'

'I didn't even make it into Halo.'

Anna laughed.

'It's not my fault that Dan has no concept of when to call it a night,' I said.

'He is very . . . ' she paused as she tried to find the right word '. . . enthusiastic.'

'I have made my plans very clear to him. We are going to drink some gin, dance to Madonna and be asleep by midnight.'

'Foolproof,' Anna said.

'Let's hope so.'

If Jamie were there, he would've told me to stop lying to myself, that I knew full well that Dan would lead me astray. And he'd be right. The next morning I'd be filled with fear and self-loathing, begging Jamie to get me some Haribo and full fat Coke from Selim down the corner shop.

A couple of months ago, I met Dan for a quiet, after-work dinner. It was a wholesome Monday night; we were drinking green tea and he was telling me all about his latest dating catastrophe.

'We go back to mine, hammered, and he asks if I have any speakers,' Dan said.

'OK.'

'I say, no. They fell off the balcony when I shagged Andy last week.'

'Of course they did.'

'Then he goes to the kitchen and starts rummaging through my cupboards.'

'Right.'

'He gets a saucepan, puts his phone in it and on comes Meat Loaf.'

'Meat Loaf?'

'Yeah, I know. But I didn't say anything because he's fit and a scientist and they're hard to come by.'

'True.'

'So, there we are, groping away, but he's got this weird, aggressive sex face on—'

'You have a thing about sex faces.'

'You know they creep me out! Anyway, he gets up from the sofa—'

'Sorry, is Meat Loaf still playing?'

'Obvs, keep up. So, we go into the bedroom and he asks me to crouch down in front of the mirror.'

'Right.'

'I do as I'm told, and I crouch . . . like, a proper yogic squat.'

'OK.'

'And then he comes to stand in front of me.'

51

'Where is this going?'

'You know what, I need wine for this. Can we get wine?'

'We said no drinking, Dan.'

'Oh, bore off, Ivy. If you're not drinking, you're at an AA meeting.'

'That makes no sense whatsoever.'

'Love – miss – hi, can we get two martinis please?' he said, gesturing at the waitress.

'That's not wine, Dan.'

'Come on, Ivy. I'm trying to inject some class into you. Anyway, stop interrupting my flow. Where was I?'

'Squatting.'

'Yes! So, he climbs under me and my arsehole is in his face.'

'There's class for you.'

'He's going at it, and I can feel his foot tapping the carpet in tune with Meat Loaf.'

'OK.'

'Then suddenly, he stops, moves his face to look up at me and says, "Have you taken a shit today?"'

'What?'

'As he looks up at me, I notice that he's got a small brown mark on his chin.'

'As in, your brown mark?'

'Yes, Ivy. My shit.'

'Bloody hell, Dan.'

'Don't judge, I had a dodgy falafel wrap for lunch and hadn't seen to it properly.'

'What is wrong with you, Daniel?'

'Anyway, then he smiles and says, "You taste amazing", and goes back to eating out my shitty arsehole.'

I gagged.

'God, I need that drink.'

I don't like martinis, but I lost count of how many we had

that night. It was after 3am when we finally stumbled through my front door. I went straight into the living room to make up the sofa bed for Dan, who had insisted on coming home with me. The next thing I knew, he was standing in front of me, saucepan in hand, playing Meat Loaf.

'You can't,' I said, trying to get the saucepan off him. 'Jamie's got a big client meeting tomorrow; he'll go ballistic.'

'No, he won't. He'll love it.'

Two minutes later, Jamie was standing in the doorway. He was not loving it.

'Why do you two always have to get so wasted together? It's a bloody Monday,' he seethed.

'Jamie, come on,' Dan cried, grabbing the neck of Jamie's T-shirt and pulling him into the living room.

He stopped dead and looked at me.

'Ivy, can we talk, please?'

I followed him into the bedroom and left Dan chuckling to himself on the sofa.

'It's a Monday, Ivy. Come on.'

'You'll laugh when I told you what happened.'

'Why do you have to resort to being nineteen-year-olds every time you get together?'

'That's not fair.'

'Come to bed, Ivy. It's late.'

'No, I'll sleep with Dan.'

'Why are you being so childish?'

'Because I am childish.'

I stormed out of the bedroom. Dan was passed out on the sofa; saliva was dripping from his mouth and making its way onto our new cushions. I turned the light off and snuggled up beside him.

The next morning, Jamie made breakfast and apologised for being so short with us.

'Don't worry, I was blotto. I can't remember a bloody thing,' Dan said, tucking into a bacon sandwich.

I went over to the kitchen and put my arms around Jamie's shoulders.

'I'm sorry for being drunk and annoying. I knew you had a big day today,' I said.

'No, I'm sorry. I argued with Dad again yesterday,' he said, hugging me.

'Oh, Jamie. I'm sorry,' I said, kissing him. 'I did think you were off when we spoke last night. What happened?'

'Usual shit, he goes on and on at me and—'

'You guys need to speak up, I can't hear you,' Dan said, smirking at us.

Jamie went to sit beside him at the table.

'Come on, talk to Uncle Dan,' he said, patting Jamie's knee. 'Controlling, manipulative fathers are my forte.'

'I sent an email to a client that was perhaps a little too premature, which Dad was cc'd into,' he said.

'I'm sure it wasn't your fault, these things happen,' I said.

'He came over from his desk and lost it at me in front of everyone, saying I can never be trusted to do anything on my own.'

'That's a bit much,' Dan said.

'It was mortifying. I felt like a fucking child.'

'He sounds like a true gent,' Dan said, licking the bacon grease off his fingers.

I gave him the eye and took Jamie's hand in mine.

'You've got to speak to your mum about this. You're so stressed. Look at the way your shoulders are hunched,' I said.

'You'll have terrible posture,' Dan quipped.

'For the sake of your happiness, and your relationship with your dad, I don't see how you can carry on working there.'

It was the umpteenth time I'd said that in recent months.

Jamie nodded.

'I'll speak to them,' he said.

'Promise?' I asked. 'Because you said that two weeks ago.'

'Ivy, I promise.'

He didn't speak to his mother, or his father. He didn't speak to anyone.

Back at the flat that Saturday afternoon, it only took a couple of hours to reorganise everything. I didn't own that much stuff, so things looked a bit bare to say the least. Anna said it was a great excuse to start again. Trouble was, I didn't want to start again.

I was sorting out the kitchen when my phone went off – a group WhatsApp notification entitled 'Bangerz', from our friend Liam. He added me and Jamie to the group and was typing.

> I've only gone and created the world's best wedding playlist!
> Are you in tonight? I've done a PowerPoint presentation with mood boards and everything!
> They're all BANGERZ!
> Is Take That 'Never Forget' a banger? Course it is, and that's why it's on the playlist.
> 'Like a Prayer', is that a banger? YES.
> And that's why it's on the world's greatest wedding playlist.
> Come the fuck on, team. Let's get on it NOW.
> I've got rum and I'm coming over.

I hadn't thought about the break-up admin; how many shared friends we were supposed to let know that it was over. In my head, it wasn't over. I stared down at the phone trying to figure out what to say. About five minutes or so went by.

Jamie is typing.

Another minute passed.

Jamie has left the conversation.

How apt.

Chapter 9

I'm coming up

In a bid to get me eating anything other than Marmite on toast, Anna signed me up to an organic food-delivery box service. In a crisis, there is always Marmite, or in Mia's case, there's pesto, but Anna was right, enough was enough. We argued over how many jars were acceptable to keep in the cupboard. I did have three, but one of them was personalised with Jamie's name, so that was obviously the first to go.

Anna wanted to stay with me until Dan arrived, but I forced her to go home to Mark. I had to start accepting the reality of the situation – me at home alone – and she had a home to get back to.

When she left, I poured myself a glass of wine, stood by the window and stared out onto the park. For some reason, I started thinking about our electric toothbrushes. I'm the sort of person who likes to have pick 'n' mix sweets for breakfast, but Jamie insisted they were better for oral hygiene, a concept that was lost on me. I could never be bothered to clean the handle, so after a while, the tooth-paste would congeal, forming thick dried clumps of paste all over it. I'd come home from work one night after another soul-destroying day in the office, and when I went to brush my teeth, I lost it.

'What's the point when it gets all over the handle every time you use it?' I asked. I had come into the bedroom and was holding up the toothbrush with one hand and pointing furiously at Jamie with the other.

He put his book down and took off his glasses.

'Ivy, what's the matter?'

'I hate this toothbrush. The handle is always dirty.'

'Just run it over warm water after you use it, it's not a big deal.'

'No, it is a big deal and I'm sick of everything always going wrong.'

I stormed back into the bathroom, sat in the bath and burst out crying.

After a couple of minutes, Jamie let himself in and sat on the toilet beside me.

'You look very silly sitting in the bath like that, Ives. Do you want me to run the water for you?'

'No, I just want to sit here.'

'OK. Are you going to tell me what the matter is ?'

'I don't know.'

'Yes, you do.'

'I wrote some minutes down wrong today and Jane had a go at me. She says I rush everything.'

'Don't pay attention to her.'

'I need something new, Jamie. This cannot be what I do with my life.'

'Stop being so hard on yourself. You know this isn't your dream career, but it pays well, and you don't take any of the work home with you.'

'I take Jane home with me. She's always there reminding me that I'm not good enough.'

'You are good enough.'

'Am I?'

'Yes. Jane is Jane. You need to find a way to not let her get to you so much.'

'That's rich coming from you. Look at you and your boss!'

'He's my dad; it's a bit different.'

I slumped back into the bath and crossed my arms against my chest.

'I know she's hard work, Ivy.'

'I'm fed up.'

'I know you are, Ives.'

He leant over the bath and kissed me.

'I want to go to bed,' I said.

'Then get out of the bath and come to bed with me.'

He got me out of the bath and led me into the bedroom, kissing my neck as he did so. I could feel myself relax with just one touch of his lips on my skin. We moved onto the bed; he pulled the hoodie over my head, put his hands on my breasts, and moved his lips to my nipples. He kissed me softly, as my hands felt the outline of his abs, and moved down to his crotch. He pulled my pyjama bottoms off and opened my legs, kissing my inner thighs and squeezing the flesh around my lower body. When his lips touched my clitoris, I grabbed his hair and cried out. His tongue ran around the folds of my vagina, the wetness increasing with every touch. I came quickly, as I always did when he touched me like that. I got him in my hand and directed him inside me. We moved in unison, his lips on my mouth, collarbone, ears. His hands all over my body. He cried out my name, and I grabbed his hair tighter, knowing he was ready to come. When he did, he fell on top of me and pulled us both to one side. We lay there for a while, my back against his sweaty torso, holding each other tightly, letting our breath settle.

When I woke the next morning, Jamie had left for work. There was a note on the kitchen table:

Now you can stop going on about that stupid toothbrush.
I love you, Welshie.
Xxx

I went into the bathroom. The handle was clean; it looked as new as when I'd first bought it. He cleaned it every day until the day he left.

The phone rang, and I jumped. It was Mam.

'Are you having a little glass of something to take the edge off, my darling?'

'Just some wine, Mam.'

'Why don't you have a gin and tonic?'

'Because Dan is bringing some over with him.'

'Good. You're never going to lose any weight like that.'

'I'm not trying to lose any weight.'

'You're always saying you'd like a slimmer waist.'

'Am I?'

'I've been a size ten all my life, Ivy. But then again, I've got good genes.'

'I share your genes, Mam.'

'Well, you've also got your father's, which is unfortunate.'

'I'm going to go now, Mam.'

'OK, darling. I love you, try to get some rest tonight.'

'I love you too, Mam.'

I put on a Madonna playlist, sat on the sofa and finished off the bottle of wine. I no longer wanted to face reality. If I didn't allow myself to stop and think, everything would be OK. I could continue in a haze of drunkenness until one day ... well, who knows.

I called Dan to check where he was. He answered the phone singing 'Come on, Ivy' to the tune of 'Come on, Eileen'.

'You sound sober,' I joked.

'I'm fine, babe. I promise I'll be there in an hour.'

'Remember the gin, please?'

'Has Mags been on at you about the wine again?'

'She's a nightmare, Dan.'

'Don't you dare say that about Margaret.'

'Go away. I'll see you soon.'

I was about to hang up on him.

'Oh, one last thing, Ives . . .'

'What is it now?'

'I might have just taken ecstasy.'

Dan arrived three hours later; the pill was starting to wear off and his face was almost back to normal. I should have known he'd be late. When Dan takes drugs, he goes off on his own for a couple of hours. He'll always come back, but you're never quite sure where he's been, or what, and who, he's been doing in that time. It's best not to ask. When he's high, his eyes go wide, he loses all control of the muscles in his face, and one side of his mouth will curl upwards, where it'll remain for the next hour or so. He looks like the Joker, and it's terrifying. I've got photographic evidence of this face, and whenever he oversteps the mark, I bring it out to remind him of the power I have over him. It's my best bargaining tool.

He stumbled into the flat, got out a bag of cocaine from his wallet and slammed it down on the table.

'No, Dan. I'm not doing that.'

'Why not?'

'It's a truth universally acknowledged that doing cocaine whilst heartbroken is a terrible idea.'

'Don't quote me that Brontë shit.'

'It's Austen.'

'It's all the same.'

'Dan, I'll be fine with gin.'

He went over to the bookshelf and got out a dark-coloured hardback, laid it on the table, then carefully dabbed what looked like a mountain of cocaine onto it. He got out his credit card and cut two large lines. I was impressed with his precision and concentration, considering the state he was in. He rolled up a £10 note and put it on a line, snorting it up in one swift go. He sniffed and dabbed his nostrils with his index finger, shaking his head ever so slightly to ensure the last bits were all eaten up.

He turned towards me.

'I think it would be wise of you to have some of this,' he said.

'You are so annoying; do you know that?'

'I thrive off it, Ivy.'

'I can't remember the last time I did coke. I don't think I'm very good at it.'

'Trust me, you will be.'

I took the note to the powder and snorted a line. It felt harsh and cold, and when it touched my tongue I was surprised at how bitter it tasted.

'Ivy, we are going to have a fabulous time tonight.'

'Are we?'

We danced the night away in the living room, spilling our drinks on the floor and stamping our feet. At one point, I went to get more gin and Dan went to the bathroom. When six songs played and he still wasn't out, I turned the music down and knocked on the door.

'Dan, are you all right in there?'

He didn't reply, but I could hear the tap running, so I went back to the lounge. A few moments later, I heard the bathroom door open. I assumed he was coming out, but when he didn't, I walked over to check on him. He was standing in the doorway, with his head between his thighs, breathing excessively loudly.

'Dan, what's wrong with you?'

'The E,' he said. 'I've come up again.'

I laughed.

'Don't you dare, Ivy. This is serious, I can't feel my face.'

I put my arms around him, walked him through to the living room and lay him down on the sofa. I sat down beside him, put his head in my lap and closed my eyes. The room was spinning, and I felt clammy and nauseous. Anna was right: enough was enough. It was time to say goodbye to drugs and Marmite on toast, and hello to organic produce and early nights in bed.

Chapter 10

Thinking about retirement

By the time Tuesday arrived, my nerves had got the better of me and I was an anxious wreck. It felt like someone was holding a very small child to my head and they were screaming repeatedly whilst hitting me with a very large hardback book. The combination did not bode well for a productive working week.

'How is Suicide Tuesday going?' Dan messaged me on my lunch break.

'What's Suicide Tuesday?'

'You're so naive. Right, so, you get on it on Saturday, you're still high on Sunday, on Monday it's wearing off and you start to feel a bit teary, and on Tuesday you want to kill yourself.'

'Why did you make me do coke?' I groaned.

'Ivy, you had two lines.'

'Is this what it feels like every time?'

'Stop whinging.'

'Thanks for your enduring support, Daniel.'

'Will I see you before you go to Wales this weekend?'

'Not if I can help it.'

I walked down to the Embankment and treated myself to a

large portion of chips from the man in the van. It was a mild afternoon for March, so I walked along the river and found a bench to sit on. I hadn't realised how tired I was, and before I knew it, I was napping. Annoyingly, I was woken by a homeless man eating the chips out of the box in my lap. I was late getting back to work, and Jane was on a mission.

'Did you get John the Gavi?' she asked.

'I got him wine, yes.'

'Is it Gavi?'

'It's white wine; the woman on the phone told me it was good.'

'Oh Ivy, this isn't good enough.'

'It's wine. I didn't think it would be an issue.'

'This is disappointing.'

'I'm sorry, but it's here now. What am I meant to do?'

'I need you to send it back and order the Gavi.'

'But the drinks are tonight; it won't arrive in time.'

'Well, you should have thought about that, shouldn't you?'

She left my desk and I put my head into my hands. Lisa shot me a look and emailed to say that her boyfriend could help us get the Gavi. I had tears in my eyes as I replied, 'THANK YOU', and called her a lifesaver; I was in no position to lose my job over an incident regarding crisp Italian grapes. She read my reply, looked directly at me and mouthed, 'Jane is a bitch.' At least Lisa was on my side.

I don't know what Lisa's boyfriend Paddy does for a living, but by 4pm that afternoon, the wine was in reception, ready to be collected. I went downstairs and was greeted by a young boy, scruffy haired and tracksuit bottomed, sitting on the crates. I said I was Ivy and that the wine was for me and he nodded, said, 'Ta, love,' and ran off. When I told Lisa about the boy, she said, 'Ah, Lynchy,' and laughed to herself. I asked her to elaborate, but she wouldn't. I also asked how we could pay Paddy back, but she said it didn't matter; he called in an overdue favour. Strange that the crates had Tesco signage all over them.

I set up the wine, crisps and dips in the communal area of the office, before taking a bottle for myself. The Town Hall started at 5pm and everyone gathered early to make the most of the free booze and snacks. I stood at the back nursing my wine while John made a speech. He thanked the sales team for their tremendous work on securing the biggest client we'd ever had, while I was livid not to even get a mention. To him, it was only admin, but I was the one who'd worked late doing all the paperwork. I asked for a pay rise but was told they couldn't look into the request until the next financial year. The relationship manager, however, was awarded a weekend away to Stockholm for the deal, on top of his bonus. All he did was what was asked of him in his job spec. I sent John daggers across the room and downed glass after glass of wine. I didn't even try to hide it. Everyone knew I was a fiancé down and everywhere I looked, people were staring at me, giving me half-smiles and cocking their heads to one side. I thought I might as well make the most of it.

Ethan stopped me as I was walking back to my desk.

'You coming out with us, tonight?' he asked.

Ethan and his team liked to go to the West End, lose about £200 each in the casino, get a KFC at 5am then pass out on the tube home. I mulled this over in my head for a split second before remembering my new-plan: organic produce and early nights in bed.

'No, I need to go home,' I said. 'And besides, I'd only get drunk and cry on you.'

'You forget I have three sisters; I'm all for tears.'

'Men cry too, Ethan.'

'Nah, real men don't cry,' he said, winking at me.

'Remind me again how old you are, Ethan?'

'I'm twenty-three, Ivy. Never too young for you.'

'You're an idiot,' I said. 'And I'm going home.'

'I'll remember this next time you need saving from Lisa and her guitar.'

'I do owe you for yesterday, thank you.'

'Your face when she started crying during the Coldplay medley. Genius.'

'Goodnight, Ethan,' I said.

'You're missing out, Ivy,' he said, downing his bottle of Peroni.

I called Dad on my way home.

'I can't do this anymore,' I said.

'Yes, you can, Ives.'

'I spent the afternoon panicking because I'd bought the wrong sort of wine. Is this what my art history degree was for?'

'Darling, as long as you're happy, that's all that matters.'

'Do I sound happy?'

'You need to pick up your paintbrush again. That always made you happy.'

'Yeah, maybe.'

'How's your friend, Lisa?'

'She's doing my head in. It's just one too many acoustic sets to handle.'

'Don't lose her, Ives. You always need one work ally.'

'Also, I think her boyfriend Paddy is a criminal.'

'Well, that's not ideal.'

'What are you and Mam doing tonight?'

'I think we're going salsa dancing.'

'I thought she said the instructor was picking on her?'

'Yeah, but she's on holiday now and they've hired a young Brazilian male teacher to cover her classes, so she's dead keen again.'

'Sounds about right.'

'I love you, darling. Don't let the bastards get you down.'

'I'll do my best.'

When I got home I put on the Christmas special of *The Office*, even though it was nearly April and I knew full well that Yazoo's 'Only You' would send me into a pit of gloom. I carried on watching regardless; the song came on and Dawn came back into the Christmas party, clutching the present from Tim. I looked over at my £80 Jo Malone room diffuser from Jamie. He was always so generous. Nobody spends that much on a room diffuser for themselves, do they? To be honest, I hadn't even known what one was.

I still hadn't heard anything from Jamie's parents. I expected a text, at least, but to be honest, I had no clue as to what the etiquette was when it came to messaging your ex in-laws. I messaged Mia and told her that, with all her spare time, she should start creative writing again, and write a rule book on how to handle break-ups gracefully, dedicating it to her best friend Ivy. She was less than enthusiastic.

I worried that Jamie's parents thought I'd done something wrong, that I could have behaved better, worked harder at our relationship. I tried to remember how I was with them, how I presented myself, all the while trying to convince myself that I'd done a good job. Deep down, I knew they loved me. Well, Cressida loved me. I don't think Will is capable of loving anything other from himself. To say our families are different is an understatement, but Jamie loved being with my family, and he made me feel welcome at his. He longed for chaos and silliness; in his house, there was mainly silence, but with us lot, we're either shouting at each other or crying with laughter – there isn't really an in-between.

The first time he met my parents was at drinks in my old local in Stoke Newington. He'd already met Anna and Mark, who loved him, but I waited a little longer before introducing him to Mam. I told her to be on her best behaviour – don't talk over everyone, don't get too drunk, and don't mention money. Obviously, this went in one ear and out the other.

'So, Jamie,' Mam said, two glasses in, 'how many holiday homes do you have?'

I couldn't help but laugh. Dad said, 'Jesus Christ, Mags,' and got up from his seat to go to the bar.

'Well,' Jamie said, hesitantly, 'we have one in Nice, and a chalet in Verbier.'

Mam nodded enthusiastically in response.

'And then of course there's the London flat,' she said.

'Yes, that's the one I live in.'

I rolled my eyes at Mam and mouthed, 'Stop it.'

'I do love Bermondsey,' Mam said. 'It's a pretty little area.'

'Yes, it is nice. But, I much prefer where Ivy lives.'

'Do you? Why?'

'The people are livelier, and louder.'

'What, you mean the crack addicts?'

'Mam!' I said, in disbelief.

Jamie laughed.

'There's a lot more going on, that's for sure,' he said.

He turned his face to look at me and squeezed my hand.

'Well, this bodes well,' Mam said.

'Yeah, it does,' Jamie said, leaning over and giving me a kiss. Mam gave me a wink and went to help Dad at the bar.

'I'm sorry,' I said. 'She can be a bit much.'

'She's brilliant,' Jamie said. 'Absolutely brilliant.'

On the walk home, he couldn't stop telling me how much he loved my parents.

'They're so ... normal,' he said.

'Normal?'

'Yes, normal.'

69

'I've never heard anyone say that about Mam before.'

'You all talk so much ... and so fast,' he said.

'Yes, but everyone in Wales is like that.'

'How do you ever have a proper conversation?'

'You don't, you just talk over each other until one of you eventually gets tired and gives up.'

'Oh, right.'

'You'll get used to it,' I said.

'Do you think your dad liked me?'

'He loved you. You love rugby and hate Arsenal; what's more to like?'

'I wish my dad was like Tony.'

'Your dad is nice enough.'

'Nice enough?'

'Sorry, it wasn't meant to come out like that.'

'You're lucky, Ivy, to have them.'

'I know.'

'And I'm lucky to have you.'

I pulled him into me and kissed him.

'I don't know what I did to deserve you, Jamie.'

He smiled, took my hand, and we carried on walking down the street.

It was so different with Jamie's family. With mine, everything was laid out on the table, but I could never work his out. I never understood his dad, how he could be so distant and lacking at home, but so rude and domineering at work. I liked his mother, but of the countless times I spent with his family, there was only one time where we spoke openly. In hindsight, we should've done it more often. Maybe then things would have been different.

The weekend after Anna found out that their first round of IVF was unsuccessful, I went to Hambleton. I was in the grand library, not reading, but staring up at all the books, waiting for something to jump out at me, when Cressida walked in.

'Can't quite decide, Ivy?' she said.

I turned around to find her standing at the back of the room in her riding get-up; her hair was messy and she had mud all over her jodhpurs. It was one of the rare moments I saw her look totally relaxed – no fuss, no make-up or uptight hairdo. She was completely natural, and she looked gorgeous.

'I've been trying to pick out a book, but nothing's jumping out at me,' I said.

'What about a bit of Jilly Cooper?'

'You look like you've come straight out of *Riders*,' I joked.

'Ah, so you have read it then?' she said, smirking.

'I haven't, no. It's not really my thing.'

'Good, and don't. It's quite poor.'

I went back to the bookshelf, running my fingers across the hardback spines. I could feel her watching me.

'I think I'm going to take a bath before dinner,' I said.

'Now, wait a second. Shall we have a glass of wine first?'

'Do you have anything stronger?'

'You don't have to ask me twice, Ivy,' she said, and walked across the room to the drinks trolley. It was my favourite piece in their home; a glamorous mid-century number laden with gilt-bronze. I fell in love with it as soon I saw it; it's the sort of thing my dad would love, so I asked Cressida where they got it from. It was an antique, and when I tried to find a replica online, the closest thing I could find was priced at a hefty £2,980. I found Dad a knock-off one on eBay for £72, and he was none the wiser.

She poured us both some whisky and invited me to sit down on the sofa with her. We were quiet for a moment or so; I kept looking down at her perfectly manicured nails, thinking about the level of upkeep that must take.

'We missed you riding today,' she said.

'Sorry, I'm being a bit useless this weekend.'

I played with the tumbler, stirring the ice around with my finger.

'You know, Wills and I tried for years before I fell pregnant with Jamie.'

'I didn't know,' I said.

'Eight years. We almost gave up.'

'That must have been hard.'

'I'm sure it was hideous, Ivy. But, if I'm honest, I can't quite remember it now.'

'That's what happens.'

'What happens?'

'How we cope. We block things out.'

'Hmmm,' she mused. 'It's not very helpful though, is it?'

'I don't know.'

'I'm of the firm belief that we must come to terms with reality, as harsh as that may be.'

'Perhaps.'

'Do you think Anna has come to terms with it?'

I knew that Jamie had told her what Anna and Mark were going through, but we'd never discussed it before now.

'I . . . I don't know.'

'And how are you in all of this?'

'I'm . . . I'm fine.'

'It's awful seeing someone you love go through something like this.'

'It's . . . it's just that it's this massive elephant in the room.'

'Have you tried talking to her?'

'Anna?'

'Yes, of course, dear.'

'I'm not very good at this sort of thing.'

'Yes, you are.'

'I'm not.'

'Well, maybe you need to try a little bit harder.'

She gave my knee a squeeze. I shifted my feet and drank what was left of my drink.

'I think we're ready for another,' she said, taking the glass off me.

'Thank you, Cressida.'

'For what?'

'For being honest.'

'You really are a breath of fresh air, darling. Now, let's ask Bea to run you a warm bath.'

Chapter 11

Those bloody Germans

There comes a point on the train journey that you hit the 'deep south' of Wales; where the accents get stronger, the banter louder, and the people drunker. Usually that's when I take my headphones out of my ears and lap up the noise in the carriage, but not even the drunken, dulcet tones of Swansea's finest could cheer me up that night. Suicide Tuesday had crept into Friday and my mood on the train was at an all-time low. I told Anna to stay in London; she needed to relax, and a weekend with Mam would be anything but relaxing.

When I got home, I found Dad in the study, Tia Maria in hand. He got up from his seat and hugged me fiercely. I could smell dry sweat on him.

'Have you not showered today?' I asked.

'Your mother was taking ages so I gave up and came downstairs.'

'Why didn't you use my bathroom?'

'You know she doesn't let me "spoil" more than one room, Ives.'

'Where is she?'

'I assume she's gone to Linda's.'

'Good,' I said. 'Some peace and quiet.'

I put my stuff down and went to sit on the floor beside his feet. The weight of the world feels much lighter when you're sitting beside Dad. His quiet energy relaxes you, unlike Mam's, which often makes you want to take a Valium.

'Can I join you?' I asked, pointing to the drinks trolley.

'Ivy, my greatest joy is sharing a Tia Maria with you.'

I got up and poured myself a glass. I shot him a look and he winked, so I poured him another. He turned the volume up on the telly; he was watching a programme called *Saxons, Vikings and the Celts*.

'Dad, what is this?'

'It's illuminating.'

'You're taking the piss.'

'Honest to God, I'm not.'

'But the title alone ... '

'It's a fascinating genetic history of the people of the British Isles.'

'Fucking hell, Dad.'

'Stop swearing so much; you sound like Gramps.'

'Sorry. How is he?'

'Up and down, my love. He'll be over the moon to see you.'

'Yeah, me too.'

'Just don't mention the nurse.'

'Is he still banging on about having a male nurse?'

'It's all he can talk about, Ivy.'

'God, he is going to do my head in this weekend, isn't he?'

I took a long sip from the crystal tumbler and tried to focus my attention on the science of our descendants around the world. After a couple of minutes, Dad spoke again.

'Your mother and I love you very much. You know that, don't you?'

'I know; I love you too.'

75

'And we both think that Jamie is a pleb.'

'That's ironic because, in the true meaning of the word, we are the plebs.'

'Don't be facetious.'

'Good word.'

'He's a complete idiot.'

'Thank you, Dad.'

He stroked my hair and bent down to give me a kiss on my head.

'You're a beauty, and he's an idiot. That's that.'

'Thanks.'

'Now shut up and watch the programme with me.'

It was the first time I'd smiled all week.

I slept fourteen hours that night; it was such a good sleep that I felt unsettled by how relaxed I was when I woke. I got up and quickly went downstairs, feeling ravenous and a tad hungover. I found Mam pottering in the kitchen.

'My darling!' she cried when she saw me. 'I'm so sorry I didn't get to see you last night. Such drama with Linda . . . her son is engaged to that awful fat girl.'

She grabbed me and started kissing me all over my face.

'Mam, stop it. You're suffocating me.'

'Darling, you look well, considering.'

'Thanks.'

'Are you OK in the spare room, my precious baby lamb?'

'Do I have a choice, Mam?'

'Not really, darling. Anyway, I'm sorry about last night, I thought I'd be home but, well, this whole saga. I feel terrible for Linda.'

'Do you feel terrible for Linda because her son's marrying someone you deem to be of larger size, or because she is in fact awful?'

'Don't do that, Ivy.'

'Do what?'

'Make me look bad.'

'Be kind, Mam. That's all.'

She was getting enough food out of the fridge to feed a small village: croissants; jams; berries; bacon; eggs; mushrooms; tomatoes and spinach.

'Who's coming over for breakfast?' I asked.

'Ivy, it's lunch. You're going to have to make this yourself. I've got so much on.'

'I'm not going to eat all of this, am I?'

'You must be hungry – you and your father polished off a good few Tia Marias last night.'

'As if you can talk!' I laughed. 'Where are you going, anyway?'

'To the golf club, darling. It's Saturday.'

'What happens on a Saturday?'

'Don't get me started. Janet and her friends always get there before us and steal the balcony seats.'

'It's not even warm enough to sit on the balcony.'

'Not today, though. Today, I will be ready.'

'Ready for what?'

'To take our seats back.'

'Right.'

'Makes my blood boil. It's like being at an all-inclusive with bloody Germans.'

'Are you referring to the incident in Greece? You're the one who got told off for trying to save four sun loungers at six in the morning.'

'Ivy, whose side are you on?'

'So, you're not coming to the hospital with me?'

'Such Euro Trash.'

'Mam!'

'Give it a rest, Ivy. I'm chock-a-block today as it is.'

77

I took a bite from the croissant and as I did she ran to grab a plate from the cupboard and promptly put it under my hand.

'I'm not spending the afternoon clearing up your mess, darling. Not today.'

'No, you've got better things to do.'

'And Olga isn't coming until Tuesday.'

'Who's Olga?'

'Olga!'

'Saying her name like that doesn't add clarity to the situation.'

'Olga is our cleaner.'

'Why do you and Dad have a cleaner?'

'Your father and I are very busy; it made sense to get help.'

'Wow, Mam.'

'Don't use that tone with me, Ivy.'

She kissed me on the forehead, grabbed her bag and ran out the conservatory door, screaming, 'I love you.'

See, Valium.

I had a couple of hours to kill before hospital visiting hours started and I was in desperate need of some endorphins, so I downloaded the David Beckham episode of *Desert Island Discs*, put on my trainers and hoped that I could last forty-two minutes. With all the cigarettes and alcohol I'd consumed over the last couple of weeks, the odds weren't in my favour.

I ran along the cycle path, struggling to navigate the mud. It had been raining heavily the night before and everything smelt of weed. Jamie would know why grass smelt like weed after it rained; he loved trivia and I was always in awe of his ability to absorb the most pointless facts. One time at his parents', we were waiting for his father to get up from his laptop when his father cried, 'I'll be with you in a jiffy.' We waited another twenty minutes or so, as was custom, before Will surfaced from the bathroom, then we all got into the Land Rover and sped off to Jamie's aunt's house. We'd been driving in complete silence, as Cressida was raging that once again Will had prioritised emails over a family day out, when Jamie said, 'You know a jiffy is an actual unit of time, not just an expression.'

'What?' I said.

'A jiffy. It's an actual unit of time, or so it is in chemistry and physics.'

'Are you sure of that?' his dad asked from the driver's seat.

'Yes. It's the time it takes light to travel one centimetre in a vacuum – about thirty-three point three five six four picoseconds.'

'Gosh, how clever,' Cressida remarked.

I shot Jamie a look and mouthed, 'You're so annoying.'

We were holding hands in the back of the car. He grinned at me and moved his hand to my crotch. I let out a small yelp.

'Is everything OK back there, darling?' Cressida asked.

'Yeah, absolutely fine,' Jamie replied.

I mouthed, 'Stop it,' at him, but the look on my face said, 'More, more.'

I ended up running to the Anchor; I thought a little pick-me-up would help to see me through the afternoon. It's custom when running this route to cheat and stop in the pub for a drink before walking home. You can't argue with tradition.

There is something about a local pub, the intimate familiarity of having your order read out to you before you've even opened your mouth. Henry and Liz have owned the Anchor for years and Henry is one of the very few people my grandfather likes, which is odd because he's English. Most of the locals only tolerate Henry because Liz is Welsh-speaking and an epic boozer. People in South Wales respect such characteristics.

I walked through the door and Liz shouted at me from the bar.

'Ivy! *Dw i heb dy weld ti ers talwn!* *Shwmae?*'

'You know I don't know what that means, Liz,' I said, giving her a hug.

'You do, babes. You know *shwmae?*'

'It's something like, "hello"?'

'You're hopeless. How are you anyway, love? Not a good couple of weeks, Mam tells me.'

'Oh god, what did she say?'

'She's been singing your praises, said you've been a real trooper.'

'Well, that's a laugh.'

I sat on the stool and she passed me a gin and tonic. I gave her the whole spiel.

'I don't know what to say to you, Ivy.'

'I am sick to death of people telling me he'll come back, that I shouldn't worry, that I need to give him time.'

'Don't listen to anyone, babes.'

'I'm trying not to.'

'Break-ups are like grief, Ives. You can do whatever it is you need to do – go on a retreat, take up a hobby, shag every man you meet – but the reality is that the only thing that will help you is time.'

'You said it took you ten years to get over your first marriage.'

'Maybe it'll take you ten years to get over this.'

'That's not helpful, Liz.'

'Ives, you're going to be fine. Sounds like he needs a bit of space, but he'll be back. I know he will.'

'OK.'

'We'll just look at this as a very big blip.'

Chapter 12

Masturbate, when you can

By the time I got back from the run (pub), I was late for the hospital. Anxiety levels had peaked – no thanks to the gin – and I was adamant that I was going to be a total mess. Liz said that all I needed to do was put one foot in front of the other, but that seemed impossible.

I messaged Mia on route to the hospital: 'I don't think I'll be any good today.'

She immediately wrote back, 'Try masturbating.'

I didn't find this funny, and she knew I wouldn't because without missing a beat, she wrote, 'Sorry, tricky to know the tone. Be strong. Don't wear mascara.'

I stood outside the entrance for a few minutes, contemplating whether to have a cigarette. I knew full well that I would; I was just delaying going inside. I had two and hated myself afterwards. I went through the doors and into the loo to spray myself with Impulse Vanilla. Gramps loathes Impulse Vanilla, which is why I like to wear it so often. Well, that and the fact that it reminds me of when I was a fourteen-year-old, misbehaving with boys.

'You're not wearing that crap again, are you, babes?' he

would say, every time he smelt it. He didn't really have a leg to stand on; his fragrance of choice being Marks and Spencer's Aramis, which isn't exactly the height of sophistication, is it?

I walked the corridors trying to delay the inevitable. I started to play a little game with myself where I would try to guess the meaning of the Welsh signs dotted around the hospital. I was wrong every time. Hospital in French is *hôpital*, so why on earth is it *ysbyty* in Welsh? Microwave in Welsh is *pipty pong*, but hospital is *ysbyty*. Where's the sense in that?

I looked for the neurosurgery ward, but it was nowhere near the stroke unit – another unfortunate turn of events. I've always wanted to date a brain surgeon, and Mia's sister Gillian had mentioned there being some very attractive doctors on her ward at St Thomas'. I put a reminder in my phone to ask Gillian where her doctor pals hang out in London. I set the reminder for Saturday 25th March 2021. There was no way it was going to take me ten years.

'Ivy, *mun*!' I heard from the reception.

It was Owen, Gramps' oldest friend. Owen is in my top ten list of all-time favourite people. He speaks in a low, baritone voice, has an almighty laugh and his accent is so strong that even I find it hard to understand him sometimes. I sped up to greet him and gave him a big hug.

'Owen, how are you?'

'Same old, babes. Same old. It's brilliant seeing you, mind.'

He took my hand and led me into the men's ward. 'Gramps is good today, fair play.'

I don't think I'm being in any way dramatic when I say that the stroke unit is the worst place in the entire world. I forced a smile at the other patients; everyone looked so fragile and I wasn't at all prepared. When Gramps saw me, his whole face lit up, and for a moment or so, the world felt right again. He was wearing an ironed polo shirt, cashmere jumper, chinos and boat shoes. I never understood boat shoes. He'd been in hospital for a week and never owned a boat.

I gave him a kiss on the forehead and took his hand in mine, but before I had the chance to say anything, Owen had launched right back into their conversation, and I couldn't get a word in edgeways. They were discussing the latest bowls gossip, which I was thrilled about because it's more dramatic than a Christmas special of *EastEnders*. There was a big match that day and Alun wasn't playing because Alun had tickets to see Swansea and Manchester United at home at Liberty Stadium. Gramps was raging.

'Yeah, I know tickets were dead hard to get, *mun*, but so what? Where's the commitment you know, babes?'

I didn't know, but I went along with it anyway.

'How long are you down for this time?' he asked.

I'm down for the weekend, I said. I'd told him the same thing the night before, when I'd called leaving London, and every day last week when we'd spoken on the phone.

'Are you still going out with that Jamie fella?' Owen asked.

I didn't know whether Gramps had forgotten to tell Owen or Owen was just winding me up, so I said no and that I'd ended it. I added that I was fine and being single in London at thirty-one is great. I don't know why I said the last bit about me enjoying single life when clearly from both my demeanour and appearance I was enjoying very little at present.

'I think it's for the best, Ives,' Owen said. 'Why you went out with an Englishman in the first place is beyond me.'

'Owen, he's from Yorkshire. You'd like it up there.'

'Would we?' Gramps asked sarcastically.

'There are no Welsh people in Hackney. I've told you this before.'

This is true; we had this conversation all the time.

'Ivy, whatever you do, just don't marry an English man, OK, babes?'

'Too bloody right, Ivan,' Owen said.

I couldn't stop myself from rising.

'Hang on, Mark's English and you seem to like him.'

'Yes, but we can't have two in the family, can we?'

'This is ridiculous,' I said, throwing my hands in the air.

Gramps winked at Owen, who laughed and went back to his Mars Bars.

I stayed with Gramps until visiting hours closed, laughing so much my belly hurt. I thought I would come out of the hospital feeling a physical and emotional wreck, but being with him was exactly what I needed. For the first time in two weeks, I felt a smidgen of hope.

I got home to a quiet house, so I treated myself to a hot bath and some of Mam's expensive wine – the Chablis that she saves for 'special occasions' i.e. a Monday, Tuesday, Wednesday. I got into the bath and closed my eyes. It was the first time since the break-up that I hadn't sobbed the moment I was alone. I was feeling smug about this when my phone went off and I started crying at the fact that it wasn't Jamie. Maybe next time, I told myself.

I walked downstairs to get another bottle from the fridge when I heard Mam and Dad come through the door. Mam was shouting my name.

'I'm in the kitchen,' I said.

They came in; Mam was tipsy and Dad looked a bit broken.

'Your father's annoyed at me,' she said, kissing me on the cheek.

'I'm not annoyed, I'm disappointed,' Dad said. He was enjoying this.

'Don't blame me, blame Linda. No, blame her son's fiancée.'

'Not again, Mam ...'

'She's going for a strapless dress. Huge mistake, Ivy.'

'It's one day. Why does everyone get so worked up about one day?'

'You didn't start any diet, Ives. You didn't have to.'

'Right, Ivy and I are going to have a Tia Maria and watch last night's *Graham Norton*. You, Margaret, are off to bed.'

'Is anyone going to ask about Gramps?' I asked.

'Oh, yes, sorry. How is he?' Mam asked.

'He was on great form. Owen was there too.'

'Oh, Owen. He's such a treasure.'

'Yeah, he really is.'

'I'm sorry I couldn't come today, darling. You know how busy I've been.'

'Did you meet Steven?' Dad asked.

'No, who's Steven?'

'Tony, stop it.' Mam said, as she went to whack him in the arm but missed and ended up hitting the cupboard instead.

'He's your grandad's bed neighbour. Just wait until you meet him and Louise,' Dad said.

'Who's Louise?' I asked.

'His daughter. She likes to go on a bit.'

'Oh, Tony. Stop it.'

'I'm only saying. I'm looking forward to Ivy reporting back,' he said, eyebrows raised.

Mam tottered off upstairs, leaving me and Dad alone. He was staring at me, eager to say something.

'Spit it out, Dad.'

'I know your mother can be difficult, but you have your way of dealing with things, and she has hers.'

'I wished she'd come today, that's all.'

'Ives, you're only here for the weekend; she is up in that hospital every day, speaking with the doctors, making sure he is comfortable. She's had a day off, that's all.'

'OK, I'm sorry,' I said.

'Give her a little bit of a break, will you?'

I nodded and we went into the other room to watch TV.

I went up to bed a little later, but I couldn't get to sleep. I lay there thinking about what Mia had said, about masturbating being calming. I closed my eyes and tried to think about something besides Jamie that might turn me on, but all I could think about was him going down on me.

'Perfect,' I whispered to myself. 'I can't even bloody masturbate.'

Chapter 13

Shake it off

I had the drowning dream again. This time, the boat sank up to the top deck where I was reading my book, allowing me to swim into the open water and onto shore. In the dream, I was scared, but it wasn't far to swim, and I knew that in the end, I would be safe. I told myself I needed to get one of those idiotic, 'what do your dreams mean?' books. Of course, I knew what the dream meant; I just thought I'd feel better with some written confirmation from WH Smith.

I went downstairs to find Mam in the living room, watching *Game of Thrones*.

'Did you know Ramsay Bolton is Welsh?' she asked.

'Iwan Rheon? Yeah, he can't be anything else with a name like that.'

'He's got a kind face, doesn't he?'

'I guess.'

'A strong surname too: Rheon.'

'Where are you going with this?'

'He'd be a good suitor.'

'Mam, nobody talks like that.'

'He's the sort of boy I want you to go for now. Someone Welsh.'

'Right. Any other trait?'

'It's a start, darling.'

I walked out the room. Despite my very best intentions, I was close to killing her.

We arrived at the hospital right on time for visiting hours, and found Gramps sitting up in bed reading the paper.

'Have you brought my shirts, Mags?' he asked.

'I brought some a couple of days ago, Dad.'

'They're dirty.'

'They're not, I can see them right there,' she said, pointing to the small cupboard next to his bed, which housed six pristine polo shirts.

'And my shoes?'

'You've got your shoes.'

'My other shoes.'

'Dad, I'm not discussing this now.'

'Bang out of order, mun.'

She ignored this and went into a rant about the golf club. Gramps had recently become upset with the 'riff-raff' clientele. In his words they were 'lowering the tone'.

'And another thing: the eggs. Don't get me started on the eggs,' Mam said, taking his hand in hers.

Gramps propped himself up in bed, as if he were about to launch an attack.

'What happened this time?' he asked.

'They were meant to be poached but they were practically hard-boiled.'

'Hard-boiled!'

'I know, Dad. I was fuming.'

'The place is going to the pits, mun.'

'It's unacceptable.'

'Not to state the obvious, but why don't you go somewhere else?' I asked.

'What, and let them win?' Mam said. 'No. Out of the question, Ivy.'

'Mags, I've said it before and I'll say it again: the fly that flies from the shit flies highest,' Gramps said.

I got up, pretending I needed the bathroom.

I walked the long route back to reception, playing the game with the Welsh signs again. I didn't get any of them right. I checked my bag and made sure I had all my supplies before walking outside. My family are fine with me smoking, but we all pretend that I don't. Every time I have a cigarette, I go through this whole palaver of getting out antibacterial gel, mints and body spray to apply after, and everyone kindly goes along with it and pretends I don't smell of rancid smoke. There's no logic to it.

I went back to the ward to find Mam at the reception; she was talking to one of the male nurses about Tuscany. She loves doing this; she will force anyone and everyone to listen to her go on about the latest holiday she's been on. I mouthed, 'Stop it,' to her and went back over to Gramps. His bed neighbour, Steven, was asleep but there was now a woman sat beside him, who introduced herself as Louise. Within a couple of minutes, she asked me where I lived.

'I live in London,' I replied.

'Oh . . . whereabouts?'

'East, a place called Hackney.'

'Not for me, London.'

I didn't know how to respond so I got my phone out and pretended to look busy, but she started up the conversation again.

'The trouble is, I don't really like people,' she said.

'OK . . . '

'And London's full of them, isn't it?'

'Full of what?'

89

'People.'

'Yes. It's a busy place.'

'And that train! Well, I can't think of anything worse.'

'The tube?'

'Yes!' she said, leaning in to me and lowering her voice as if she was about to share her deepest, darkest secret.

'You know, I was down there one time, years ago now ... I had my suitcase with me ... I remember it well because I'd just bought a new one from TK Maxx; it had a pink handle, and I had tied a white ribbon to it. You know, so I could tell it was mine.'

I nodded, not knowing where on earth this was going.

'Anyway, not a single soul helped me.'

'That's a shame,' I said.

'I couldn't believe it.'

'People are in a rush, aren't they?'

'A rush! It's rude is what it is.'

'Well—'

'And then there's the coffee. Now, I go down to Bar Italia for my coffee, see. I've known Paolo for years and his father knew my father well.'

She paused and nodded to herself.

I looked over to Gramps, who was avoiding all eye contact.

'Oh yes, Paolo makes the best coffee.'

I didn't know what to say, so I simply nodded my head in agreement.

'You know where the coffee comes from, you know?'

Again, more nodding.

'None of this Starbucks malarkey. Can you believe they can charge four pounds for a coffee? Four quid! And you know they never spell my name right. It's not hard is it – L.O.U.I.S.E.'

She sighed deeply before starting again.

'And Paolo knows you, you know, love? We're a community.

People know my family name. It's Thomas, if my father hasn't already told you.'

'Lovely name, Thomas,' I said.

Christ, Dad certainly wasn't wrong about her going on.

'That's another thing. My friend Tanya said you don't have an Asda down here?'

'That's not strictly true, we do have some—'

'No Asda!' she interrupted. 'Where am I meant to do my weekly shop?'

'Louise!'

It was Steven; he was still lying down, and his back was turned towards us, but the voice definitely came from his bed.

'Oh Dad, you're up,' Louise said.

'Course I'm bloody up. Your voice is like a foghorn, Lou.'

'I'm only talking to . . .' She looked at me to get my name.

'It's Ivy,' I said.

'See, I'm only talking to Ivy.'

'Ivy doesn't want to hear you go on about bloody Paolo. You never shut up about him, mun!'

Louise blushed and started faffing with her handbag.

I stifled a laugh and in came Mam with the doctor.

'Can we bring the curtain around, so we can discuss your grandfather's charts in privacy?' the doctor said.

'Yes, that would be great,' I said.

I thanked Louise for the chat and closed the curtain around us.

'Ivy, your mother tells me you'd like to speak to me about your grandfather and his care?'

'Yes, that would be good,' I said.

'He is making good progress. We have to monitor his blood pressure closely, but it's stable.'

'Good.'

'He's getting the best care that we can give him.'

For some reason, this comment annoyed me.

'Why say "that we can give him"?'

'I'm sorry, I don't follow?'

'Well, what if your care isn't even that good, but that's just the best you can do? What does that even mean?'

'He is getting the very best treatment, I assure you.'

'And what about physiotherapy?'

'He's having intensive physiotherapy.'

'Yes, but how many times a week, a day?'

'Currently, about two times a week.'

'That's not very intensive, is it?'

Mam opened her mouth but stopped herself before she said anything.

'What? Mam, it's not intensive. Sorry, but, why isn't he having more sessions?'

'Ivy, calm down, mun,' Gramps said, holding my hand to his chest.

'I am calm. But that's not a lot, is it?'

'We have a lot of patients undergoing physiotherapy and these are our resources at present.'

I looked at the doctor, who was trying his very best, and at Gramps, who just wanted me to stop asking questions.

'OK. OK.'

'Is there anything else I can help with?'

'No, thank you.'

'If you have any further questions, please come and ask either myself or one of the nurses. We're here to help.'

The doctor opened the curtain and left. Louise was nowhere to be seen and Steven was sitting in silence eating his jelly. He smiled at me, this lovely, warm smile, and my heart sank. Gramps pulled me over so that I was sitting on the bed next to him. I lay my head on his chest.

'Come on, babes. Have a *cwtch*,' he said.

'Sorry,' I said, and looked at Mam for a bit of reassurance. She didn't say anything, which made me feel even worse.

'I'm fine. Look at me! Fit as a fiddle, aren't I?' Gramps said.

'Yeah. Sorry.'

'Don't be so tense, mun.'

'I'm not tense,' I said.

Mam said we should go as I had a train to catch. I held Gramps close and tried my hardest to look positive. I told him I'd be down in a few weeks, with Anna, and he assured me he'd be back home by then. He couldn't wait any longer to watch *Sleepless in Seattle*.

We got into the car and I burst out crying. I couldn't handle the doctor standing there telling us there was no improvement, that this was it. How long would this be it for?

Mam held me as I sobbed onto her shoulder and apologised for my behaviour. I know they were only doing their best; it just didn't look like their best was that good.

Taylor Swift came on the radio and Mam started to sing along. I watched her as she got all the words wrong, before telling her that she sounded like a drowned cat. She looked at me and mouthed, 'You bitch,' and we burst out laughing.

I started the engine and we drove off home. 'Dad was right about Louise,' I said.

'What do you mean?'

'She doesn't half go on.'

'She just wants a chat, darling.'

'A chat? I had her whole life story, Mam. She told me the colour of her suitcase.'

'You can be so judgemental sometimes, darling.'

'I'm not being judgemental! Dad said the same thing.'

'Your father? Why doesn't he like Louise?'

'We've had this conversation, Mam.'

'No, we haven't'

'We have, last night.'

'No, I would've remembered.'

'You don't remember?'

'Ivy, you always do this,' she said, getting into a huff.

'What do I do?'

'You make things up to make me look bad.'

Chapter 14

18 days, 12 hours and 14 minutes

'It's a shame you can't keep the ring,' Mia said.

'In what world would it be OK for me to keep the ring?'

'You and I both know it'd make a gorgeous necklace.'

'Mia, I'm not keeping the ring.'

'What if I kept it?'

'Mia, stop it.'

'Fine, have it your way. This was my one chance for a killer rock, Ivy. My one chance.'

I said goodbye and hung up the phone. Mark came in from the kitchen.

'Here, see if this'll help,' he said, passing me a glass of wine. I took a large gulp. It did help.

'So, I talked to my uncle.'

'Oh God, he's going to throw me out, isn't he? I'm going to be homeless.'

'Ivy, you're not going to be homeless.'

'I'm going to be out on the streets, destitute, doing meth—'

'Where'd the meth come from?'

'Mia and I just watched Louis Theroux's documentary.'

'It's so good, isn't it? I love that man.'

I nodded in agreement.

'How am I going to cover Jamie's rent?'

'Aaron said he'll take five hundred.'

'What? Are you joking?'

'He was jilted at the altar, remember? He's sympathetic.'

'Wasn't he jilted at the altar because his fiancée Claire found sexy texts to another woman on his phone?'

'Do you want to stay in the flat or not, Ivy?'

'Yes! I've always liked Aaron . . .'

'Come on, he's not so bad.'

'Didn't he also shag his best friend's pregnant sister in—'

'Ivy!'

'OK, I'll stop. I'm very grateful.'

'It's easier if he has someone he knows living in it. Plus, he's minted. Just pay the rent on time and don't piss off the neighbours.'

'I can do that.'

Mark raised an eyebrow.

'You might need to take him out for dinner next time he's back from Dubai.'

'Fine. I can manage one dinner with him. You've got to come, too.'

'Are you paying?'

'Guess I'll have to.'

'Don't let him choose the restaurant.'

'Thanks, Mark. The thought of moving . . . I can't . . .'

'I know, don't worry.'

'In the spirit of being amazing and doing very kind things for me, can you also give Jamie my ring back, please?'

'God, Ivy. Anything else?' he joked. 'If that's what you want, of course.'

'I know he's away with work, so you could drop it off at the office—'

'How do you know he's away with work?'

'He put it in the shared calendar.'

'And you still check said calendar?'

'It's synced to my phone, Mark; it's out of my hands.'

He raised another eyebrow.

'OK, Ivy. Whatever you need.'

I took another gulp of wine.

'I can't believe it's been—'

'Eighteen days, twelve hours and—' I check my watch '—fourteen minutes?'

'Right. Well. That's that then.'

I looked across at Mark and felt an overwhelming sense of gratitude towards him. I felt the tears start to come.

'Mark?'

'Oh, no. Please don't start crying on me, I've had very little sleep and—'

'Just shut up. I need to say this,' I said, clearing my throat. 'You are a wonderful, wonderful man. Thank you.'

There was nothing else to say, so he turned the television back on and we sat in silence, nursing our drinks.

Mark was the only one who let me sit in silence. I didn't have to be active, or present, or avoid any elephants. Everyone else talked too much and sometimes all a person needs is to sit in silence and wallow. Well, that and have someone you trust pour you several glasses of wine until you felt numb and fell asleep.

I'd read an article about break-ups and the importance of taking back ownership of things you used to do together as a couple. For Jamie and me, that meant me cooking. I loved cooking for him, and it wasn't just because of the praise – give the man a plate of beans and oven chips and he'd be eternally grateful. I loved the effort of it all, the patience, time and love it required. It didn't feel right doing all that when I was the only one eating it.

I was trying my best with the organic food-delivery box, but the reality was that I had zero energy and I couldn't be bothered to make anything. I needed to get my act together, so I went to the bookshelf and picked out one of my Nigella Lawson cookbooks – if she couldn't revive me, nobody could. I landed on squid spaghetti, because I was craving carbs and I thought the squid would help make me feel more sophisticated. Plus, Nigella called it 'gangster food', which I found amusing.

Despite my best efforts, taking back ownership was proving to be difficult, and the following day, I had a complete meltdown in the dairy aisle of the supermarket. I couldn't find the right cheese, and I lost it. I ran out of the shop empty-handed and rang Mia. I couldn't get the words out; I just kept repeating 'pecorino romano' over and over again.

'At least do it in front of the onions, nobody would've thought anything of it,' she said.

'It doesn't work like that; they need to be chopped.'

'Really?'

'Yes.' I said, grateful for yet another one of her gaffes.

'You're coming to ours tomorrow night, right?'

The last thing I wanted to do was go to a party with a bunch of actors. She sensed my reticence and pleaded with me.

'I don't want to be around people, Mia. I look like shit.'

'That could never be true.'

'And I need to drink less.'

'Don't do that; don't make all these promises to yourself.'

'I can't remember the last time I went to bed sober.'

'I can't remember the last time I could fit into my denim cut-offs, but nobody likes a skinny bitch, Ivy.'

'What does that even mean?'

'I'm making "liquid cocaine", your favourite.'

'It's not my favourite.'

'Champagne and gin are your favourite.'

'I like them both, yes. But not together, in one drink.'

'Well, now you're just being difficult.'

The next morning, I had to have a word with myself and shut down the pity party. I looked in the mirror, mouthed 'get a fucking grip' and went for a run on the canal. I then paid £7 for a blue majik lychee boba juice because the woman in front of me in the queue ordered it and she had that J Lo glow that real people can only dream of. No, I don't know what majik is. Or boba, for that matter.

I went to Anna and Mark's for dinner before the party.

Mark greeted me at the front door.

'Oh good, it's you again,' he said.

'Sorry,' I said. 'Your wife invited me over.'

'Did she now,' Mark said, walking back into the living room.

'Ivy, good. You can help me chop,' Anna said, coming out of the kitchen.

'Mark's pleased I'm back again,' I said.

'Mark, come on. You heard about the supermarket saga. She needs all the help she can get.'

'Great, I'm your pity project.'

'Shut up and sit down.'

'I thought you wanted me to help you chop.'

'Changed my mind, you take forever in the kitchen and I'm starving.'

I sat on the sofa while Anna finished up the cooking, with Mark sat in silence in the armchair beside me.

'Mark, don't just sit there reading; talk to Ivy,' Anna said from the kitchen.

'Anna, I'm watching TV,' Mark replied.

'Ivy needs company right now and you're being boring.'

I mouthed, 'Sorry,' at him and turned up the television volume.

Anna came into the living room with a glass of wine for me and a pint of squash for her.

'When is your appointment?' I asked, as she sat down beside me.

'It's next week. It's just a conversation to talk through our options.'

'Options for IVF, yes?'

'Yes.'

'How are you both feeling about it all?'

Mark looked up from his book and smiled at Anna.

'Well, it's bullshit, isn't it? But there we go,' she said.

'It's total bullshit,' Mark said.

'I could murder a wine.'

'You're allowed to drink, aren't you?' I asked.

'It's more about me feeling that I'm doing everything I can to help move things along.'

She let out a big sigh, shrugged her shoulders and sank back into the sofa.

There we were, just a couple of thirty-something women, trying to navigate our own terrain of shit.

I arrived at Mia's and the first person I recognised was Noah's friend Rob. Rob works in radio and thinks that he's God's gift to women just because he made a 'Best of David Bowie' playlist that featured in *The New York Times*. I was assessing the room when Mia came up behind me, grabbed my hand and led me upstairs to the main bathroom. It's a little oasis, filled with big, leafy plants, candles, incense and oils: the perfect hiding place and my favourite room in the house.

'Why were you staring at Rob?' she asked, as she got out a book from the shelf called *The Art of Mixing* and went to sit in the bath. She pulled out a cardholder from her pocket and took out a £5 note and a Waitrose loyalty card.

'Mia, it's not even double digits yet.'

'It's a house party, Ivy. Stop judging me.'

'I'm not judging ... and I wasn't staring at Rob.'

She got out a packet of cocaine from her bra and started distributing it onto the book.

'He is fit though, isn't he?' she said.

'It's unsettling that someone can be so fit and so annoying at the same time.'

'I know, it's baffling.'

'Last time I saw him, he talked at me for about seven hours about Neurofunk,' I said.

'That's not a word.'

'Apparently it is; I had to look it up afterwards.'

'God, he's the worst.'

'I honestly didn't know whether to rip his clothes off or punch him in the face.'

'So tricky, isn't it?' she said, passing the book to me.

'Not for me, thank you.'

'As you wish, Ives,' she said, before inhaling the line and lying back in the bath.

'Nice nails by the way,' she said.

'I did them myself! And I did a deep conditioner. I'm practically a new woman.'

She lit a cigarette and sank deeper into the tub.

'Do you think you'll shag him tonight?' she asked.

'Who?'

'Rob! Keep up, Ivy.'

'No, God no. Too soon. I can't even masturbate at the moment.'

'Christ, that is bad.'

'I know.'

'Stay clear of all the actors tonight.'

'Everyone's an actor. You're an actor.'

101

'Well, no. I'm currently a barmaid and a telesales executive.'

'You've got so many talents, haven't you?'

'Look, it's going to be really, really shit for a while. Then it will be less shit, and hopefully, one day in the not-so-distant future, it will be sort of OK.'

'That's the best advice you've ever given me.'

'It's the coke talking. Now come sit in the bath with me.'

After putting the world to rights in Noah's dead aunt's bath, we went to join the others downstairs. I clocked Noah in the kitchen and spent most of the evening following him around; he was warm and kind, and not in the patronising way that everyone else was. More importantly, he made sure I didn't spend too much time with fit, annoying Rob. I kept looking over at him and being repulsed by his arrogance but then a second later I'd be thinking about what his hands would feel like on my bare breasts. It was a confusing time.

After drinking several glasses of Mia's deathly 'liquid cocaine', I took myself home. I could feel myself getting teary and nobody wants to see a woman cry, let alone at a party. I couldn't sleep that night; I needed the loo too much. I finally got up at 8am, determined to have a productive day. I needed new photo frames and object d'art that Jamie would have never approved of. To be honest, I don't approve of object d'art either, it's pointless tat, but the stark white walls were depressing and I needed something to keep me out of the pub.

Chapter 15

Meatballs to go

Anyone of sound mind would have realised that going to IKEA on a Sunday morning with a three-week hangover was, in fact, a terrible idea. But then again, I wasn't exactly 'firing on all cylinders', as Gramps would say.

I got there early and stood in the car park waiting for it to open. I overheard someone say that it's a shame how there aren't any IKEA shops in central London locations, but why on earth would you want to be reminded of a place like IKEA on a more regular basis? There was a man beside me talking to his wife about how excited he was about the hotdogs. Is this what we have become?

A few more smug-marrieds arrived and we all waited together in the dreary car park. I was wearing Jamie's old rugby jumper, which would make me look cute in an all-American high-school girlfriend sort of way had it not been for my sunken cheeks, greasy hair and anxious gait. I had such high hopes for the day, but the reality was that I couldn't be bothered to shower and I stank of booze.

I rang Dan, desperate to etch a plan.

'You're waiting for IKEA to open?' he asked.

'Yes, I'm in the car park.'

'This is getting really sad.'

'Sad?'

'Yes, as in pathetic.'

'I know what sad means, Dan.'

'You need a change of scenery, Ives.'

'I know! I'm trying. But one minute I'm glowing from all the juices and serums and overpriced crap that everyone's been forcing me to try, and the next I'm feeling nauseous after sinking two bottles of wine and chain-smoking till I can't breathe properly. It's relentless.'

'Babe, it's been three weeks. Give yourself a break. Listen, next week, we'll have a chilled one and do some boot camp. It will sort you right out.'

'I'm not paying twenty pounds for someone from the military to shout at me for an hour.'

'Well, that attitude isn't going to get you anywhere.'

'And when did you start doing boot camp?'

'I do it every Saturday, thanks very much.'

'*Every* Saturday?'

'Yes! On Friday I have a tuna poke and quinoa salad and I'm in bed by eleven with a Kiehl's clay mask. I do boot camp on Saturday morning, then hit the sauna and steam room before my disco nap.'

'Disco nap?'

'Yes, to get me charged up for Halo.'

'That sounds exhausting.'

'Exhausting or not, we're doing the nine am class next Saturday.'

'Fine, I'll book it today.'

'You know I'm right.'

'Yes, I know. Thank you.'

I picked up a few photo frames before making my way to

the café to get some food. I was determined to cook that day, so I picked up some of their 'famous' Swedish meatballs to go into a ragu. I knew that by calling them 'famous' they were going to be awful, but I was trying to stay upbeat in the face of adversity.

On the train home, I started getting stomach cramps. I got off the train without further delay, having suspected I'd followed through. I ran into a public toilet, where I sat clutching my stomach until my bowels opened and I finally had some release. It was a new low. I was too scared to get back on public transport, so I ordered an Uber and told him to step on it. As soon as I got home I threw my bags on the floor and called Mam, who picked up the phone in tears.

'Mam, what's wrong?' I asked.

'It's Khaleesi.'

'What?'

'Daenerys Targaryen.'

'I know who she is, but what's wrong?'

'Khal Drogo died.'

'You know he dies; you've watched it before.'

'It takes on a new meaning when you watch it again.'

'I can't have this conversation with you now, Mam.'

'Darling, what's wrong, you sound tense?'

'I *am* tense.'

'What's happened? Did Jamie ring you?'

'No, he didn't. He won't.'

'Oh, my precious baby lamb.'

'Stop calling me that.'

'OK, darling.'

'I'm going to go.'

'Not before you tell me what's wrong.'

'I had to run off the train earlier because I almost followed through.'

'Oh, darling. I am sorry.'

'I'm thirty-one, my fiancé has left me, and I'm basically incontinent.'

'It's far from ideal.'

'I need something to go right.'

'It will, it will.'

'Will it?'

'Yes, of course. Your father and I were just planning our holiday to Loch Lomond.'

'I am not coming with you.'

'Darling, you sound very angry.'

'I'm going to go now.'

'OK, I love you.'

'Yeah, love you too, Mam. Bye.'

I never went to the toilet in front of Jamie and when I told Mia this she said it was odd. Apparently, going to the loo in front of each other was an inevitable step in your journey together as a couple. My thoughts were, why would you ever want your sexual partner to see you wipe your bum? What good could come of that? I'd vowed never to go to the toilet in front of him; I was going to keep things classy, sexy and dignified.

Keeping things classy was harder than I thought, and quite early on in our relationship, I made a complete tit of myself. I had just started working for Jane and the Christmas party season was upon us. It was the first place I'd worked where they had money to take us out and I'd been warned to take it easy. Jamie said that for every glass of wine I had, I should have a glass of water – hydration was key to longevity. Nobody wants to be the drunken new girl who everyone makes fun of the day after the Christmas party. I wore a velvet dress with sheer black tights and knee-high boots – conservative, but stylish. I was feeling the most confident I'd ever felt and it showed; I was glowing. Probably due to all the sex Jamie and I were having.

Things in work were going well. The directors liked me, Jane was yet to show her true imperious self and Lisa hadn't started guitar lessons yet.

Considering it was their lives I was managing, not hers, I didn't seem to mind her self-importance and micro-managing so much – not yet, anyway. I had an inkling that she was a difficult and complicated woman but in no way did I realise what a total psychopath she was. This was when I was trying to see the good in everyone. Anna said that I needed to make more of an effort with Jane, and I was trying, but the woman brought her own herbal tea bags to the Christmas lunch and didn't eat any of the food. Enough was enough.

At the Christmas lunch, I was sat in-between Lisa, who was telling me that music was her true vocation, not accounts, and Gerald, who I'd recently caught staring at the Domino's menu on his computer screen for a full sixty minutes. I had little option but to drink, and I drank fast. We were in a pub in London Bridge, the name of which I have blanked out, and, like most pubs during the Christmas season, it got to 4pm and the place was heaving with merry working folk in crap Christmas jumpers and cheap reindeer headbands. By 6pm I'd had two Jägerbombs; by 7pm I'd drank what seemed like a pint of Baileys, and by 8pm, Lisa had us all on mulled wine. I could feel my legs going from under me. I could never take a Jägerbomb, let alone two. This is what happens when you try to fit in.

I spent a lot of time on the dance floor being swung around by Gerald who, it turns out, does a cracking rendition of 'Do They Know It's Christmas?'. By 9pm, I couldn't see straight.

I did an Irish exit and left the pub in spectacular speed, grabbing my bags and shouting, 'I love you,' to Lisa, who was crying into Gerald's lap about her latest row with Paddy. I wanted to call a taxi but I couldn't for the life of me figure out how to use my phone. So, I walked down Bermondsey High Street, towards Jamie's flat.

When I arrived outside his building, I pressed all the flat numbers, screaming his name, until the door opened and there, in his lounge pants and university rugby jumper, was the man himself.

'Ivy, what the hell are you doing out here? You're going to freeze to death,' he said, pulling me into the corridor and wrapping his arms around me. I closed my eyes and tried to find comfort in his chest, but everything started spinning, so I quickly moved away for fear I was going to be sick in his face.

'I didn't drink,' I said.

'I think that's a lie, Ives.'

'No,' I said. 'Water. I didn't drink any water.'

'Ivy, try not to burp in my face like that.'

'I'm hiccupping, Jamie.'

'You're burping, Ivy.'

When we got upstairs he sat me on the sofa and told me not to move, while he got a blanket to wrap over me, a pint of water and some paracetamol.

'Do you think it's odd that Jane brought her own tea bags to lunch?' I asked.

'Yeah, that is odd.'

'I think Gerald fancies me.'

'He's only human, Ivy.'

'Do you hate me?'

'No, I don't hate you.'

I got up and walked to the bathroom, but when I went to sit down on the toilet I couldn't work out how to take my tights off, and before I realised, it was too late. A bit of warm pee trickled down my legs and I knew right there and then that I was going to be sick. The sink was too far away, so I did the only thing I could do, and threw up in the bath. I was too drunk to clean any of it up, so I lay on the bathroom floor, closed my eyes and passed out.

Jamie wasn't in bed when I woke up the next morning. From the looks of things, he'd put me in the shower, but I had no recollection of anything after passing out on the bathroom floor. I pulled the covers over me and wished that I could crawl into a dark hole and never surface again, but when I looked over at the clock, I was already forty minutes late for work, so I sprung to action and ran into the living room. Jamie was nowhere to be seen, but there was a note on the kitchen table:

There's a box of Rennie in the cabinet and a bottle of Lucozade in the fridge. Take two Rennie with the Lucozade and you'll be right as rain.

I'll ring you later, Welshie.

xx

PS: I love you, and you owe me dinner.

There I was, navigating the cascades of romantic courtship and thriving.

Chapter 16

Richard Curtis

I bought the dream book and for £12.99 I was told that dreams featuring drowning are caused by fear and anxiety. Also, I might have been feeling overwhelmed. What a capital investment that was.

The nights were getting longer and the only real company I sought was Anna's. I went by one night after work to find her in the garden, her bare legs propped on the table, trying to soak up the last of the day's sun. She was playing with her hair the way she does when she's overthinking. She used to do this before exams; she would spend hours weaving her long auburn hair through her fingers. She'd scrunch her forehead up in an intense frown as she tried to learn yet another Carol Ann Duffy poem off by heart. She's ever so beautiful, especially when in deep concentration mode.

I stood by the window for a minute and watched her, until she caught my eye in the reflection.

'Ivy, I can see you staring, you weirdo,' she said.

I went over and gave her a kiss on the cheek.

'What were you thinking about?' I asked her.

'My inhospitable womb.'

I couldn't help but laugh.

'What's in the bag?' Anna asked.

'Well, one – wait for it – a dream book.'

'What on earth possessed you to buy that?'

'And two ... Rosé from Aldi, the one Mam was on about.'

'You brought Aldi rosé all the way up from Wales?'

'Well, yeah. Mam insisted. I can't keep it at mine, I'll just drink it, and you're not boozing, so this works.'

'I cannot believe you brought a five ninety-nine bottle of wine all the way from Wales.'

'Mam got me a case! It's good wine. She gave me some more fancy conditioner too.'

'You'd have us thinking you're living on the breadline.'

'Well, you'd think not being able to stomach anything would save me some money.'

'Has it?'

'No, it's mostly wine. Some gin, and now boot camp.'

'It'll be good for you. Don't you get bored running all the time?'

'Running is free, and nobody shouts at me.'

'Why don't you come to yoga with me?'

'I'm not into yoga.'

'You've never been to yoga.'

I pulled up a chair and sat down beside her.

'Dan said I was becoming pathetic.'

Anna laughed.

'The worst thing is, he's right. I know it's only been a month but I'm even beginning to annoy myself.'

Anna gave me a faux-sympathetic look.

'Also, and maybe you don't want to hear this ... '

'Go on ... '

'I can't masturbate.'

'What?' Anna laughed.

111

'I can't. I've tried, and I can't.'

'I think that's normal when you're feeling sad.'

'Is it?'

'Yeah. What about porn?'

'Anna, we are not having this conversation.'

'Oh, come on. Watch some porn.'

'I don't watch porn.'

'Never?'

'No, never.'

'Are you being serious?'

'Yes, don't look at me like that! I'm serious.'

'I always took you for a porn sort of person.'

'Can we change the subject, please?'

'Fine,' Anna said, laughing.

'Where is Mark tonight?'

'Down in Peckham. I told him he needed to get drunk, for the both of us.'

We sat in silence for a bit, Anna playing with her hair.

'How are you feeling about everything?' I asked.

'Not great.'

'I'm sorry, Anna. It's the worst.'

'The language these people use. It's so unhelpful. I mean, is my womb *actually* unfriendly? Is it, Ivy?'

'No, I'd say it's very friendly indeed.'

'Well, exactly. Inhospitable? I'll give them fucking inhospitable.'

'Try not to let it—'

'Could they make me feel like less of a failure?'

'I'm sorry, Anna. I don't know what to say.'

'I want a glass of wine and a baby. That's all.'

'That seems like an acceptable request,' I said.

When I got home later that night, I tried to masturbate, but being heartbroken and worrying about my sister's fertility didn't put me in the sexiest of moods. I didn't want to ask Anna what porn she watched because then I would start thinking about her and Mark watching porn together, and that's not a territory I wanted to delve into. There was only one thing left for me to do: boot camp.

The next morning, I met Dan in Regent's Park at 8.30am. He liked to arrive early; he said it was important to build up a positive mentality, stretch and familiarise myself with the new surroundings.

'Getting into the right mindset is so important, Ivy,' Dan said, as he clutched his protein shake. 'This isn't just a one-hour fitness class, you are going to move your muscles like you've never moved them before, creating a surge of growth hormones, which will in turn expand your mental fitness.'

'Sorry, what?' I said, dumbfounded.

'Ivy, get the fuck on board or get back on the tube to Hackney.'

'I am on board! But, considering in ten hours you'll be gurning your jaw off in Halo, I find it hard to take this routine seriously.'

'I am a complex, well-rounded individual,' he said. 'Also, ten hours? Are you kidding me? You know I never step foot in Halo before midnight.'

It was going to be a trying morning.

Dan had mentioned that the instructor Gabe was more motivational than drill-sergeant, which suited me fine. He was encouraging, but not too shouty, and didn't come right up to my face like I've seen them do on TV. When Gabe asked me if I was going to be OK using a high intensity mixture of kettle-bells, sandbags, and free weights, I said yes, of course. Despite my diet, which might mirror that of a moody fifteen-year-old, I consider myself fit. I played lots of sports in school and I run – not as regularly as I used to, but the thought is there.

However, what became apparent quite quickly was that, no, running the odd three to four miles once a week in-between smoking several packs of cigarettes doesn't give you the right to say that you can absolutely handle a 'total transformative body series' that takes your heart rate to such heights that you feel like it's going to burst out of your chest.

There was no way I was going to let Dan know that every time I did a burpee, I could feel my knee pop, or that, after the ninth squat, there was a tingling in my lower spine that made my whole back feel tight. Through mountain climbers, jumping jacks, air squats, squat thrusts and jump squats (why are there so many squats?), I put on a brave face and survived the whole sixty minutes.

'Ives, you are killing it,' Dan said, during the cool down.

We were lying on the grass, finally, and I was staring at the masses of grey clouds in the sky, praying for the rain to come and cool me down while trying my best to breathe through all the muscle pain and heartburn.

'I know!' I lied.

'I am impressed, babe. I thought you'd be shit, to be honest.'

'I've been trying,' I said, slowly. 'I've smoked much less this week, and I've barely drank any wine.'

'So proud of you. You should come back with me next week.'

I scrambled to find an appropriate excuse. My left calf was twitching. Why was it twitching?

'You know ... I might stick to running.'

'That's so dull and lonely!'

'Yeah, but ... now that I'm in the flat on my own ... and ... covering all the rent, I need to find cheap activities to do.'

'I thought you said Aaron was charging you pittance?'

'I mean yes ... it's much less ... but you know ... with the bills.'

'Shit, yeah, of course. Running it is then, babe.'

Thank the fucking Lord.

I put on a positive face for Gabe and thanked him for his support. Dan wanted to stay on with some of the others in the class and get some breakfast, but I needed to get myself home to a dark room and a cool flannel. I was sweating profusely and my whole face was blotchy and red.

I sat on the tube and listed reasons to be proud of myself:

I don't like mornings.

It's a Saturday, and I was awake at 7am.

It was picking with rain, a bit cold and any sane person would have stayed in bed.

I didn't complain ... not even once.

I lied about liking the class to make people feel better about their own life choices.

This will get me one step closer to looking like J Lo.

I didn't vomit, despite five near misses.

I didn't cry.

I didn't kill Gabe.

I didn't kill Dan.

Sitting there, excessively panting on the tube home, I felt like a new woman. An enormous sense of well-being washed over me; if I could achieve this, I could achieve anything.

Mark ran a marathon once and said that afterwards you forget the gruelling early morning runs in the rain, the boredom of staying in every weekend when your mates are out on the piss, the complete overhaul of your diet. Instead, all you can think of is: I ran a fucking marathon. I am a fucking warrior. This is how I felt after those arduous sixty minutes. It didn't matter that, on several occasions, I had to swallow my own vomit. No. I *was* a warrior.

I did go home and cry when a re-run of *Top Gear*, Jamie's favourite TV show, came on the telly, but that's neither here nor there. This was progress.

Chapter 17

Dorset with Hugh Grant

Even though my calves were on fire and I couldn't lift my arms up past chest height, I was starting to feel like things were on the up. After the best night's sleep I'd had in weeks, I called Mia to tell her about my reinvigorated state of mind and she suggested we spend the following weekend in Dorset, where Noah's mum lives. Mia is very much an all-or-nothing sort of girl, and she loved the idea of a wholesome getaway. There'd be home-cooked food and fresh sea air and my mother wouldn't be there. It was a win-win situation.

Mia's very close to Noah's family. His father died when he was young and his mother, Lucy, never remarried, which Mia said was a waste because she was very attractive for a middle-aged woman, which is sort of a compliment, I suppose. His older brother is a bomb disposal expert who also found time to row the Atlantic Ocean. Sadly, he got married after the row to a ridiculously attractive woman and is now off the market. I'd like to think that if he was single and in Dorset that weekend, he would have overlooked my desperation and intense loneliness, and we'd have embarked on a long and passionate affair.

Noah's mum lives in an incredible cottage with huge

exposed timber ceilings, fireplaces in every room and books everywhere. When I say everywhere, I really mean everywhere: I counted twenty-seven in my bathroom alone. There's a beautiful wildflower meadow out the back where Mia likes to get stoned, though I told her we would be doing no such thing that weekend. Lucy was also under strict instructions not to get any wine in. As Mia put it, 'We're going to be bored out of our minds.'

Getting out of London was a godsend. I was walking around on tenterhooks, petrified of bumping into Jamie. I had everything to say, and nothing to say. I agreed with Anna and Mia in that, although this was very much his decision, I needed time and space away from him to try figure out what I wanted. But it was hard, so hard in fact that seeing him was all I could think about. It consumed my every thought, and I had no idea what to do about it. So, I did nothing.

We drove to Dorset after work on Friday night, and went straight to bed. I'd been looking forward to waking up to a view of the sea, with the salty air coming through the windows. It was such a peaceful morning, all I could hear was the distant squawking of seagulls. It was a far cry from my usual wake up call of police sirens and chattering cockneys.

We spent the day reading the papers, doing puzzles and playing cards. We cooked soup with vegetables from the community garden and Lucy made us cookies from leftover pulp in her juicer. To think, only a week ago I had diarrhoea on the tube.

Lucy made us a vegan Pad Thai for dinner before she went out to play bridge. By 8pm I was ready for bed; my soul was nourished and I was exhausted by all the goodness and virtue, but Mia had other ideas and wanted to put a film on.

'Oh, oh! *Bridesmaids!*' she squealed.

'Something non-wedding related, please,' I said.

'*My Big Fat Greek Wedding?*'

'Mia ...'

'*Runaway Bride?*'

'Come on ...'

'*Bride Wars?*'

'Shut it.'

'*Father of the Bride?*'

'Stop!'

'*Four Weddings and a Funeral.*'

'Fine, go on then.'

I couldn't say no to Hugh Grant.

We drank green tea and discussed the many merits of John Hannah and how it's difficult to write upper-class characters with empathy, but if anyone could do it, Richard Curtis could.

The next day we woke early and went for a walk down to the beach. When I was younger I would always go to the beach with Gramps; he said there wasn't a problem in the world that couldn't be solved by watching the waves, and he was right. We used to laugh that we could taste fish and chips on our lips. Being by the sea brought me such comfort that I started making solo journeys to the beach whenever I had something on my mind. I felt very far from him that weekend; Dorset could never replicate the Gower and as much as Mia tried, she just wasn't as insulting or condescending as Gramps.

We walked for a couple of hours along the beach, holding hands. Even Mia was taken aback by the beauty of it all; she managed a whole five minutes without talking a hundred miles an hour at me. It was the most gorgeous day. We might have been starving, but we were zen.

When we got back to London that Sunday night, Mia dropped me off in Highgate and I ordered an Uber home. Doing nothing is very tiring, and I was looking forward to getting into bed and starting the week off on the right foot.

When was the last time I didn't skip six alarms and went into work on time? When was the last time I went into work without a slightly boozy aroma on me? This would be the week.

I was dropping off in the back seat when the driver asked me if I needed home insurance. I was about to tell him that I wasn't in the mood for mindless chat when I remembered that this was Uber, and I had a strong 4.7 rating to maintain.

'I'm all sorted for insurance, thank you,' I said.

'You own the house?'

'I rent it.'

'Do you know if your landlord has insurance?'

'I assume he does.'

'You don't have personal insurance, for you and your family?'

'I don't have a family. I mean, I don't have children.'

'Oh, you must be very young?'

'You're very kind. I'm thirty-one.'

'Thirty-one and no family?'

'Yes.'

'Are you single?'

'I am.'

'I am single too.'

'That's . . . good.'

'Do you think I am attractive?'

'I'm sure you're a lovely person.'

'My average is four point eight rating. That's very good.'

'That is good, well done.'

'I am also a landlord.'

'Brilliant.'

'I meet a lot of women in Uber.'

'I'm sure you do.'

'Can you give me a good rating?'

And just like that, my zen was gone.

Chapter 18

Athleisure

Six weeks went by and I was starting to see Jamie differently. I kept thinking about all the times I went to Hambleton. He never came down to Wales that much. Did he make as much effort with my family as I thought he did? We came from such different backgrounds. Was it possible to end up with someone from a completely different world to you? Was the sex even that good? I thought it was but, if I looked at it objectively, he didn't even go down on me that much. What if our married life was one blow job after the other, whilst I had to take myself off to the bathroom and get going with the shower head?

I'd planned another weekend in Wales, and Anna was coming back with me this time. She was about to start taking daily hormone injections, so I watched a YouTube video of how to administer the shots, hoping I could help her out. The comments below the video only wound me up even further. It was all, 'It's going to be a breeze!' and, 'All it takes is confidence.' I hate it when people use the word 'breeze' in idiom format. It takes a lot more than mere confidence to stab someone in the flesh with a needle. The internet is full of shit.

Mam was in good spirits when we arrived home on

Friday night, but that was because she'd been on the white wine spritzers since noon. Linda had decided that they were going to focus their efforts on raising awareness for Alice in Wonderland Syndrome and, to kick off their first campaign meeting, they drank four bottles of wine between the six of them. As Anna pointed out, Alice in Wonderland Syndrome is a temporary condition often associated with brain tumours, so why didn't they focus their energy on raising funds for a brain tumour research charity instead? Mam's response was, 'They have enough money as it is,' so that was that.

I woke on Saturday morning midway through the drowning dream. Taken right out of the scene in *Titanic*, I was Jack, Jamie was Rose, and he let go of my hand and smiled as he watched me sink to the bottom of the sea. I woke up in a pool of sweat, barely able to breathe. It was only a matter of time before he started to permeate my subconscious.

I went downstairs to find Anna and Mam watching *Game of Thrones*.

'I've been looking forward to a *cwtch* all morning,' Mam said, as I came into the living room.

I gave her a hug and walked back out towards the kitchen. She followed behind me.

'What's wrong with your hair?' she asked, sizing me up as I put the kettle on.

I put the kettle down and tried to remain calm.

'Nothing, why?'

'It looks quite greasy, darling.'

'I've just woken up.'

'You must wash it before we go out.'

'I'm going for a run.'

'Why don't you come to yoga with me and Anna?'

'You're doing yoga?'

'I might.'

'You've never done yoga in your life, Mam.'

'Fine then, why don't you and me have a little walk around the shops while she does whatever it is they do in there.'

'Practice.'

'What, darling?'

'They practice yoga.'

'Well, whatever it is they do, count me out.'

I looked her up and down and laughed.

'What are you smirking at now, Ivy?'

'Are you wearing Lululemon trousers?'

'Yes! Aren't they fabulous?'

'Mam, that's a yoga brand.'

'Darling, it's athleisure.'

'That's not a thing though, is it?'

'Ivy, I've had it up to here with you today.'

I left the house as fast as I could and ran all the way to the Anchor. I knocked on the door, calling for Liz and Henry, and finally, Liz came out the back.

'I wasn't expecting to see you today,' Liz said.

'I need a bit of space, that's all. Can you sit with me? Is that OK?'

'I'd love nothing more, *cariad*.'

We sat in the garden, the sun was shining and every man and his dog seemed to be on their way to the beach. I would've stayed in that garden forever if I could.

'How's your mother doing?'

'I think she's OK.'

'What do you mean "you think"?'

'Well, I think.'

'Try asking her how she is, Ives. Must be hellish with Gramps still in hospital.'

I tried to remember the last time I asked Mam how she was. I couldn't recall a thing.

123

I'd lost track of time when Anna called, asking where I was. I forgot that I said I would drive us to the hospital. We'd had a couple of gins, so I asked Liz to get me a can of Coke and a bag of crisps for the ride home, and she called me a taxi.

I got home to find Anna in the kitchen on the phone to Mark. She gave me a stern look and mouthed, 'Get in the shower,' so I ran upstairs to get ready. She came in as I was drying my hair.

'I want you to hear me out for a second, OK?'

'OK.'

'I don't know what you're going through, but you've got to give me a bit more here.'

'What do you mean?'

'You can't go out for a run and come back pissed four hours later.'

'I've only had two gins!'

'Liz has no concept of measures; you've probably tallied about twelve with her pouring.'

'OK, I'm sorry.'

'I want us to do stuff together, but you're never here.'

'I am here.'

'No, you're not. Any excuse and you're out the door.'

'I'm sorry, OK?'

'You've got to try.'

'I am trying.'

'Try harder. I'm here reading all I can about ovary stimulation, waiting for you to take me to the hospital to see my sick grandad. Come on, Ivy.'

'OK. OK. I'm sorry.'

'I don't care if you go out and see Liz; I want nothing more than to sit with you both and set the world to right.'

'I know.'

'Just be here, OK?'

'OK. I'm sorry, Anna.'

Anna had to drive because, as she'd predicted, the gins were starting to take effect and I was quite tipsy. I inhaled another bag of crisps in the car as I told Anna about my hospital game. Walking to the stroke ward, Anna got one word correct, *brechdanau*, meaning sandwiches, though I'm convinced she got help from the dinner lady in the canteen.

We found Gramps sitting up reading the papers. He wore a crisp checked shirt, with a yellow cashmere jumper and smart navy trousers. His boat shoes were placed neatly under his bed. Thankfully, Louise was nowhere in sight.

'My loves!' he shouted, as he saw us come through the ward.

He moved the papers and chocolate biscuits to one side, as Anna got up onto the bed and sat next to him.

'Tell me everything, girls,' he said, beaming at us both.

'Why are you dressed for a christening, Gramps?' I laughed.

'Don't be so bloody cheeky, Ives. Some of us take pride in what we wear.'

'You look dead smart,' Anna said, as she cuddled up into him.

'They're bastards here, Anna. Steven keeps taking my biscuits.'

'I don't think that's true,' I said.

'It bloody well is, Ives. Look at him, the sod; bet they're under his pillow.'

'Gramps, you literally just moved about six empty packets when we came in.'

'I did not.'

'OK, fine. Let's change the subject. How's physiotherapy going?' Anna asked.

'Shit, mun. I can't be arsed.'

'That's the spirit,' I said.

Anna put on her positive voice.

'Gramps, the more you put in, the more you'll get out and the sooner you'll be able to go home.'

'That's what these sods keep saying.'

'Well, they have a point.'

'And I can never get the *Sun*.'

'We'll bring you the *Sunday Times* tomorrow,' I said.

'I don't want that liberal bullshit. I'll take the *Mail on Sunday*.'

'Fine, we'll bring you that.'

'See what good old Boris has been up to,' Gramps said.

'Please don't,' Anna said.

'What?' said Gramps, smirking.

'Why do you have to say his name so affectionately?'

'I don't know what you're talking about.'

'Stop being so annoying,' I said.

'Yes, stop it. And stop with the swearing,' Anna said.

'God, you two are the worst. Where's your mother?'

'At the garden centre, with Dad.'

'Your mother, gardening?'

'Dad says she's not happy with the gardener.'

'She can't sack another one, mun.'

'She'll be here tomorrow.'

'No, tell her not to bother. I only saw her yesterday.'

'That's nice, Gramps.'

'Too many sodding people come here as it is.'

Chapter 19

Maybe I should shave my legs?

On Sunday night we all sat down to watch *Countryfile*; there was an episode about South Wales on, and Mam wanted to see if she knew the people in it. In her words, 'I know practically everybody there is to know down here.' There was a very handsome farmer being interviewed and Mam remarked that he looked like the sort of person who wouldn't break a young girl's heart. I saw Anna bite her tongue and go back to her book.

'Ivy, what's this Tinder business everyone's on about?' Mam asked, pausing the programme so that everyone had her full attention.

'It's a dating app,' I said.

'I see,' she said.

I knew what was coming next.

'Ivy, do you think you could go on Tinder?' Mam asked.

'How can I possibly go on Tinder when I don't even know my left from my right?' I joked.

'Remember, your left hand makes an L . . .' Anna said, and I threw a cushion at her to shut her up.

'Darling, don't put yourself down like that,' Mam said.

'It was a joke, Mam.'

'You've got lots of lovely qualities.'

'Thanks.'

'Mam, what do you think Ivy's qualities are?' Anna asked, knowing this would rile me up.

'She's very pretty. Tony, isn't Ivy pretty?'

'Ives, you're a beauty.'

'Thanks, everyone,' I said.

'And you've got my genes ... mostly.'

'Here we go ... ' Anna laughed.

'What? I'm just saying.'

That night, Dad and I sat together drinking Tia Maria, listening to records and talking about Gramps' bizarre fondness for Michael Gove. Anna and Mam were in the kitchen talking to Mark; I don't think he anticipated Mam being on the call, but then again, he had no choice. I could hear them laughing down the hallway and Dad remarked how relaxed Anna seemed, considering. I went to bed that night with a genuine smile on my face. As I lay there trying to get to sleep, I started to think about Tinder. It had only been six weeks and I was in no way ready to get back on the horse, but I did think it might be a good idea to start shaving my legs again. I could go out, with Mia as my wing-woman, and have a bit of a flirt. How bad could it be? I was confident that I could muster a conversation with a member of the opposite sex, but nothing more than that. I needed to know that I still had it. I needed people other than my parents to tell me that I still had it.

The next day, we got the train back to London. We went to see Gramps before we left, he was on fantastic form, flirting with the nurses and rowing with Steven over who was the greatest Welsh kicker of all time. We saw him get up and go to the toilet and, though wobbly, it was a far better sight than I'd anticipated. He gave us a packet of biscuits for the train journey and told us to stop picking on Mam. Things were on the up.

I should have checked my inbox on the train home so that the rage wasn't so intense when I got into the office the next morning. But, I didn't, and so I opened Outlook to find thirty-three new emails from Jane. I'd taken one day of annual leave; need I say more? She'd looked through all my open projects and commented on every single one, asking me why this wasn't finished, why I'd not done that. I tried not to let it get to me and went to distract myself with making tea, but Lisa caught me walking to the kitchen and followed me in. She had bought a new guitar. She was going to play me a new song at lunch. What did I think about her new skirt? I responded in my head with a, 'Christ. Please don't. Too short.'

At about midday, I clocked Gerald going into the kitchen to heat up a McDonald's. Within minutes the whole place stank of French fries and I knew it wouldn't be too long before Jane came in. She waltzed through in a matter of seconds and I berated myself for underestimating how much of a control freak she is.

'Gerald, what are you eating?' she asked, cornering him by the microwave.

'McDonald's,' he said, shovelling multiple fries into his mouth.

'Could you not have chosen a more appropriate lunch?'

'What?'

'You can't go heating up McDonald's like that. The whole office smells.'

'Jim had fish pie yesterday.'

'Fish pie is acceptable.'

'What's wrong with McDonald's?'

'It's offensive.'

'Jane, it's my lunch.'

'Can you kindly take it outside; I'm starting to feel sick.'

'You can't make me do that.'

'I can't, no, but John can.'

'John's not even here.'

'I have called him to let him know and he has asked you to kindly take your McDonald's outside.'

'Fine, Jane. Fine.'

'Thank you, Gerald.'

Ethan went over to Gerald and suggested they go to the pub.

'Ivy, coming with?' he asked.

'I can't chance it; she's sent me thirteen new emails in the past hour alone.'

Ethan mouthed, 'Gutted,' and off they went. I saw Lisa get her guitar out and kicked myself for not having an escape route. Within seconds, Jane was back.

'John has asked that you only play your guitar in the creative space,' Jane told Lisa.

'But it's lunch; you said I could play at lunch.'

'Not today, Lisa. Not today,' Jane snapped, as she went back into the kitchen, grabbed a very small avocado and walked to her desk. Lisa whispered, 'Bitch,' and while I tried to look sympathetic, I couldn't have been happier with the outcome.

I put on Kylie Minogue's *Desert Island Discs* and went for a walk. What would my interview be like? Would I mention Jamie? No, I would have moved on by then and he would be an insignificant blip in my history. Then again, I'd be livid if he didn't mention me. Of course, he would have to mention me; I would be the amazing lover that got away.

I left work bang on 5.30pm and decided to walk all the way home. I rang Mam and listened to her moan about Linda's new diet regime, then I called Mia to make plans for the weekend. Noah had offered to cook us dinner before we went out, much to Mia's dismay, who still thinks eating anything before a night out is cheating. We were going to head into Soho and have a few cocktails before meeting Dan and moving onto a club that catered for homosexual men and needy woman – Mia's terminology, not mine. I made it clear to Mia that the cocktail part of the evening was where I would try to have a two-minute conversation with a man. But once those two minutes were up, I would need to move swiftly onto a safe place with no heterosexual men in sight, dance for a few hours, and be in bed by 1am. It was the perfect plan.

I walked home through Shoreditch, feeling smug about my organisational skills, and that's when I saw him. He was standing by the traffic lights, holding a woman's hand. I stopped dead, unable to take my eyes off them. He turned to face her, moving her hair away from her face and tucking it behind her ears. She was pretty, very pretty, with Amazonian legs and toned arms like she did light weights for hours on end every day. I saw him lean into her face and I ran behind the bus stop to shield myself. When I looked back out again, there they were – kissing. It wasn't a small, polite, one-off kiss. It was a 'I'm taking you home right now' sort of kiss. His hand was on the back of her neck and she had one arm on his back, tugging at his jacket and pulling him in closer. I couldn't take my eyes off them. It must have only been a few seconds, but when their lips parted I could see her laugh and when he turned in my direction, he was laughing too. I stared at him, the tears welling up in my eyes, and then I ran. I ran as far as I could before my chest couldn't take it and I had to lean against a lamppost with my head between my thighs. I'd bought him that jacket. I'd been with him when he'd got those shoes and I knew all too well what shape his face made when he smiled.

I sat on a bench for over an hour, paralysed with the fear of seeing them again. I couldn't even bring myself to compose a text or make a phone call. All I remember thinking about was

131

the day he'd proposed to me. His smile. The same smile he'd just shown her. You don't smile like that with someone you've just met. That wasn't a 'we've been on a couple of dates' smile. That was a 'we know each other' smile. How long had they been smiling at each other like that for?

I walked to Anna's. When she opened the door and saw me, her lips made an 'O' shape.

'Jamie. I just saw him kissing . . .' and before the rest of the words could come out, my knees buckled and I fell onto the shoe rack sobbing.

Chapter 20

If looks could kill

I wanted to physically hurt him. Anna kept saying how good it was to be angry; I was entering the next stage of grief, and the positive in all of this was that I was moving forward. She had a point – I'd been going through the motions, but there was always a little bit of hope in the back of my mind.

I drank the contents of their fridge. Anna stayed up with me, not wanting to leave me alone, but by 1am I told her to get to bed and lied that I would be right behind her. Excessive boozing meant I would pass out drunk, instead of lying awake in wild panic. It did mean I would wake up with a blinding headache, but I could handle that.

My mind was playing havoc with me and my eyes were wide open. I kept thinking about his smile. I've always trusted that niggling feeling deep down in the pits of my stomach – the feeling that tells you when something isn't right. Here it was again, and I knew. I knew this wasn't a woman he'd been on a few casual dates with since we'd broken up. That would be strange enough. No, this wasn't new. This had had time to develop. Those were the faces of two people falling in love.

I fell asleep in my clothes on their sofa and woke with

Anna sitting over me. I wasn't immediately crying when I woke up; there were two minutes of grace before I went into full meltdown mode, something I was grateful for. But when I did start crying, I couldn't stop and it was then, while snot was streaming out of my nose and onto Anna's shoulder, that I had the faint recollection of leaving Jamie a voicemail. I don't know what time I called, how long I spoke for, or what I said, but I knew what I'd done. I jumped up from the sofa to find my phone, and there it was – a text sent at 3.57am: 'I fucking hate you. Who the fuck is she?' I let out a loud groan, walked back over to Anna and showed her the message.

'Good,' she said, throwing the phone onto the sofa behind her.

'What do you mean "good"?'

'I'm sorry, Ivy, but he deserves it.'

'I didn't want to do that.'

'What does it matter?'

'I don't want to be that person.'

'What person?'

'The person who leaves their ex drunk voicemails.'

'He should know how much he's hurt you.'

'You've changed your tune. You're the one who said to give him space.'

'That was before. He can't go parading his new girlfriend around where we live, like it's all fucking fine.'

'We don't have monopoly over East London, Anna.'

'Ivy—'

'And she may not be his girlfriend—'

'Ivy, stop it. Stop standing up for him.'

I didn't have anything to say.

'Look at what he's done,' she said.

I couldn't argue with that.

I told Jane I had more stomach issues and called in sick. Back

134

home, I went into the drawer in the bedroom and found our box; I'd kept photos, cards, the odd Post-it note – things to remind me that we were once an us. I couldn't bring myself to throw them away when he moved out, but at that moment I emptied the entire contents onto the floor before shredding everything into tiny pieces. When I was done, I hoovered everywhere, then I got all the cleaning products out from under the kitchen sink and cleaned the entire bedroom. I then bleached the bathroom, before moving onto the living room and kitchen. I didn't stop for breath and, a couple of hours later, the place was spotless. When I was done, I put on my trainers and ran out the front door. I was about a mile in when my phone beeped with a message. I knew it was him.

'Please can we talk? I can explain . . .' was the first line.

'Can I see you? Tonight?' came second.

I thought about my reply. I wanted to compose a dignified response, apologising for the drunken call. But then, I couldn't get his cocksure smile out of my head, and I changed my mind. I started typing, prodding the screen.

'Do you think I'm stupid?'

'Please can we meet after work?' he replied.

'Go fuck yourself.'

'Please, Ivy. I can explain.'

I waited a couple of minutes then wrote, 'I hope you take a long hard look at yourself. Don't ever contact me again.'

I pressed send, took a deep breath, then started running again. I ran for an hour before I stopped at the pub and ordered a bottle of wine.

Jamie surprised me once with afternoon tea at the Ritz. It was right before Christmas and I was feeling terribly pleased with myself that, despite recently peeing all over his bathroom floor, he really did love me. I was still buying overpriced underwear sets, but I wasn't giving so many blow jobs, perhaps every other week, which is still too much in my opinion. Mia insisted I borrow some of her clothes for the occasion; my usual baggy jeans, plain T-shirt and scuffed flats weren't remotely sexy and it was about time I started making some effort. Her words, not mine. So instead, for my surprise date at the Ritz, I was wearing red suede knee-length boots, a silk black camisole, skin-tight leather trousers and a vintage leopard print coat. My lips were painted siren red and I had Mam's sparkly gold clutch with me, which she'd forced upon me earlier that month after being appalled that I had no, 'Proper accessories for the festive season.' She was treating my going out with Jamie as if it were my debut into the upper echelons of British society. I was just excited to be having regular sex.

Everything was going fine until we walked into the Ritz, and, suddenly, everywhere around me were middle-aged women who looked like Jamie's mother, and I, in comparison, looked like a Soho call girl. I started pulling at my top to make sure my boobs weren't out and Jamie had to tell me to stop fussing. Everyone was in pearls and tweed and knee-length pencil skirts, or they were children. Actually, the children were also in pearls and tweed and knee-length pencil skirts. We were taken to our seats and when the waiter passed me a menu I let out an audible, 'Bloody hell,' as I read the price: £76 for champagne afternoon tea. For a start, this was mis-leading – don't put 'champagne' in the title when all you get is one glass of the stuff. And secondly, the traditional afternoon tea is £57, which means they're charging £19 for one measly glass of fizz. What sort of world do we live in?

With it being a surprise and all, I hadn't known that we were going for afternoon tea, so I'd already eaten four slices of toast that morning at Mia's whilst rummaging through her wardrobe. But, I did my best and, not wanting to waste Jamie's money on cucumber and egg, I asked for extra Scottish salmon and an unhealthy amount of Cornish clotted cream scones. Mia's leather trousers were already far too tight and the zip was beginning to dig into my belly button. Jamie kept insisting that we have more champagne but I put my foot down and said that the bubbles were making me full. Of course, this was a lie. The truth was that I knew all too well how much a bottle of champagne cost and this was a colossal waste of money.

There was a Camilla Parker-Bowles lookalike sitting at the table next to us with her daughter. The girl had a pretty pink bow in her hair and a cream cashmere jumper on, with big colourful gems sown into the Peter Pan collar. She caught me smiling at her and she waved her cute little hand at me. I waved back, and as I did, her mother turned to face me, gave me a filthy look, and told her daughter to put her hands away.

I wanted Jamie to tell me that I looked gorgeous, that I shouldn't worry about what anybody else thought, but he didn't and, as the meal went on, I started to question whether we were right for each other at all. The Ritz isn't me and if he thought it was me then did he really know me? This was very much his world, or rather his mother's. Was he trying to turn me into Cressida Langdon? I excused myself to the bathroom and spent a long time on the toilet contemplating what could be worse than becoming another Cressida. While she was lovely, she was also bit of a bore, and, as Mam says, there's nothing worse than being a bore.

By the time I got back to the table, Jamie had paid the bill, so I tried to look impressed as I thanked him. He helped me put on my coat and said we better get going or we'd be late for the next surprise. I hoped to God it didn't involve more sandwiches.

We were standing in silence at the traffic lights by the Ritz, waiting to cross the road, when he turned to me.

'You hated that, didn't you?'

'I didn't hate it, I promise,' I lied.

'You did and you can say so.'

'It's just . . . ' I tried to get out of it but it was no use.

'You spent the best part of two hundred pounds on bread, Jamie.'

He laughed and leant in to kiss me.

'I knew it. Mum said you'd love afternoon tea, but I knew you'd think it was—'

'A bit stuffy?'

'A bit stuffy, yes,' he said.

'The thought is lovely but—'

'I should never listen to my mother.'

He moved closer to me, putting one hand on the back of my neck and the other on my bum, and when we kissed I felt like my whole body was on fire. He pulled away and pressed the crossing button again. We stood side by side, bodies touching, grinning like there were coat-hangers fixed in our mouths. He put his arm around my shoulders and I put my hand in his back pocket, my favourite place to rest it. The cars came to a halt and the green man started flashing in front of us. I went to walk, but he turned to face me and stopped me from doing so.

'Ivy,' he said, 'I think we should move in together.'

I looked up at him and said, 'Yes, I think so too.'

We kissed for what seemed like hours and when he finally pulled away, there it was – that smile.

Chapter 21

Picking up

It was Saturday afternoon and I was in the Quiet Lady doing a line of cocaine with a total stranger. I saw her go in to the bathroom, and, having spent a while in there, clocked that she might have some on her. I hadn't planned it, but it was 4pm and I was drunker than I wanted to be. This shouldn't have come as a huge surprise, considering I'd ran five miles that morning and barely managed half my Marmite sandwich, but I wasn't in the right headspace to plan. In my warped logic, taking drugs meant there'd be less chance of crying and I was determined to get through the day without another embarrassing public episode of heartache. I'd been surprised at how much I'd cried over the past two months. Mia said that our bodies were almost 60 per cent water, so it made perfect sense that I was so teary. I still don't quite understand how that fits, but at the time it made me feel better.

My new toilet friend was gorgeous and looked like she was having the time of her life, with a bunch of girlfriends all as equally captivating. I wondered if people looked at me and thought I was happy. I looked like I had the potential to be happy. Mam had recently treated me to a whole new host of products, having been worried I was letting myself go – always a helpful comment – and so my skin and hair were looking marginally better. Also, my new dress made my boobs look much bigger than they were, which is always nice. We complimented each other's outfits, she said she loved my lipstick and then I asked her where she got the coke from. She had a number, she said; I would have to text him and say I was Sasha's friend, then Sasha would message him and say, 'I've given your number to Ivy.' It was all very coordinated and efficient and after a few minutes I had arranged to meet Trevor, though of course Trevor wasn't his real name. He asked what I wanted and I wrote, 'One bag of coke please! Thank you xxxx.' He replied with, 'Next time, say 1C,' and I wrote, 'SORRY!!! Thanks SO much xxx.' I was a total natural.

I went back to the group and told Mia what I'd done. She said she never picked up – what if they realised who she was and sold her story to the tabloids? No, picking up was Noah's job. I had to remind her at this point that she had done one awful advert for an unknown vegetarian sausage brand four years ago, where she'd featured for all of three seconds, and so the likelihood of her being recognised as that famous barmaid/ telesales executive was slim to none. Also, the likelihood of a drug dealer selling their story to the tabloids is quite low.

Twenty minutes later, I was meeting Trevor down a backstreet. He said he'd be in a black Peugeot with the headlights on and so I nervously walked towards the car that fit that description best and knocked on the window. The man inside rolled it down and asked me for my name.

'Ivy Carwen Edwards,' I said, as confidently as I think I've ever said my name, before apologising for revealing my full identity.

I was surprised at how normal 'Trevor' looked. He didn't have a buzz cut, he wasn't wearing any jewellery and he didn't have any gold teeth. He looked rather nice, like he could be someone's dad. I got in the car and he started driving off.

'I've not done this before,' I said, pulling a face at him in the rear-view mirror.

'What do you want?'

'Cocaine please, thanks so much.'

'How much?'

'Just the one please, thank you.'

'OK. Just gimme two minutes to find another place to stop.'

I sat back in my seat and smiled to myself. I couldn't believe that I was pulling this off.

'Busy day?' I asked.

He didn't respond.

'Do you stick round here or go all over?'

He mumbled something inaudible.

'Must be nice to work for yourself, I bet.'

He didn't respond.

'Do you get a lot of women picking up drugs from you?'

'What the fuck is this, *Question Time*?'

'Sorry, sorry.'

'OK, here we go,' he said, as he pulled over. I handed him sixty pounds and he gave me a tiny bag of snow-white powder.

'Thank you ... Trevor?'

'Sure, Trevor it is.'

I told Mia it had been a roaring success despite the interrogating questions, and we went into the toilet to get going.

'Do you have anyone you can just shag?' Mia asked, as she cut up two lines for us on the toilet seat.

'I don't think so, no.'

'What about Adam?'

'Trace said he's got a really small penis and if it's just sex then it needs to be good, at least.'

'You can have good sex with someone with a small penis.'

141

'Name me one time where that's been true.'

'Um . . .'

'Go on . . .'

'Got it – Eric!'

'You only liked Eric because he went down on you for hours. It doesn't count.'

'Yeah, you're right.'

I wanted to have sex with the least amount of effort and sadly there was nobody I knew who could fulfil that wish. We listed off university flings who I could get in touch with over Facebook, but that required effort and, as I said, I didn't want to make any. I spent far too much time hanging out with jobbing actors and there was no way I was going to listen to someone bang on about their creative heartache for hours on end before I even got a boob grab.

Later that night, I was stood by the bar trying to suss out the potential, when Rob came in and squeezed beside me. He was wearing a denim shirt with shiny silver buttons and flower embroidery on the shoulders, with a ripped black T-shirt underneath and skinny black jeans. Around his neck he wore two silver pendants hanging on a frayed shoelace. His hair was a mess and he smelt a bit damp. He said hello and gave me a kiss on the cheek and when he did I was sure that his lips lingered there for just a second too long.

We moved from pub to pub and I moved onto whisky. After my third double measure, I went outside for yet another cigarette. I needed an excuse to take myself out of the conversation, which had moved onto politics and why the campaign to stop Brexit mustn't make us lose sight of the real issues concerning the country – a classic Saturday night out with those lot. A minute later, Rob came out the door and stood beside me. He offered me a light and when he lit my cigarette, he kept eye contact for a little longer than I was comfortable with. Something in me stirred and I realised I was turned on. I looked at him with confusion and then thought, screw it, why not. From that moment on, even though he irritated the hell out of me, I was going to try to have sex with him.

We smoked our cigarettes and chatted about nothing. When I laughed, I did my best to graze a part of his body – stomach, thigh, arm, whatever was nearest. I think it was working, because when we went back inside he held the door open for me and put his hand on the small of my back as we walked in. We went to the bar and stood close enough together that his thigh was touching mine. He paid for my drink and when I started walking back to the group, he grabbed my arm and asked me to hang back with him a little longer. He offered me some of his coke and I told him I didn't need it, I had my own; something I thought made me sound cool and sexy. Then he grabbed my hand and led me to the disabled toilets. I locked the door behind us and stood against it as he got his card and note out and started cutting up the powder. He did the first line then ushered me over and I crouched down by the toilet to do mine. I got up and wiped my nose. He was staring at me.

'Why are you looking at me like that?' I asked, in my very best 'casual but sexy' tone.

'You look great tonight.'

'Thanks,' I said, grinning at him.

He moved towards me and I put my hand on his chest; he was more muscular than I expected and I desperately wanted to see him topless. He grinned, moved his face into mine and kissed me softly. His lips were wet and he tasted like cigarettes, but then again so did I. He pulled my body up against his and started to gently sweep his tongue against my lips. His hands glided to the sides of my neck and onto the back of my head, his fingers tightening in my hair. I opened my mouth a little more and then suddenly, in a completely bizarre turn of events, he started whirling his tongue around my mouth in endless circular motions. I didn't know what to do; I gripped both sides of his face with my hands in a strategic move that I thought would control the tempo of his routine, but he kept going at it and I felt like I was drowning in his mouth. I pulled away, not wanting to show him that whirling his tongue around my mouth at lightning speed wasn't the sexiest manoeuvre. He moved his head a little lower and started to kiss my collarbone, parting his lips ever so slightly and grazing his tongue against my skin. The whirlpool tongue action had left me bemused, but there he was on my chest, knowing exactly what to do, and it felt fantastic.

Despite the rocky start, I was determined to have sex with him. I was high and drunk and I needed to do something to make me feel like I existed.

Chapter 22

Lay Lady Lay

Rob's flat was like something out of the 1800s. There were candles burning everywhere and musky smells lingered throughout. The floorboards creaked and he had a small canary in a cage in the living room called Morrissey. I went to sit on his bed; a profound stench of cigarettes came off the sheets and I gagged a little. I was sure Rob came from money, so I was confused as to why he lived in a hovel. I mused over this as he went to the kitchen to pour us some drinks, and it dawned on me that this is what 'bohemian' children of the uber-rich do: they live in squalor, wear ripped clothes from charity shops and always have a dubious smell lingering around them. But, check their current account, and they'll be at least a few thousand pounds in there.

There was a copy of Jack Kerouac's *On the Road* by the bed, as well as poems by Bob Dylan and a record player with Jeff Buckley's *Grace* on it. Everywhere I looked there were things scattered haphazardly, as if to give the impression that he was terribly creative. I didn't know what to do with myself so I kept crossing and uncrossing my legs to see if I could find a point of comfort, but there was none. I also didn't know what to do with my hair – do you leave it down or does that just get in the way when you're on top? Would I even be on top? What would my first move be? I had, it seemed, lost the ability to behave as a functioning adult. To busy myself, I went to put a record on. As I did, he walked in, whisky tumblers in hand.

'Don't touch that, Ivy. It's a family piece,' he said.

'Oh, sorry.'

'Let me put on some Dylan.'

I rolled my eyes behind his back; the last thing that was going to put me in the mood was Bob Dylan.

He sat down on the bed, went into the drawer and got out a bag of MDMA. He licked his finger and put it in the bag so that the crystals stuck to his fingertips. I leaned in and put my mouth around his finger and sucked, not breaking eye contact. It tasted metallic and bitter and I tried not to let my face show that I found it hideous. I licked my finger and got some for him too, before he put the bag back in the drawer. He moved the hair away from my neck and put his lips against my collarbone. His fingers traced the top of my thigh under my dress, then up to my belly, caressing my skin. When his hand got to my breasts I let out a little moan and tilted my head back in pleasure, but then he grabbed my hair and pulled my face into his and started sticking his whirlpool tongue in my mouth, and the moment was lost. I closed my eyes and tried to think about better kisses I had experienced, but all that came into my head was Jamie. I started to get a bit teary, so I pushed him away from me and onto the bed so that I was on top and could have more control.

'I can't wait to fuck you,' he said, which should have been sexy but for some reason, the way he stressed the word 'fuck' irritated me and I found myself annoyed. I tried to think of when his lips were on my chest and then I realised that, except for my mouth, everywhere he kissed me felt amazing, so I would have to be honest and guide him through it. In that spirit, I went to kiss him and as soon as he shoved his tongue in my mouth, I pulled back and told him to go slower.

'Why? Don't you like it fast?' he asked.

'I like it when you kiss me slowly, without ...'

'Without what?'

'Without so much tongue ...'

'OK.'

He kissed me again.

'No, go slower ... with less tongue.'

'I love it when you tell me what to do.'

He sat up so that I was straddling him and pulled my dress over my head. He kissed my breasts as I fumbled with his belt and put my hands into his boxers. He was big, not so big it was frightening but big enough that I did a mental high five to myself. His hand moved in-between my legs and I could feel myself getting hotter.

'I want you,' he said, as he bit my nipple and slid his fingers inside me. He began circling my clitoris and I knew I was going to come within minutes. My legs went tense and I started getting cramp in my calf but all I could do was close my eyes as his fingers moved faster. When I came, I opened my eyes and he was staring right at me, looking very pleased with himself.

'You're good at that,' I told him.

'You turn me on so much, Ivy.'

I went to pull off his jeans.

'Can you get a condom?' I asked.

'Do we need one?'

'Yes, of course we need one.'

'I'm clean, Ivy.'

'How do I know that?' I laughed.

'Because I am.'

147

'Rob, please. I'm not an idiot. I know you've shagged half of East London.'

'I've not shagged half of East London.'

'You have and stop ruining the moment even more than you already are. Go get a condom.'

He went into the drawer next to his bed and put a condom on without breaking eye contact with me. I climbed back on top of him and he put his hands on my back and steadied himself inside me. He started slow, making sure I was OK and for a few seconds there, I didn't think of Jamie. I felt alive and in control and even though the alertness and oversensitivity was probably down to the considerable amount of Class A drugs we'd taken, I didn't care. I deserved this. He waited for me to come again, which I thought was very polite but then again, he's posh and posh people have impeccable manners. When he came, his whole body tightened and he gripped me so hard that I thought I was going to get bruises. It was exactly what my vagina needed.

We lay in silence for a while afterwards; me nestled into his armpit, his hands running through my hair. It all felt familiar and relaxing until I realised I had to leave. I didn't want to see him in broad daylight and I certainly didn't want to have to make conversation sober.

'I need to go,' I said, as I pulled myself off him and went to find my dress.

'Don't go, Ivy. Have another drink.'

'It's four am. I need to go.'

He leant up and moved towards me, kissing my belly button and grabbing my bare bum with his hands.

'You look so great,' he said, kissing the tops of my thighs.

'Thank you, heartache is an excellent diet.'

He went quiet.

'Oh shit, sorry. That wasn't funny.'

'No, sorry, I, um . . .'

'Sorry, can we forget I just said that? It was stupid.'

I went to kiss him and my hands went straight to his crotch. He was hard again, so I climbed on top of him and before I knew it, we were at it all over again.

Chapter 23

Anthony Michael Hall

I got home just before 8am. I was so pleased with myself for having sex and not crying; I could feel my vagina thanking me. I opened the front door and there were two pairs of men's shoes in the hallway. I could hear laughter in the living room – laughter that could only belong to one person. I opened the door and saw Dan and an attractive blond man kneeling on the floor; my sofa was on its side and they were trying to screw one of the legs back in.

'Dan?'

'Babe! Sorry! I thought you'd be home.'

'What the hell are you doing here?'

'Hi, I'm Tim,' the blond man said, as he came towards me and held his hand out to shake mine.

'Hi Tim,' I said, giving him a look of, 'Who are you and why are you in my flat?'

I turned to Dan. 'What the fuck?'

'Don't look at me like that, I have spare keys.'

'Which are for emergencies . . .'

'Can I get you a little drink?'

'It's my flat!'

'Darling, don't be angry. Come sit down.'

'Where?'

'Oh ... sorry, your sofa's a bit broken.'

'Yeah, I can see that.'

'We can fix it. Tim's good at DIY, aren't you, Tim?'

'Brilliant at it.'

'Right. Thanks for that, Tim. Dan?'

'So, we were in Soho but the vibe was off, not the right crowd at all; you'd have hated it.'

He looked at Tim for approval.

'Oh yeah, so off,' Tim said.

'Anyway, we went back to mine but the neighbours knocked on the door complaining about the music, so I grabbed your keys and we came here.'

'Dan!'

'Ivy, I thought you'd be back here with Mia! You weren't answering your phone! What did you expect me to do?'

'What about your house, Tim? I assume you have a home?'

'Not an option, babe. I live with my parents.'

'Right. And my sofa?'

'I did a little dance on it and the back leg fell off.'

'Dan!'

'We can fix it.'

'Oh, for fuck's sake.'

'Ivy, don't be mad at me!'

'I'm not mad. You're impossible.'

I told him to make me a cup of tea while I changed into my pyjamas. We sat on the floor and I told them all about Rob and how happy my vagina was.

'I am so proud of you,' Dan said.

'It's so fabulous,' replied Tim, nodding in agreement beside Dan, like an adorable little puppy.

'To Ivy's happy vagina,' we cheered.

I finally got into bed at about 10am. Tim was in the bathroom and I made Dan promise me that they wouldn't shag on my sofa. Broken or not, I wasn't going to allow jizz on my soft furnishings.

I woke at 4pm with a thick head and a scratchy throat. I downed a pint of water and then composed texts to my sister and Mia to tell them about Rob. 'YAY ME' was written a lot. I got out of bed and walked into the living room to find Dan on the sofa.

'Darling!' he said, sweeping his hands out dramatically.

'Have you slept?' I asked.

'Um, I've been busy,' he said, gesturing around the flat.

He'd cleaned everywhere – you could lick the skirting boards.

'You didn't have to do this,' I said.

'I did, your sofa's fucked.'

'Oh, Dan,' I said, as I went to look at it. There were books holding it up on one side, so it was steady, at least.

'And I cleaned the bathroom. I think I pissed on the floor in the night.'

'God, I'm so glad you came over.'

'I bought breakfast too.'

'It's after four in the afternoon.'

'And?'

'This is lovely, thank you. Well, the sofa situation isn't ideal, but there we are.'

'I thought we could watch *Titanic*.'

'I dreamt about *Titanic* the other week.'

'Sex dreams about Leo? Tell me more!'

'No, I can't. It's too dramatic for a come down.'

'Who said anyone was coming down?'

'I'm not doing drugs, Dan. It's a Sunday.'

'Well, you're in luck, because I ran out. But I notice you have whisky . . . '

'What is wrong with you?'

'Shut it, you know you love me.'

We had fried eggs on toast washed down with a couple of pints of orange juice. Dan swears by orange juice after a night of drug taking and I was desperate to lose the metallic taste from my mouth.

Halfway through *Titanic*, Dan suggested a drink to settle our stomachs. After protesting for all of five seconds, I gave in and poured us both a whisky. I knew this was going to be a mistake, as I'd drank so much of it the night before. The rule goes that you never match the same drink the next day. Another pearl of wisdom from Mam.

After *Titanic*, we put on *The Breakfast Club*. Dan said it was 'more than just a movie' and when I called him dramatic, he didn't speak to me for a whole hour. After much discussion about who was the greatest cast member in all the John Hughes films, he finally left my flat at 2am and I stumbled into bed.

I woke mid drowning dream – just before I died – and started to make notes of all the nasty things I wanted to say and do to Jamie. I admitted defeat and got out of bed at 7.30am. I messaged Jane to tell her I was sick and wouldn't be coming in to work. I felt like I was back in school, in Maths class, failing all over again. But there was no way I could face her disappointment. Her response was a trite, 'Please log it with HR and we'll discuss tomorrow.' I thought about texting Anna to see if she could go for lunch, but I suspected she wouldn't be impressed with me skipping work again. In a bid to ease the self-loathing, I forced myself to go for a run. I only managed about eleven metres before I turned around, walked back home and crawled back into bed.

I waited until lunchtime to ring Mam, pretending I was on my break. She was in one her frantic moods and I couldn't get a word in edgeways. Dad's seventieth birthday was coming up and the organisation was being done with military precision. She had bought no less than seventeen dresses for the occasion, sending Anna and me photos of her modelling every one. Dad had no idea the extent of her planning, but of course, it being Mam, he knew all too well that she was going to go 'full mental', as Anna and I called it. I was to blame for this; if the wedding were still on she'd be much less intense about the whole thing. Now she had nothing to focus on, which was terrible news for the rest of us. You'd have thought that Gramps being in hospital would be enough of a distraction, but it wasn't.

Mam had been to various caterers and sampled what seemed like hundreds of food options for the party. Dad's favourite is steak and kidney pie, but there she was looking at tiger prawn crostini and polenta chips. When she told Anna that she was going with white sprouting broccoli and vinaigrette for one of the canapés, Anna told her that perhaps she'd gone a little off-piste. Mam swore at her and said she was ruining her flow.

'Also, darling, I bought you a little something,' she said, after exhausting all the menu options to me.

'I don't need anything, Mam.'

'Well, either way, I got you some earrings.'

'Oh, Mam. Thank you.'

'From that jewellery shop you like in Cardiff.'

'Mam, you shouldn't have.'

'It's my pleasure, darling. But please don't tell your father.'

'I'll try not to mention it.'

'And I bought you some new tops, too.'

'I don't need any new tops.'

'I disagree, darling.'

'OK ...'

'Your clothes are all a bit ... baggy.'

'They're not, and anyway, what's wrong with baggy?'

'You look a bit like ...'

'Like what?'

'Well, like a lesbian.'

'You cannot say that.'

'Why?'

'It's insensitive.'

'Don't give me that, Ives. Your father and I have lots of gay friends.'

'Name one gay friend.'

'Patrick. Patrick is gay,' she said, after a long pause.

'Who is Patrick?'

'Patrick! He works with Nicky.'

'This is the first time you've ever mentioned either of them.'

'Oh, for goodness' sake. I am sick and tired of your interrogations, Ivy.'

Chapter 24

The elderly

I went into work the next day and caught a glimpse of Jane in her office, staring at me as I walked to my desk. She was standing motionless, holding a bowl and fork up to her mouth, probably containing the four cherry tomatoes she allowed herself to eat for breakfast. I sat down at my desk and took a couple of biscuits out from my drawer. Lisa waved at me and then put on the 90s song 'I'm Horny'. She started shaking her shoulders and mouthing the words, beckoning me to join in. I might have been more inclined to appreciate the song choice had it not been 9.43am on a Tuesday in the office, but there we go.

'Lisa, this is mega bants!' Ethan said, laughing. I gave him the finger and went back to my emails.

About a minute later, Jane walked over and demanded Lisa change the song.

'Ivy, can you come into my office at ten am, please?' she asked.

I nodded.

I counted the minutes and bit my nails while I awaited my sentence. When the time came, I took a notepad and pen with me and knocked on her office door. There was one lone cherry tomato on her plate. She made eye contact with me and didn't lose it until I sat down.

'I want to discuss your performance,' she said.

'I'm sorry about yesterday. Stomach issues, again.'

'I think you'll agree with me when I say that your work ethic is not what it used to be.'

'OK.'

'On top of being late and calling in sick often—'

'It's only been a couple of times and—'

'Let me finish, please.'

'OK.'

'I'm giving you the benefit of the doubt, Ivy. The team loves you, but your performance has slipped.'

'Right.'

'You must make more of an effort.'

'You know there have been some changes in my personal life.'

'Everyone falls on hard times, Ivy. Me included.'

'I just thought . . .'

'It's not an excuse.'

'Right.'

'I want to agree an action plan.'

'OK.'

'I've written it up. I want you to read it and agree to the points. Then we can review it in three months.'

'OK.'

'This shouldn't come as a surprise, Ivy. I expected better from you. We all did.'

I didn't expect anything of myself, so the fact that I failed her expectations meant very little to me. I thought I was doing OK, and socially, things in the office had never been better. Ethan and the sales team had much more respect for me since I started drinking with them at lunchtime, and I'd bonded

157

with Gerald over my newfound love of greasy fast food before noon. I mulled over Jane's comments throughout the day and concluded that I was doing the best I could with what I had, and that was fine. Thankfully, Jane left for an appointment at 4pm, so I snuck out early and walked all the way to Anna's.

'What do you smell of?' she asked, as she greeted me at the front door.

'Bitterness? Booze?'

She asked me if I wanted a glass of squash but I poured myself a large wine instead.

'You look thin, Ives,' she said, looking me up and down.

'I'm not exactly on top of the world, am I?'

She scowled at me before taking a bite of her Deliciously Ella bar.

'Stop staring at me, you're weirding me out.'

'Stay for dinner?' she said. 'Mark's out tonight.'

'He's sick of me, isn't he?'

'No, darling. Of course not.'

'You're lying.'

'We just need some more alone time; it's hard when there's so much going on.'

'Ah, I hear you loud and clear.'

'Don't be like that. You know I'm here for you, but . . . '

'I know, sorry.'

'Don't be sorry, just—'

'Don't come over every other day?'

'Yeah,' she said.

'Got you.'

'Anyway, I'm making vegetable lasagne, so please stay.'

'Why the vegetable bit?'

'I'm trying to eat less meat, aren't I?'

'Are you?'

'Don't be annoying.'

'Sorry. How are you?'

'I'm fine. They're gathering my eggs this week.'

'That sounds ... horrible.'

'I feel like an experiment.'

'It'll all be worth it in the end.'

'Will it?'

'I don't know. We've got to be positive.'

'I know, I'm trying. It's just ... '

'Really shit?'

'Yeah. It's really shit.'

I didn't feel like eating the lasagne but I knew she'd go off on one if I didn't. Gramps called halfway through dinner to tell us his new physiotherapist was, 'Fine, but talked too much.' With any luck, he said, he'd be home in the next couple of weeks. This was optimistic to say the least, considering he needed help to wash himself and couldn't walk more than a few steps unsupported, but we went along with it anyway. It was exhausting being so positive.

'I think you should start volunteering,' Anna said, as I was loading the dishwasher.

I took a sip of my wine and thought about the nicest way to tell her that this was a terrible idea.

'I'm being serious, Ivy.'

'But, with who?'

'Old people.'

'Old people?'

'Yes, what's wrong with that?'

'What would I do with old people?'

'I don't know, chat to them?'

'Where is this coming from?'

'Look, don't get defensive before I've said anything—'

'Here it comes ... '

'Ivy, come on. Mark and I are worried about you.'

'I am fine!'

'You're not fine.'

'No, I'm not fine, but that in itself is fine. It's not even been three months, Anna.'

'I know. I just think you'd benefit from helping others when you're in need of help yourself.'

'That sounds so wanky. Where did you read that?'

'I'm trying to help.'

'Where would I even start?'

Anna had done a lot of research into this; she put it down to needing something to focus on other than the daily injections and tests, which was fair enough. There were a dozen befriending services nearby, and all I'd need to do is take part in a small induction before I was permitted to volunteer at a care home. As Anna showed me the websites, I started to think that this wasn't such a bad idea after all. It would keep me out of the pub at the very least and, having put up with Gramps all my life, I was very equipped at dealing with lonely old people.

I rang Mia on the way home to tell her about my new venture, but she was too preoccupied with the new season of *Love Island* starting.

'I'm going to set up a WhatsApp group for us all again,' she said.

I hate WhatsApp groups. 167 notifications every night? No thank you.

She sensed my reticence.

'What? Why aren't you excited?'

'I am excited.'

'You don't seem it.'

'I've sort of got a lot on my mind right now, Mia.'

'But it's *Love Island* season. Our season.'

'Mia, let's get some perspective. Only two weeks ago I saw Jamie snogging a girl's face off.'

'I thought it was more of a lingering kiss?'

'No, it was a snog. A huge, wet, passionate, sexy snog.'

'Because sometimes lingering kisses can just be out of politeness.'

'Can they?'

'I don't know. I'm just making stuff up at this point.'

'Right, I'm going to go.'

'Yeah, me too. Noah and I are watching *The Crown*.'

'I can't watch that,' I said.

'Why?'

'I started watching it with Jamie.'

'So?'

'I can't watch it on my own now, can I?'

'Why not?'

'Well, it would make me sad.'

'This conversation is sad. Get over it, Ivy.'

When I got home I ran a bath and brought my iPad in to reclaim *The Crown*, but I started thinking about Rob and if I should message him. I could say something funny about Dan and the broken sofa, but I think he found Dan tedious. I could talk to him about vegetable lasagne – he was on a strict plant-based diet – but that didn't seem so sexy for our first phone interaction. While I was composing a message, I thought about his fingers inside me, and I reached for the iPad. It was time: I was ready to watch porn.

I can't put my finger on why, but I chose lesbian porn; the chat was appalling, but I liked the breasts and there were no oversized veiny cocks in sight, which made it a little more bearable. The video was just getting started when I got a message on my phone. It was Rob.

'When can I see you next?' he wrote, with a wink emoji.

I sank into the bath grinning from ear to ear and pressed play on the video.

Chapter 25

Viva la Cliff

'I'm thinking about throwing a dinner party?' Mam said.

'Why?' I asked.

'Linda always throws dinner parties.'

'Don't you think you should focus on Dad's party?'

'Us women can do it all, Ivy. Hashtag "me too" and all that.'

'That's not what it's used for.'

'Is it not?'

'No.'

'Oh. Oh, right. I better go change the flyers.'

'Anything else, Mam?'

'Yes, your grandfather is coming out of hospital.'

When it came to Gramps' progress, we didn't have a lot to go on. Mam was only interested in discussing the attractiveness of the male nurses and all Dad said after a visit was that he was doing his best to avoid Louise. During the last visit, she told him about the time she went on the coach to Birmingham, to see Peter Kay, but they broke down on the bus for seven hours. Dad said the conversation itself felt like it had taken much longer than that.

I got off the phone with Mam and went straight to ring Gramps, who was apathetic about the whole thing.

'I've been stitched up, Ives,' he said.

'How?'

'Should've been out months ago.'

'You haven't even been in hospital that long.'

'Don't be so patronising, babes.'

He was going to be out in a couple of weeks, meaning he'd be at Dad's seventieth. We'd be able to sit in the corner and make fun of Mam's friends all night. I couldn't wait.

As soon as we got off the phone, I went to ring Jamie. Habits were hard to break and I was desperate to hear his voice. Instead, I poured myself a glass of wine and opened my volunteering pack. Anna had put me in touch with her friend, Vic, who volunteered at a care home in Islington. I went along to an induction, a two-hour talk about the charity and how they helped organise social outings for the elderly. Vic said there would be alcohol involved, which was great news. Plus, Rob thought it was a real turn on that I was giving up my time to help others. It was a win-win situation. Rob and I had seen each other twice since I first went to his flat and on both occasions, I spent 70 per cent of the time getting angry at the speed of which his tongue moved, and 30 per cent of the time enjoying myself. We can't have it all though, can we?

The first weekend in June, I met Vic and ten other volunteers at Stratford station. When the coach arrived from the care home, the first person to appear was a man called Bill, who shimmied off the bus and started singing 'Viva Las Vegas'. It was going to be a good day.

Vic introduced me to Maude and within a minute I knew I was going to be fine. Maude had a hunched back and walked very slowly. She wore tiny brown Velcro shoes, thick cream socks pulled up to her knees, a long brown skirt and an over-sized blue cardigan. She carried a cute little leather handbag with her, just like the Queen's, with two knitting needles sticking out the top.

Maude kept remarking that this was the most excited she'd been in years, which only made me love her more. She was having the time of her life and we hadn't even left the bus station yet. I helped her onto the new bus, strapped her in and sat down beside her. She got out her knitting needles, before putting them down on her lap.

'You don't mind, pet, do you?'

'The knitting? No, of course not.'

'It's just I'm making a little cardi for my friend Judith's new granddaughter, but I'm quite a bit behind schedule.'

'Knit away, Maude.'

'I can talk and knit, you know. Ask me anything, I'm an open book, me.'

Maude had lived in Islington all her life. Her mother died when she was eight and she was brought up by her dad, a West London boy who worked as a lift engineer. She was very proud of the fact that he used to fix the fancy art deco lift in Selfridges, which meant he mingled with lots of celebrities. He was once in a lift with Lauren Bacall and when he came home to tell Maude, she shrieked with delight and asked him to regale every detail about the glamorous actress. Ever since, every morning when she went in front of the mirror, she would try and mimic Miss Bacall's shiny, bouncy curls. She said the trick was in the parting, which started exactly at the arch of her brow. When I told her I couldn't remember the last time I did anything other than put my hair up in a messy bun, she looked horrified at my lack of effort. I asked her to tell me more about how she managed to master the signature wave and, luckily for me, she seemed to forget about my laziness.

We went on a mini tour of London, which I thought was unnecessary considering the O2 was less than five miles away from Stratford. But Maude was enjoying herself, and that's all that mattered.

We stood at the main entrance of the O2 holding hands and gazing up at the big glass windows. Maude was in awe; she couldn't remember the last time she'd seen anyone sing live and Bill's escapades on the karaoke machine in their old people's home didn't count. She asked me where the merchandise stand was.

'I've been saving up, dear,' she said.

'Bloody hell,' I said, as we got to the desk.

'What's wrong?'

'Nothing.'

Twenty-five quid for a teddy bear wearing a T-shirt with the slogan, 'never underestimate a woman who listens to Cliff Richard'. It was quite something.

Maude asked me to get her purse out of her bag. She opened the zip and took out four pristine £20 notes and £8 in 50p coins.

'Maude, we won't need all that,' I said, trying to get her to put her cash away.

'I've saved it, pet.'

'Yes, but . . . '

She looked at me anxiously as I thought of what to say next.

'You can't spend all of that.'

'Why?'

'It's eighty pounds, Maude.'

'Eighty-eight, dear.'

'Well, exactly, that's a lot of money.'

'But, I saved it.'

'Yes, but, do you mean to spend all of it?'

'Of course I do.'

I whispered Jesus Christ under my breath and signalled someone over to serve us.

Maude was ecstatic with her teddy bear, tea towel, calendar and ballpoint pen. When Maude handed her money over she asked me why I was taking so long to pick something out for myself, and when I couldn't think of an excuse quick enough, I blurted out, 'The magnet!' and parted with £7.

I had no clue how Cliff managed to look so great, but there he was on stage, in skinny black jeans, a garish shirt and a black leather waistcoat, and he looked phenomenal. Maude was singing away and clapping her hands. I put my arm around her and as she shouted, 'This is fantastic, pet!', I don't know if it was the merchandise or Maude's enthusiasm, but I got out of my seat and danced to all the hits with her. Vic was in front of us and turned around laughing.

'You two are like a pair of naughty schoolgirls,' she said.

Maude clapped her hands and carried on singing 'Sweet Little Sixteen'. It was the best Saturday I could remember.

When the concert finished, Maude was crying.

'I am so lucky, dear,' she said.

'No, I'm lucky. Thank you, Maude,' I said, and I meant it.

On the bus home, Maude asked me if I was courting. I didn't want to spoil the day by mentioning Jamie, so I said that I wasn't, and changed the subject. As they dropped the volunteers off at Stratford, I hugged her again and thanked her for a wonderful evening.

'Promise me you'll come and visit, dear?' she said, holding my hand.

'Maude, you won't be able to get rid of me.'

I couldn't wait to tell Mia that she had been replaced by a seventy-seven-year-old woman with a penchant for asexual popstars. I got out my phone and, as I did, Anna rang.

'Anna, you need to meet Maude!'

'Ivy—'

'She's the most amazing woman.'

'Ivy . . .'

'What's wrong? Why is your voice like that?'

'It didn't work.'

'What didn't work?'

'I'm not pregnant.'

Chapter 26

Where's all this grief going?

I went straight to Anna's and found her on the bathroom floor, leaning on the bath, smoking a cigarette. I'd not seen Anna smoke in about a decade.

'I'm so sorry,' I said, as I crouched over her and gave her a hug.

I sat down beside her and lit myself one too. She rolled over and put her head into my lap and started sobbing. Mark put his head around the bathroom door, passed me an ashtray, and closed the door on us.

Anna was obsessed with reading stories about women's experiences of IVF. She trawled through thousands of web pages and tens of books. It was like winning the lottery, or so it seemed. Yes, Couple Z might have won £10,000, but Couple X spent £100,000 on lottery tickets over the years and now they were bitter, broke and alone. I told her to stay away from blogs. They all featured smug-marrieds making unhelpful comments like, 'Don't worry, you guys will be next, we know it!' But they didn't know it. It was all rubbish. Why was everyone selling so much false hope? Why couldn't we all be honest with each other: this was a gruelling, emotional horror show. Anna met a woman in the waiting room of the fertility clinic a little while ago, and they became friends for a few weeks, but in the end, Anna gave up. It was all-consuming enough already, she couldn't handle being burdened with someone else's heartache too.

'If it makes you feel better, I had a dream last night that I couldn't kiss anymore,' I said, as she lit another cigarette.

'Where did that come from?' she laughed.

'I can't stop thinking about kissing. It's because of Rob.'

'I thought you were having fun?'

'It's too much work. He's like a thirsty dog.'

'That does make me feel better, thank you.'

'See, told you.'

'I'm glad you're having an equally shit time.'

'Yup, still one fiancé down.'

'And I'm still childless.'

'I feel like someone's died.'

'Yeah, me too.'

It was a kind of death. Grief is a highly calibrated thing and I didn't know where either of us were at or how we were going to move onto the next level. We just had to do what Liz said, and try to put one foot in front of the other.

I kissed Anna on the forehead and went into the living room to find Mark.

He was sitting in the dark, staring out of the window. There was an empty bottle of beer and a couple of used tissues by his side.

'Mark?'

He turned to face me but didn't say anything.

'I'm going to go home, but let me know if you need anything, OK?'

'We'll be fine, Ivy.'

'I know, but ring me if you need help.'

'I know how to take care of this.'

'I know ... I ... I'm trying to help.'

'I know. You've done enough, thank you.'

He turned to look back out the window.

I toyed with the idea of going over to hug him, but I thought it would make things worse. I said goodbye and walked out the door.

I walked home via the kebab shop; I'd been making frequent visits to this outlet and was pleased to see a familiar face as I walked in.

'Hi Selim,' I said, as I got to the counter.

'Ivy! You want a can?'

'Yes, please. Full fat.'

'I know! Chips and Doner?'

'Yes, thank you.'

'Extra salad?'

'No, what's the point.'

'OK, sit down and wait.'

I sat down on the table and lit a cigarette.

'Ivy, you can't do that in here!'

'Shit, sorry,' I said as I went to stand by the door.

'I give you extra chips.'

'Thanks, Selim.'

'And vinegar on top.'

'Always vinegar on first.'

'Why you so about the vinegar?'

'Selim, why would you put vinegar on after the salt?'

'I don't know.'

'The vinegar goes first, so it can soak up all the salt.'

'I know, I know.'

'Thank you, Selim.'

'You OK?'

'I've been better.'

'You be good to yourself, Ivy. The Coke's on me.'

The next day, Mia suggested we go to Hampstead Heath. We lay in the sunshine on some dusty, ugly blanket that she'd stolen from the prop room at the National Theatre. She was in a state because Noah's ex-girlfriend Clara had just been cast in a new play at the Royal Court.

'I hate her,' she said, as she took her top off to get more rays.

'Mia, your bra is see-through.'

'Yeah?'

'There are children everywhere.'

She ignored me.

'Ivy, she's a dick.'

'Why is she a dick?'

'We hate her.'

'That's a bit dramatic—'

'But we have to go see this play.'

'What? No, we don't.'

'We do. I'm texting her now.'

'Mia!'

'She needs to think I'm OK with this.'

'Why?'

'It's imperative.'

'It's not imperative.'

'Why are you so negative all the time?'

'Why are you so mental all the time?'

Mia and Clara were in the same year at drama school, always up against each other for the lead role. It didn't help that they looked similar, they both had blue eyes, but Clara was slightly taller and had thick, delicious blonde hair, whilst Mia's was always a bit wild. Also, she was 'less in-your-face'. I would never, ever tell Mia this. Mia had done amazingly well after graduating and landed herself a supporting role on Broadway. I went out to see her and cried every time she walked on stage; she was mesmerising. She stayed in New York for two years and we threw the biggest welcome home party when she moved back to London. Her agent was so optimistic; there was no stopping her. But, when she'd been back six months and hadn't got a single job, she started to worry. She worked in a pub in Putney for a while, and every Monday she would line up at the Royal Court to get cheap theatre tickets. She became obsessed, and the more anxious she got about the jobs, the less auditions she seemed to get. Meanwhile, Clara's career skyrocketed. She made her professional debut as Desdemona with the Royal Shakespeare Company and she smashed it. I went to go see it with Anna and I couldn't take my eyes off her. I never told Mia; she'd never speak to me again if she found out. You can imagine how thrilled she was when she met Noah and found out he'd dated Clara for a while. Even if it was years ago, it was enough to make Mia's jealousy go into overdrive.

We stayed on the Heath all afternoon, sinking a couple of bottles of rosé and singing along to Radio 1. At one point, Mia got up and performed a solo rendition of Beyoncé's 'Halo', but when people started staring, I had to pull at her shorts to get her to sit back down again.

'By the way, the boys are having a party on Friday,' she said, as she sat back down beside me. 'It's my own fault.'

'What is?'

'The party. I accidentally picked up four hundred pounds of drugs yesterday.'

This wasn't the first time this had happened. Mia needed glasses but refused to get her eyes tested because she was convinced they wouldn't suit her. We were at her thirtieth last year when she ordered £400 worth of drugs and had to borrow £360 from everyone at the party to pay for it all. I never did get that £24.30 back.

I was telling her what a total idiot she was when Gramps called.

'Hiya babes. You OK?'

'Great, Gramps; what's going on?'

'Everyone's doing my head in.'

'Well, you'll be out soon.'

'They gave me cold custard today. The bastards.'

'Gramps, your language.'

'Your mother is driving me up the wall too, Ives.'

'What's she done now?'

'This party, it's getting over the top, mun.'

'Well, it's Dad's seventieth—'

'Don't I know!' he interrupted. 'I'm wearing my new shoes.'

'Will you be my first dance?'

'Of course.'

'Tell your mother I want Nat King Cole, mun.'

'I'll make sure you get it.'

'I miss you, Ivy.'

'I miss you too, Gramps. One month left.'

'Counting down the days, babes.'

Chapter 27

Contemplating the environment

'What do you think Mam's first comment will be?' Anna asked. We were sitting in the back of the taxi, Mark, Anna and I, on the way back to my parents' house for the big birthday party. I'd been doing my best to give them both space, after what Mark said back at their flat, but the truth is that I'd been looking forward to this weekend more than anything. I felt like I was part of something special when I was with them.

'My jumper, she hates this jumper,' Mark said.

'My hair,' I said.

'Yeah, always your hair,' Mark agreed.

'She'll be all over me like a rash,' Anna said.

'I don't know what's worse – the attention or the criticism,' I said.

'If she mentions that Highland water again, I am going to lose it.'

'What?' asked Mark.

'Didn't you hear? There's a spring in Scotland that's going to get Anna pregnant.'

'It's just another ploy to get us to go to Loch Lomond.'

'I thought we agreed we weren't doing that?' Mark said, with a worried look on his face.

We let ourselves in and I went straight to the fridge, getting out various types of cheese, grapes, crackers and a bottle of wine. We sat in silence and scoffed our faces. This was the only peace and quiet we'd be getting over the next few days and we were going to savour every bit of it. We got a good twenty minutes of calm in before we heard Mam shout, 'Darlings!' and run down the stairs. She greeted us in her bathrobe with a face mask on.

'You weren't meant to be here until eleven pm,' she said.

'We caught the earlier train, I did text.'

'I was having a lovely glass of Chablis in the bath.'

'Where's Dad?'

'Your father's in the loft listening to Alan Bennett.'

'Course he is.'

'Oh, my precious baby lamb, come here,' she said, opening her arms to greet me.

She stroked my hair then quickly released me from her embrace. She stood in front of me at arm's length, eyeing me up and down.

'Darling, is everything OK?' she asked.

'Yeah, fine,' I said, putting a wedge of Stilton in my mouth.

'That shirt's a cry for help.'

'Mam!' Anna said, laughing.

'I knew I should've gone with Ivy's shirt,' Mark said.

'Look, girls, if I don't say it, nobody will.'

'You're impossible, Mam,' Anna said.

'Don't make me laugh, I'll break the face mask.'

The next morning, I went downstairs to find Mam smoking in the garden. She was trying to be secretive about it, so when she caught me looking at her through the window, she threw it on the grass and pretended to attend to the dahlias.

'You don't have to hide,' I said to her, as she came back into the kitchen.

'Ivy, this party will be the end of me.'

'It'll be great.'

'I can't begin to tell you how busy I am.'

'Can I do anything?'

'Linda's already lost two helium balloons. We're on our third number seven.'

'Right.'

'They're ten ninety-nine a pop, Ivy.'

'Why are you spending ten ninety-nine on one balloon?'

'Ivy, stop asking me questions. I need space to think.'

'Right, well, you do that. I'm going for a run.'

'Hang on, I wanted us to go for a walk later.'

'I thought you were busy?'

'I got us all new water bottles for Loch Lomond. We can trial them out.'

'I'm not going to Loch Lomond, and you hate walking.'

'Look how fabulous they are.'

She opened the cupboard and there they were: three in rose gold for the girls, two in black for the boys.

'Mia's got one of these; aren't they twenty-five pounds each?'

'Sweat proof, leak proof, BPA free.'

'What's BPA?'

'I'm not sure.'

'You bought five of these?'

'Yes. One each.'

'You spent a hundred and twenty-five pounds on water bottles?'

'It's an investment . . . for us, for the environment.'

'I'm going,' I said, quickly putting on my trainers.

'OK, darling, and don't mention this to your father!'

I called Gramps to tell him I'd be over after my run. I ran

down to the beach and sat down on the sand to catch my breath. The water was still, glistening in the sunshine. There were children playing by the shore, buckets and spades in hand. There were young boys on boards, frustrated with the lack of surf, and teenage girls in skimpy bikinis ogling for their attention. I had sex for the first time on this beach; I was fifteen and his name was Lloyd. I met him in the car park one summer. He was seventeen and drove a yellow Vauxhall Corso, which made me think he was the coolest boy in the world. We snogged for hours in his car and for the first three weeks, all he did was touch my left breast. On week four, he moved onto my right breast, and that's when I told him I wanted to lose my virginity to him. I knew he'd slept with three girls, but he had a face like Heath Ledger and he listened to Blink 182. Nothing else mattered. Mam banned me from going out that night after I got a C in my maths test, but I snuck out and met him in his car at the end of the road. Mam had recently returned from Edinburgh after a girls' weekend away with a posh tartan blanket and, in an act of teenage rebellion, I stole it on the way out. We were going to have sex on it and there was nothing she could do about it.

The sex was forgettable, as all sex is when you're a teenager, but he was kind. He always had Polo mints on him and bags of Cadbury Wispa bars in the car. Those were simpler times.

By the time I got to Gramps' I was knackered and my knee was starting to twinge. I knocked on the front door and put my hand on the window to steady myself as I took some deep breaths. I could see him walk towards the door, stick in hand, smiling. He unlocked the door and I grabbed hold of him, almost knocking him over.

'Come on, babes. You'll embarrass me, mun.'

'I've missed you so much.'

'Come on in, you softie.'

I walked into the living room and there it was – *Sleepless in Seattle,* all set up ready for us to watch. I gave him another hug and almost toppled him over.

'You stink, mun.'

'Sorry, it's sweat, I've been for a run.'

'I can see that, Ives.'

'Need to catch my breath a bit. Do you have any squash?'

'You know where it is.'

I came back in and sat down beside him.

'Haven't been running in a while.'

'Don't be stupid, babes. It's the fags, mun.'

'I'm not smoking.'

'You're your mother's daughter. You're smoking.'

'Fine.'

'I don't want to see you with that shit this weekend, OK?'

'OK.'

'Don't sulk like that.'

'I'm not sulking. Put the film on!'

We sat arm in arm watching it, laughing and crying at the same bits we always did. The last time I watched this, I thought, I was engaged.

Chapter 28

Changing rooms

The next day, we went shopping to find me a suitable dress for the party. Mam kept saying she didn't mind paying 'through the nose' for an outfit because it would mean I'd look less, 'washed out'. She was quite wrong.

'I should've kept my graduation dress,' I said.

'Oh no, you were much bigger then,' Mam replied.

'That's helpful, thanks.'

She was staring at my stomach, so I knew where this was going.

'You know where all that sugar goes?'

'Where?'

'To your gut, darling.'

'Mam, what are you on about?'

'Alcohol. You should have at least three days off a week.'

I looked at Anna to save me from the conversation, but she put her hands up in despair.

'When did you last have a day off?'

'I'm not talking about me. I'm lucky.'

'Right.'

'I've always been naturally thin.'

I shot Anna another look.

'Can we get a move on, Mam?' she said.

'All I'm saying is that when you get to my age, you'll be wishing you listened to my advice.'

'What exactly is your advice?'

'Darling, I'm just saying.'

I looked at my reflection in the mirror; my face was a little bloated. Truth be told, everything was a little bloated.

'Right, let's go,' I said. 'This is painful.'

Mam made dramatic, audible sighs as we made our way out.

'What's wrong now?' Anna asked.

'I can't bear it,' she said, walking out of the shop.

'What?'

'Those changing rooms ... so local authority.'

We got home and I tried to think of things to do to keep me away from Mam. You'd have sworn she was planning the inauguration of the next president the way she was going about everything. I assumed that all her years organising piss-ups for charities would come in handy for such an occasion, but no.

I wasn't allowed anywhere near Dad; he was reorganising his vinyls and had requested not to be disturbed. He told us he would be taking dinner alone in the loft, some 'quiet reflection' time before his milestone birthday, which of course was code for, 'I need to get away from your mother.' I rang Gramps, who said that I was only allowed to come over if I could guarantee Mam wouldn't come with me. She'd called him earlier that morning and said he was only allowed to pick clothes for the party from his new, post-hospital wardrobe. Under no circumstances was he allowed to wear anything that he'd worn to previous social occasions. This was a clear sign that she was losing it, because everyone who knows my grand-father knows he almost never wears the same item of clothing twice. He's like Princess Margaret without the chain-smoking.

Come to think of it, they have a lot in common: unpredictable, rebellious and incredibly spoilt. Her comment annoyed him and he wanted to be as far away from her as possible, which very much worked in my favour.

I found him in the garden. He was leaning against the wall, glaring at the children playing on their skateboards.

'What are you doing?' I asked as I approached him.

'It's not Travellers' Awareness Month.'

'What?'

'They can sod off and get their own patch.'

'Who?'

'The little shits,' he said, waving his stick at the children.

'Get away from the wall and stop swearing, Gramps.'

'Don't use that tone with me, Ivy.'

'What tone?'

'*That* tone, young lady!'

'I give up,' I said, and walked into the house.

He came indoors and sat down beside me, looking a bit sheepish.

'What's gotten into you today?' I asked.

'My leg's giving me *gyp*.'

'Grief, you mean.'

'*Gyp*, Ives!'

'Stop going out into the garden then.'

He was tense. I almost pressed the issue, but feared I would rile him up even more, so I went to put on *Homes Under the Hammer.* Property programmes are another great way to diffuse family tension. We sat in silence, but he kept shaking his head and sighing. After a while, I couldn't stand it any longer and asked him what the matter was.

'Boys are shits, Ives.'

'They are if they're six years old, Gramps.'

'We can be selfish, us men.'

'What are you on about?'

'Nothing, ignore me.'

I saw his face scan mine; he was contemplating what to say next, something I hardly ever saw him do. Usually he just came right out and said whatever was in his head, regardless of who was the target. He took my hand.

'How are things with Jamie, babes?'

'There's nothing to talk about.'

'You haven't heard anything?'

'No,' I lied.

'I worry about you, babes.'

'I'm fine, I promise.'

'You're taking care of yourself, aren't you?'

'Yes! Honestly.'

'You'd tell me otherwise, right?'

'You know I would. Can we just watch TV, please?'

At least three times a week I would wake mid-dream, gasping for air, panicking in a pool of sweat. I wasn't alone on the boat anymore – he was there, watching me drown. As I sank deeper into the abyss, she would appear. She'd come up behind him, put her arm around his waist and they'd watch me drown together.

It took me ages to get back to sleep, and as luck would have it, it seemed that every time I started to drift back off again, my alarm would wake me, and it would be time to get up for work. It was a relentless cycle that made me fear going to sleep. I started staying up as late as I could to ensure that when I got to bed I'd be tired enough to drop off right away. But that never happened; I just lay there, running over all the different scenarios in my head. I imagined bumping into him on the tube, in the park, on the street. I went through every plausible scenario. I wanted to make sure that the next time I saw him, I was ready. I wrote down all the different things I would say, and would practise them at 3am, over a cigarette and, usually, a small glass of whisky. Next time, I'd be ready.

Of course, I didn't tell Gramps any of this; it would only worry him.

I got back home just in time for dinner. Anna made beef Wellington, but Mam refused to have any pastry because she was trying to lose another three pounds before the party. We told her this would be impossible, but she said we were being negative and stormed off into the living room to watch *Game of Thrones*. I took my dinner and joined her. I knew she was worked up – we are never, ever allowed to eat dinner in the living room.

'I'm sick of everyone having a go at me,' she said.

'Nobody is having a go, Mam.'

'Anna deliberately made beef Wellington when I told her not to.'

'I think that's unfair. She's been off meat for weeks and you know it's her favourite.'

'What about my favourite?'

'It's a bit difficult to cook a family meal when you're only eating broccoli.'

'Whose side are you on, Ivy?'

I wanted to cheer her up, so I suggested she show me her dress options for the party. One of Mam's favourite things to do is try on all her party outfits in front of me and Anna and pretend she's on the runway. She'll go full throttle: hair, make-up and all the accessories.

Mam had whittled it down to seven potential outfits for Dad's party. Not wanting to stop there, she had also picked out three potential outfits for Dad, which all looked the exact same to me, but I knew better than to comment. Dad had made that mistake and Mam, horrified, had refused to speak to him all afternoon. As she'd put it, 'How can you not know the difference between celestial and imperial blue?'

She tried on each individual outfit; matching underwear, dress, shoes, handbag and jewellery. I got my phone out and put on the Stones, her favourite, and pretended I was MC at London Fashion Week. She sauntered down the length of the room, stopping at each end to give me a twirl. On outfit five, Dad walked upstairs, popped his head around the door and wolf-whistled, which set her off even more. She was swaying her hips and flinging her handbag over her shoulder, working the crowd (albeit only me and Dad) like a real pro. We cheered her on and when all seven outfits had been paraded, we gave her a standing ovation. After her final bow, Dad went over to give her a kiss.

'Get off me, Tony!' she cried as he nuzzled his face into her neck. She gave him a kiss on the cheek then went to take off the final pair of shoes. Dad gave me a wink and walked out the door before turning back.

'Mags?'

'Oh, what now?'

'You are taking some of these back, yeah?'

'Of course, the tags are still on. See?' she said, showing him the labels.

'Good . . . just checking.'

'You've got no intention of returning any of these, do you?' I asked when Dad was safely out of the room.

'Ivy, you'll keep your mouth shut if you know what's good for you.'

I laughed, told her I loved her, and walked back downstairs.

Chapter 29

One in a million

On the morning of the party, everyone was on high alert. Nobody wanted to put a foot wrong in front of Mam, who'd been awake since 4am. As usual, she'd been pottering so loudly about the house that she'd woken the rest of us all up, and by 6am, when we really couldn't stand it any longer, we all got out of bed. I tried to make breakfast, but she took the bowl away from me as I was emptying cereal into it. She told Anna she wasn't allowed coffee because it might stain (not sure where) and Dad wasn't allowed to put on the TV because she needed to concentrate (not sure what on). It was a harmonious environment.

I downloaded Cilla Black's episode of *Desert Island Discs* and told myself it was going to be OK; I would come out of Mam's pre-party meltdown unscathed. Even though my knee had electric currents shooting through it, I put on my trainers and went for a run. Anything, and I mean anything, was preferable to staying inside with her.

I was walking up the back garden when I saw Anna in the window; she was in my old room, now the nursery. I walked back into the house and up the stairs, knocking on the bedroom door as I entered, not wanting to startle her.

'I told her to keep it up,' she said. 'I can't bear the thought of her taking it all down.'

I looked around the room; it was the first time I'd stopped to take it all in. Last time I went in, I was too angry about my stuff having disappeared (still no word of that).

The wallpaper was decorated with pink, blue and yellow hot air balloons, with little bears in each one who were waving down at us. The room was decked out with the latest Silver Cross gear: a gorgeous cream cot with matching drawers and changing table, with individual knobs with various animals on them. Dad had put up shelves on both walls to house all our favourite books: *The Very Hungry Caterpillar, Dear Zoo, Guess How Much I Love You* and enough Roald Dahl to last a lifetime.

I started to cry.

'Don't you dare,' Anna said, taking me in her arms.

'Why aren't you crying?' I asked.

'I think I'm at the end of my tears.'

'Mia said our bodies are sixty per cent water, so it makes sense that we can cry so much.'

'Mia's an idiot.'

'Yeah, she is.'

Mam would've loved putting that room together. She'd have been so proud at how beautiful it was. I'd not even bothered to ask her how she was feeling, walking past this room every day, being reminded of what wasn't happening.

'One more time, that's what we said,' Anna said, breaking the silence.

'Yeah, one more time.'

'Don't tell me it's going to be OK.'

'I wouldn't dare.'

'I hate when people say that.'

'Yeah, me too.'

'What do they know anyway?'

'Nothing, that's what.'

I walked downstairs to the living room where Mam was engrossed in yet another episode of *Game of Thrones*.

'I thought you were rushed off your feet?' I said, as I went to sit down beside her.

'It's bedlam, Ives. I need a little half hour to myself.'

I kissed her on the cheek and pulled her in close to me.

'What's that for?' she asked.

'Nothing.'

'Don't tell me you've lost one of your new earrings?'

'No, Mam.'

'I need everything to be perfect today, Ives.'

'I love you, that's all.'

'My precious baby lamb, I love you too.'

'Let's go upstairs and get ready together?'

'Now you're talking,' she said. 'I'll grab the champers, you get Anna.'

We all got ready in Mam and Dad's room. Mam pretended that she was annoyed at me for stealing her accessories and new make-up products (as if I can afford a sixty pound face cream) and I finally found an outfit, one of Anna's oldies. While Mam was disappointed that I wasn't wearing anything new for the occasion, she was pleased that my 'swimmer's frame' was masked by the off-the-shoulder cut of the jumpsuit. At last, everyone was happy. On a side note, I've never been a swimmer.

We arrived at the cricket club at 5pm. Mam had set up all the decorations the night before, so we had a full two hours to refold napkins and rearrange the confetti on the tables. Thank God we arrived early. Dad and Mark were still out playing golf. Golfing gets you out of everything.

Linda arrived shortly after us.

'Linda, you're late!' Mam shouted at her. She was carrying two enormous gold helium balloons.

'These have been the end of me, Mags,' she said, walking towards us and air-kissing Mam.

'Darling girl, how are you?' she asked, tilting her head and pouting her lips in an infuriatingly patronising manner.

'I'm doing great, thanks.'

'You look thin, are you eating?'

'She eats everything,' Mam said.

'My heart goes out to you, darling.'

'Thanks. How are you? Congratulations on Lewis' engagement.'

'I was so embarrassed about the timing, what with you and Jamie.'

'Linda, it's OK.'

'You will find someone.'

'Thanks.'

'Get right back on that horse.'

'Sure,' I said, looking for Anna for help. She'd gone off somewhere, on purpose, I bet.

'You are stronger than you think.'

'Thanks, Linda.'

'And Jamie? Well, I can't even,' she said, throwing her hands up in the air dramatically.

'Right. Can I get you a drink?'

'No, no. Now, you take as much time as you need. But not too much time, of course. You want a family.'

'I'm going to get a drink, Linda.'

'You poor, poor love.'

This conversation happened in various forms throughout the night. Nobody asked Anna if she was OK; they completely avoided any baby talk, which she was thrilled about. She said it was the first time in a long while that she felt relaxed in a group of people and thanked me for having such a shit-show of a life that the focus was now on me. I was glad to be of help.

Everyone received strict instructions to arrive for 7pm, as Dad was making his grand entrance at 7.15pm sharp. He picked Gramps up after golf and took him for a pint, another opportunity for them both to moan about Mam. Once the guests started arriving, Mam was in her element, mingling with everyone, being complimented on her outfit, how nice Anna and I looked, how great the room was done out. She was loving it.

Fair play to her, the canapés were a hit; roast beef with horseradish, pork belly skewers, triple cooked chips and lobster rolls. They had five different lagers on tap, various types of Welsh gin, endless bottles of Tia Maria and copious amounts of whisky. It was 100 per cent Dad. Well, aside from the excessive use of confetti and shimmery banners, which was more Mam.

Just before Dad and Gramps were due to arrive, everyone stood by the bar armed with confetti canons and party poppers. As they walked through the door, we all cheered, bottles popped, and everyone went into a stellar rendition of 'Happy Birthday' in Welsh, even though nobody in the room spoke the language. I went to take Gramps off Dad's arm and, as we walked away, Dad bowed to the whole room, before gesturing for Mam to come over. They kissed and hugged, and everyone erupted in wolf whistles. I'd never seen them happier. I looked over to Anna and Mark, who were chanting, 'Mags, Mags, Mags,' and I looked at Gramps standing beside me, with a tear running down his cheek. He turned and faced me, I smiled and gave his hand a squeeze. For a split second, it didn't feel like anyone was missing.

Mark was DJ for the evening, a job he took very seriously, while Anna and I sat beside Gramps, laughing as he insulted all of Mam's friends. Linda 'looked shabby' (she was wearing a beautiful floral wrap dress and looked lovely), her son Lewis was, 'thick as shit' (he's a junior doctor) and his fiancée was, 'a commoner from the valleys' (everyone is common to Gramps). Just before 10pm, when he was about to go home, Mam asked Mark to put on Nat King Cole's 'Unforgettable'. She came over to us, looked at Gramps and said, 'Ivan Thomas, I might not be as good a dancer as Mam was, but you owe me one.'

He couldn't stand so well, so he steadied himself against the table as he took her hands in his. She did twirls around him while Anna and I stood beside them, cheering him on. As the song ended, she grabbed his cheeks and kissed them both.

'I love you, babes,' he told her.

'I love you more,' she said.

When the song finished, Dad asked everyone to quiet down for him to say a few words. He started with how Mam made him buy a new outfit, and their argument about the various shades of blue. He asked the men in the room to put their hands up if they knew the difference between powder blue and marine blue, and Gramps was the only one to raise a hand. That got a big laugh.

'I'm so glad to have my two girls here tonight,' he said, pint in hand. 'I miss them all the time, mind. I hate that they don't live down the road from us, but they're probably very happy about that, ha! You're both such beautiful, kind girls. I'm so proud of you both, I really am. You also worry me sick, but that's another story! Thank you for being so good to your old dad; your mother and I love you both very much.

'And Mark, listen, you're not allowed to come down again, not after that performance on the golf course. Jesus, you make me look eighty-five, not seventy. It's my birthday, you sod. No, Mark, you know how grateful I am for everything you do for Anna. With Anna of course comes Ivy. You deserve a medal for putting up with those two, ha. Thank you, I mean that.'

He made everyone raise a glass.

'Right, who's next. Ah, there we go – Ivan! Dad, it wouldn't be a party without you, and I'm chuffed to bits you're on the mend. Don't forget, you owe me a dance, and I'm picking the bloody song this time.'

Everyone cheered and whooped.

'Now then, last, but not least, my beautiful Margaret. Mags, I don't know what I did to deserve you, but you are the single greatest thing to ever happen to me.'

Everyone said, 'Ahhh,' in unison.

'You are a total nightmare, haha, but, God, how I love you. You're one in a million, Mags, and I wake up every day a better man because of you.'

He started welling up. Mam ran over to him and kissed him all over his face and everyone started clapping. I leant into Anna and told her how lucky we were.

'I wouldn't have it any other way, Ivy.'

Chapter 30

Virginia Woolf

While everyone was telling me that it was important to get myself out there and try to talk to a member of the opposite sex, I was losing sleep over the *Love Island* final and had little time or energy to do much else. I'd barely seen Rob, mainly because I didn't want to drink bitter coffee from an organic farm in Guatemala and listen to the realness of Nick Cave for three hours before he went down on me. What I wanted was to drink a bottle of cheap rosé in the sunshine with an older, European gentleman who kissed me like there was no tomorrow and didn't try to spend the evening discussing why *Skeleton Tree* is one of the most important albums of our time. It's not like I was asking for much.

I watched the *Love Island* final with Maude. I'd been to see her a few times since the Cliff outing, and whilst I was reluctant to take her down the rabbit hole that is *Daily Mail* Showbiz, it was important that she was up to date with everything to minimise the amount of questions asked when the show was on. So, despite everyone's disapproval (Mia called me a sell-out, which I said was hypocritical as last week I saw her looking at photos of Kate Moss on there),

I downloaded the app and went through the main themes with her. You'd think a TV show about a bunch of twenty-somethings snogging and shagging in a villa would be easy to follow, but it's quite complex. Maude was enthralled; I was thrilled.

Maude had become interested in my love life, or lack thereof. I tried to avoid the conversation as best I could but she kept pressing me. How could a lovely woman like me still be single? It was tricky to convey to her that while I was happy to be felt up in a public toilet, I was in no way ready to go on a real date. I don't think they did casual in Maude's day, and my situation was very, very casual.

I was starting to forget intimate details about Jamie, things I swore I knew inside out just weeks before. I could remember little things I did, like the way I held his hand, or how I stroked the back of his neck when I was bored, but I couldn't remember the contours of his face, or how exactly the muscles on his back moved when he put a shirt on. I could remember when he wrote 'you are annoying' on the bathroom mirror with my new lipstick, after we'd fallen out about how many potatoes were acceptable for a six-man roast. But him, physically, I couldn't picture it.

Mark heard that Jamie was back in his own flat, in Bermondsey, so I refused to go anywhere near the Borough of Southwark. The only thing I could think about was whether she was in the flat with him. I couldn't bear the actual details of his living situation, so everyone went out of their way to avoid the topic at all costs. Well, everyone aside from Mia and Dan, who have far too much to say about everything.

It was approaching August, when London and Londoners are at their best, and I'd arranged to go over to Noah and Mia's to cook them Sunday lunch. I was trying to make plans on Sundays that involved me doing something practical in a bid to make it home before 5am. That morning, I'd come in at 4.25am, which I was very proud of.

I woke that Sunday to Beyoncé's 'Sorry'. Mia had changed the alarm tone on my phone, her theory being that waking up to a song about female empowerment and sexual confidence would help set my day off to the right start. I must admit, it did help.

I let myself in and found Mia sunbathing in the back garden, drinking an Aperol spritz. She was wearing layers upon layers of gold jewellery, a pink turban wrapped around her head, white men's briefs, and a ripped T-shirt. I told her she was becoming a caricature of herself and went to put the oven on. I heard Noah rehearsing his lines from the living room, so I went in to say hello. He was standing by the fireplace, with one leg mounted onto a wingback Chesterfield chair, smoking from a shiny silver holder. He was rocking a paisley dress with blue Dr Marten boots.

'What on earth are you wearing?' I asked.

'It's my auntie's.'

'Is that not a bit weird?'

'No, why?'

'She's dead.'

'Yeah, so?'

'I don't know, you're wearing a dead woman's clothes ... it's creepy.'

'Ives, don't be so narrow-minded.'

He waved me out of the living room, so I went back into the kitchen. Mia was crouched over the oven.

'Don't touch that, Mia.'

'I'm putting it on oven mode.'

'It was on oven mode.'

'No, that's grill.'

'No, that's oven.'

'Squiggly lines mean grill?'

'Yes.'

'Well, that explains a lot.'

I turned the oven back to the correct setting and told her to sit down and pour me a glass of wine. I often wonder how Mia functions as an adult; her lack of common sense and shocking culinary skills being two characteristics that never cease to amaze me. I think that constant sense of restlessness is down to her being an actor, and summer, being famously dry for acting gigs, is the worst for this.

We listened to Cerys Matthews' show on the radio while I cooked, with Mia humming along beside me, pretending to know all the jazz songs. Mia likes to listen to highbrow programmes to convince herself that she is more cultured than she really is. She always says, 'Be the woman you know you can be,' or something like that. She had recently convinced herself that she looked like Virginia Woolf and wouldn't shut up about it. She had a habit of aligning herself with famous women, another sign of boredom, and she'd gone through quite a diverse list in 2019 alone: Virginia, Zooey Deschanel, Jessica Biel, a young Cherie Blair and, lastly, Winona Ryder. I did point out that all these women had completely different colouring to her, but she said I was missing the point.

As she demanded I inspect her nose from a side angle, Noah came in, took one look at me and mouthed, 'Here we go again.' That man deserves a medal.

I got distracted by all the wine, so the dinner wasn't my best, but it felt nice to have achieved something on a Sunday. After dinner, with Noah retired to the attic to rehearse his lines, Mia and I sat down to watch a film.

'I've booked tickets to see Clara's play,' she said, as we were flicking through Netflix.

'You're not seriously going?' I asked.

'You are too.'

'Mia!'

'Ives, come on. I need you.'

'It's all a bit weird, Mia.'

'Come on, it'll be fun,' she pleaded.

'When is it?'

'Thirsty Thursday. We'll go out after.'

'Do I have to?'

'Yes,' she said, as she got up and came to sit beside me.

'Now, let me show you her Instagram feed . . . '

Clara's social media feed was a world unto its own. Her ability to multi-task was remarkable and her hair had that level of volume I could only dream of. Here's Clara in this season's finest fashion, both ethically sourced and chic, eating sustainable produce while holding a friend's baby and reading her lines. Mia was seething with jealousy and had a bitchy comment to support every photo. There were juice diets ('Sponsored, obviously'), headstands ('This isn't PE'), and lots of gluten-free, vegan, sugar-free, no added palm oil cookies ('Just eat a Jaffa Cake, why don't you'). If you scroll deep enough, you'll find an old photo of Clara and Noah, which Mia sometimes tortures herself with. They are sitting in St James' Park; her legs are on top of his and his arm is around her shoulders. It looks like he is whispering into her ear. The caption reads: 'Summer vibes with Noah #lovethisboy #summer #insta #London #blessed #friendship #flowers #park.' I can't associate myself with anyone who uses #blessed in a non-ironic fashion.

I planned to leave by 7pm to get a good night's sleep before work the next day, but wine turned into gin and I found myself in a taxi on route home at 10.30pm.

I was dozing off when my phone woke me up. It was Gramps.

'Didn't wake you, did I, babes?'

'No, I'm just coming home.'

'On a Sunday!'

'I've not been drinking!' I lied. 'What are you doing?'

'Just sitting in bed, looking at photos of us all in Disneyland.'

'Was that when Anna threw a tantrum because she was too short for Space Mountain?'

'Yes, you ran on before her and she screamed for days.'

'Can we go back for my birthday?'

'Don't be stupid, babes. You're too old.'

'You're never too old for Disney, Gramps.'

'Joking, I am. Let's do it.'

'I want to go to Tenerife again, too.'

'I'll take you somewhere classier next time, babes.'

'What's wrong with Tenerife?'

'It's all lads on tour now, isn't it?'

'Where on earth did you get that from?' I asked, laughing.

'Owen's grandson went last week, and Owen said they kept shouting "lads, lads, lads" to each other in the airport. Owen was terrified, poor sod.'

'Can't wait to hear about that holiday.'

'Bloody idiots they all are, mun.'

'Did you see Mam today?'

'She's doing my head in with all these exercises.'

'Well, you're meant to do them.'

'They're dead hard, babes.'

'I know, but they'll help you get better.'

'Fair play, she does look after me.'

'I'm going to have to go, Gramps, my taxi's pulling up,' I lied. I was starting to feel nauseous and needed to breathe out the window.

'I'll ring you in the morning.'

'Yes, babes, that'd be lovely. Love you.'

'Love you more, Gramps.'

'I really do miss our holidays, Ives.'

'Me too. As soon as you're better, we'll go somewhere nice. I promise.'

Chapter 31

The theatre, darling

I was late to meet Mia at the Royal Court. I went out for a couple of drinks with Ethan's team during lunch, thinking Jane had gone for the day. But, unluckily for me, she hadn't, and I felt so guilty about coming back to work thirty minutes late that I stayed till 7pm to make up the time. It's difficult to be productive in work when all you've had all day is a bottle of wine and some pork scratchings. I was doing my very best to look busy when in fact I was googling nice restaurants for Anna and Mark to visit when they were on holiday in Italy. I called her when I got off at Sloane Square for a quick chat, forgetting how close the theatre is to the station, making myself even later than I already was.

'Send my love to Mia, bet she's in a right state about tonight,' Anna said.

'It's her own fault we're even going; she's such a narcissist.'

'Either way, it's good of you to indulge her.'

'Have you packed?'

'Sort of, thanks for letting me borrow so much. I'm so bored of my wardrobe.'

'Don't thank me, Mam bought it all. She said now that I'm single I need to make an effort.'

'That sounds like her.'

'What am I going to do without you?'

'Ives, it's three weeks.'

'Three whole weeks!'

'We need this, Ives.'

'I know. You can tell Mark I promise not to hound you with calls and texts.'

'Please don't, darling.'

'I was only joking.'

'I'm not sure you were.'

'Hey! I've been better.'

'I know.' She laughed.

'You're going to have the most amazing time.'

'I honestly can't wait. I'm going to drink all the wine and eat all the pasta.'

'Urgh, I hate you. Send me postcards at every stop.'

'Nobody sends postcards anymore, Ives.'

'I like it, it's romantic.'

'Fine, you'll get postcards.'

'One with you and the Pope.'

'Do you think if I meet him he'll miraculously make me fall pregnant?'

'It's worth a try.'

'I think so too.'

I got off the phone, already missing her. She needed this trip; it was an echo chamber in London, everyone was tiptoeing around them and avoiding the conversation. She said the next attempt would be their last, but nobody believed that.

I got off the phone and ran downstairs to the theatre bar. Mia wanted us to be there early so we could have a drink before going in. What she called 'loosening up'. I found her holding court at the bar, drinking a martini. She was wearing leopard print kitten heels, black leather cigarette trousers and a red cardigan. It had little hearts sewn into it and was wrapped around her shoulders revealing her slender arms. She looked sensational. I walked over to her, embarrassed by my shabby appearance.

'You look amazing,' I said as I hugged her.

'I know, wait until you see my arse in these trousers,' she said, waving at the barman to get me a drink. I whispered into her ear that I'd rather catch up on our own, but she'd spotted some friends and refused to shy away from the crowd. She wanted news to get back to Clara that Mia Bradley had arrived and was looking fabulous. To be fair, I didn't think that Clara would care one bit whether Mia had arrived or not. But, I was there to be supportive.

I felt out of place so naturally I drank quite fast. There I was, surrounded by dozens of people in a noisy basement bar in one of London's most popular theatres, and I was acutely aware that I was alone. There were groups of artists using their hands to gesticulate about the current political and socioeconomic climate, loved-up couples with their hands all over each other, and newly formed couples with no idea what to do with their hands. It was one of the rare occasions where I felt my single status. There were limited occasions where I felt outnumbered; I didn't count Anna and Mark. I was so used to their way of being with each other that I didn't notice their displays of affection, which is a good thing, considering how much time I spent with them. All I could do was hide behind a glass of wine and pretend to be on my phone. Well, I wasn't pretending, I was texting Mam – we were still mourning the death of *Love Island*.

I fell asleep within minutes of the play starting. The air was hot and the play was boring. I am a deep sleeper, quiet as a mouse, so when the play finished ninety minutes later, I assumed Mia was none the wiser.

'She is so good,' she said to me, as Clara did the final curtain call.

'Yeah,' I replied.

'Her face! So much going on, yet so subtle.'

'Yeah,' I said, stifling a yawn.

'The way she carried that final scene.'

'Hmmm.'

'What was your favourite bit?'

'Eh?'

'You need to go up to her at the bar and tell her what bit you liked best.'

'Why do I have to do that?'

'Well, I'm not doing it.'

'I liked it all.'

'What about the bit with the paedophile uncle?'

'Yeah . . . intense.'

'You are a lying piece of shit, there was no paedophile uncle!'

'Mia!'

'I knew you were asleep!'

'Why did your mind go to "paedophile uncle"? What is wrong with you?'

'Oh, don't give me that, Ivy.'

'Mia, I'm tired.'

'No, you're hungover, there's a difference. Where's your stamina?'

'Sorry.'

'Shut up and buy me a drink.'

We went to the bar and Mia asked the waiter to get me a 'Corpse Reviver', which is essentially 99 per cent absinthe. We got news that all the cast was going to Lulu's, a private members' club in Soho, and Mia insisted we go along too. Neither of us had membership but Mia was adamant we could get in because Noah once acted in a play with Jude Law and

Jude's nephew would be out tonight and he had a secret soft spot for her.

The club itself is nothing to write home about; lots of old mismatched chairs, middle-aged white people and young hosts in skimpy outfits. Mia kept pointing people out to me: he wrote the latest *Star Wars* script, he commissions dramas for Channel 4, that girl won 'Brit to Watch'. I had no clue who any of them were. Noah's friends came to join us but I told Mia I'd had enough and wanted to leave. Just as I was getting my coat, Mia tugged at my arm and ordered me to sit back down again. Clara had arrived.

'Oh my god, babe!' Clara screamed, as she ran towards us.

Mia quickly got out of her seat to greet her.

'Darling, you were phenom!' she squealed.

'That means so much, I wasn't feeling it tonight.'

'No! You were incredible!'

'Thanks, Mee Mee,' she said, taking Mia's hand. 'You look amazing!'

'No, you do! You're so thin, I love it.'

'Ah, I love you!'

'It's so good to see you!'

'You too, we must do lunch!'

'Yes! My shout, to celebrate the play.'

'You're such a babe, Mia.'

'Let me get you a drink?'

'Don't bother, my agent's over there. I'll go say hi then come join you?'

'Perf.'

Clara walked away, leaving me bemused as to what I'd just witnessed.

'So, we're saying "perf" now, are we, Mee Mee?' I said.

'Shut up, I'm being nice.'

'And "phenom"?'

'I always say "phenom".'

'Where are you taking her for lunch?'

'Pizza Express. Two for one on mains; that's all the bitch deserves.'

'You're an awful human being.'

'I know,' she said, with delight.

Clara came back and sat at the other end of the table. She was next to someone called Davey, who I assumed was a male model – horrendous dress sense, perfect whiter than white teeth, great bone structure – and spent most of the night flirting with him. She seemed to be getting bored, because she asked Mia to escort her to the bathroom, and they walked off together holding hands. I got up to follow them; there was no way I was being left alone with Davey. His face didn't move and his eyebrows were too high. You can't trust a person who looks like that.

'How well do you know Davey?' Clara asked Mia, as they touched up their make-up in the mirror.

'Oh, we go way back. He's great.'

'Is he single?'

'Yes, one hundred per cent single.'

'Oh my god, perf. He is so hot.'

'Oh my god, so hot.'

'I hate wasting my time chatting to men only to find out they're in a relationship.'

'I know, it's the worst.'

'Thanks, babe. Wish me luck,' she said, as she rushed back to shiny-faced Davey.

I shot Mia a look.

'You're being very pally,' I said.

Mia laughed.

'Davey's gay,' she said.

'You're going to hell, Mia.'

Chapter 32

A bigger one, this time

I had it all planned. I was going to have an early night, go for a run in the morning and then hit bottomless brunch with Dan. We had originally planned to go out in Vauxhall, but I felt that the Borough of Lambeth was too close to the Borough of Southwark, where Jamie lived, so I made Dan book somewhere in Soho instead.

I was drifting off to sleep when the phone rang.

'Ivy, are you at home?'

'Yeah.'

'Are you with anyone?'

'No, why?'

She started to speak again, but her voice broke.

'Mam, what's wrong?'

Silence.

'It's your grandfather . . .'

'God, what's he done now?' I asked, with a laugh.

I could hear Mam's breath down the phone, short and shallow. My chest tightened.

'Mam, what's the matter?'

'I'm so sorry, darling.'

'What? What is it?'

'He had another stroke . . .'

I got up from the sofa and turned the TV off.

'But, I talked to him yesterday . . .'

'I know you did, darling.'

'Is he back in the hospital? I'll book the train, I'll come down first thing in the morning.'

'Ivy, it was a bigger one this time.'

I walked to the kitchen and steadied myself against the fridge.

'No,' I said, shaking my head. 'He's been eating all the bananas. They said potassium would help with strokes.'

'I know . . .'

'What are you saying?'

My voice was quivering. I dropped down to the floor.

'My darling girl.'

Mam started to cry. I shook my head, this wasn't happening.

'He was getting better.'

'He was, but—'

'We spoke yesterday, Mam. Yesterday.'

'Owen found him.'

'No.'

My body started to shake as the tears streamed down my face.

'When?' I asked.

'This morning. He went over with the papers . . .'

I held my hand up to ward off her words. I was suddenly unable to breathe.

I've never feared my own grief. I knew that if someone close to me died, it would be awful, but, for some reason, I always thought I'd be able to cope. I'd be the strong one, the one who held everyone together.

I sat against that fridge, with Mam on the end of the phone, telling me that she loved me, that Gramps loved me.

Everything stood still. I was unanchored, helpless, completely alone. I've never known pain like it – like there wasn't a hope left in the world.

When Gramps was first hospitalised, I contemplated how I'd feel if this were to happen, how different life might be. It's never the same, though, is it? In fact, life itself remains the same, but you, in the most resolute way, are altered for life.

I wanted to run all the way home to Wales. The last time I spoke with Gramps, we argued. He banged on about Pauline and her Jehovah's Witness leaflets and I told him to stop whinging about every little thing in his life. He called me spoilt, I called him an old grump and he cut the conversation short. Later that night, he called me to apologise, saying he was tired of being stuck in the house all day and missed being able to do things for himself. He said he was sorry for getting so worked up, but he was in pain. I told him to be patient, that he'd be better soon. It would all be OK. I don't know what I would've said had I known it would be the last time we'd speak, but I know it wouldn't involve Pauline's campaign for the Jehovah's Witnesses. In fact, I do know. I'd have told him that I wouldn't have survived the past five months without him. That I loved him with all my heart. That he was the best friend I ever had.

I stayed on the phone to Mam for over an hour.

'Your father managed to catch Anna before the flight,' she said.

I hadn't thought of Anna; all I could think about was Gramps, watching Sky Sports, eating a banana, waiting for Owen to come over.

'She's on the train back from Gatwick.'

Just like that, there went the three-week holiday. There went time to relax, to reconnect as a couple, to drink all the Aperol spritz on the Amalfi Coast.

I got off the phone with Mam and walked out the door.

I walked on autopilot, down to the canal. I stopped to sit down in the beer garden of a pub; I couldn't see straight from the tears. I could feel the mascara clogging my eyelashes, the black stains on my cheeks from the tears. A woman asked if I needed help and I didn't even bother to look up at her. The couple sitting on the table next to me moved out from their seats and went inside. I walked down to the canal and screamed. A man got off his bike, touched my arm and asked me if I was OK. What a ridiculous thing to ask a woman who's standing alone in the dark, screaming.

I got my phone out, desperate to ring Jamie, and that's when Trevor messaged.

> Hi guys, we are all working now delivering the
> best around London.
>   Weekend deals
>   X2c = 110
>   X3s = 100
>   X3m = 90
>   And we have also started to sell Cali skunk
> and the best hash.

I called Trevor, then I went to find a cash machine and took out £110. I waited by the pavement and leant against the lamppost as I finished off the cigarettes.

I don't know how much time went by, but I got a phone call, asking where I was. I ran to find the right street, got in the back of the car and asked for two bags of coke.

'You're late,' he said, throwing his cigarette butt onto the pavement.

'Sorry,' I mumbled.

'I'm double parked, for fuck's sake.'

'I said I'm sorry, OK?'

He didn't say anything. I could feel his gaze in the rear-view mirror. I avoided eye contact.

'Why aren't we moving?' I asked.

'Is everything all right?'

'Yes, I'm fine.'

My voice was wavering, I cleared my throat and started biting the skin around my thumb.

'You don't look fine.'

'I said I'm fine.'

'If you say so.'

I cleared my throat again.

'I want two bags.'

I wiped my face with my sleeve and brushed the hair off my face. He said nothing, as he turned on the engine and drove a little further down the street.

He lit another cigarette and offered me one. I said no, thank you.

He parked up opposite a school and turned off the engine.

I was crying again.

He spun around in the front seat so that he was facing me, with his arm resting on the back of the chair.

'Are you sure you want those two bags?'

I leant my head against the window. It was difficult to breathe.

'You need to take a deep breath,' he said. He reached his hand out, but didn't know where to land it.

We sat in silence. I kept thinking, what would Gramps make of all this?

'I don't want the coke,' I finally said.

'You're lucky I'm in a sympathetic mood.' He laughed. 'Time is money.'

I didn't reply.

'Listen, let me drive you home. Where do you live?'

'I need to get to my sister's.'

'Where's your sister's?'

'She won't be home yet . . . '

'Well, you can't stay in here all night.'

'I'm aware of that.'

'So, tell me where she lives . . . '

I could feel the panic rising in me.

'Hello?'

'Stop asking me so many questions!'

'I'm not fucking—'

'Christ, now who's *Question Time*?'

'*Question Time*? What? Look, I'm not selling you anything, so either you get out now and walk to your sister's, which I wouldn't advise in your state, or, I drive you there. What will it be?'

'I'm sorry,' I said.

'There's no need to be sorry.'

He rooted around his bag and pulled out a packet of tissues. He passed them to me and told me to take a deep breath.

'Can I have that cigarette now, please?' I asked him.

'Yeah, sure.'

I lit the cigarette and slumped back in the seat.

'He died.'

'Who died?'

'Gramps . . . I don't understand it.'

'I'm sorry. Death is shit, mate.'

'What if he never knew how much I loved him?'

'They always do.'

'I've never had anyone die before.'

'You'll get over it.'

I wound the window down to get some air. My body didn't feel like my own; everything seemed to slow down, like I was wading through honey.

210

'Do you want some water?' he asked.

'Yes, thank you.'

He passed me a bottle of Fiji water. An odd brand choice for a drug dealer.

'Can I start the car now?'

'Yes,' I said, as I lay down on the back seat, curled up in a ball and tried to forget I existed.

A little while later, we arrived at Anna's.

'Thanks for not throwing me out,' I said as I got out of the car.

'Yeah, no worries. Hey, listen, if things improve next week I'll give you a discount, my treat.'

Yeah, that'll be just what I need.

Chapter 33

Knickerbocker glory

Gramps and Mam were very good at betting – strategic, calm, didn't get ahead of themselves. They'd go through all the predictions, reviewing tips and in-depth analysis from the experts, before putting together a 1-2-3 verdict for each race. They'd do this at Gramps' house and create a big mess; there'd be papers all over the floor and cold cups of tea alongside half-eaten packets of biscuits. Anna dubbed it the War Room. I once made the mistake of answering my phone to Jamie, and Gramps got out of his seat, grabbed the phone off me and hurled it across the room. Mam said it was my own fault. Dad knew better than to interfere, but Anna and I loved to get involved. It was so dramatic, so tense. Not even planning my own wedding day came close to that level of organisation.

Gramps wasn't a big drinker, and he didn't like drunks. On race day, he would look me and Anna in the eye and make us promise to take it easy. One step out of line, and that'd be it. Mam said a little alcohol helped settle her nerves, but even she didn't drink a lot on race days; she didn't want it to affect her concentration.

Anna and I would sit in silence, cups of wine in hand, as Mam and Gramps shouted profanities at the horses. Afterwards, we would stop at the fish and chip shop and Gramps would order a large battered sausage, chips, mushy peas and a pickled egg, despite constant protests about the smell. Mam would refuse to eat anything. 'Far too greasy,' she'd say, shaking her head in disgust as we ordered enough food to feed a small village. Her favourite line was always, 'I can't believe you're going for a large portion of chips, Ives.' We'd go back to Mam and Dad's house afterwards, sit in the kitchen and listen to the race analysis on the radio as we devoured the food. I'm not that fussed about horses and I don't really care for betting, but those were some of the best days of my life.

It wasn't long before Anna and Mark were back from the airport.

Anna and I sat in silence, while Mark brought out Ben & Jerry's ice cream, the Phish Food one, Anna's favourite. He started to reminisce about the time we had ice cream and jelly back home in Wales and Gramps refused to eat it. He couldn't believe that we'd spent money on 'second-rate dessert' when the country's finest, Joe's, was right on our doorstep. As soon as Gramps said it, Anna pushed her bowl aside and said, 'Come on, I'll drive,' and we all got in the car, drove down to Joe's and had the best ice cream we'd ever tasted. Joe's is to South Wales what Greggs is to Northerners: an institution. It's our Mecca, the holy grail of desserts. Gramps always went for a Knickerbocker Glory with nuts and chocolate sprinkles on top, while the rest of us kept it simple: three scoops in a carton. No need for faff. Nobody knows what it is about Joe's, but Gramps was always right: everything else is second-rate.

I went out like a light that night. When I woke, Anna was beside me, her arm across my body, her face nestled into my back. My shirt was soaking from where she'd been crying. I turned around to face her and wrapped my arms around her.

'It's going to be OK,' I said.

Was it?

I went into the kitchen to find Mark making a full breakfast for us all. He looked broken, but as soon as he saw me, he straightened himself up, and walked towards me with open arms.

'Eat some breakfast, Ivy. Even if you don't want to.'

'Thank you.'

'I'll get everything sorted for Wales, don't worry. Just eat.'

I wondered how he managed to keep everything together. He was always so calm and collected whilst everyone around him was falling to pieces. Mark's parents died when he was a teenager, and Gramps always said how remarkable it was that someone who'd experienced such trauma could be so normal. He wasn't holding onto any regressed emotions, no anger, anxiety or guilt. He went above and beyond for us, always. Gramps used to joke that Mark was like Michael Caine, calm on the surface but 'paddling like the dickens underneath'. Maybe that was true, but, whatever the case, we wouldn't have got through that day without him.

We caught the train down to Wales that morning and Dad met us at the station. It had only been a day, but he looked terrible. All these lines had shot up around his eyes and his grey stubble made him look about ninety-five, not seventy.

We went into the house and up the stairs to find Mam lying on the bed, hugging a pillow and crying into it. Anna got the infamous tartan blanket out and wrapped it over her, then we both lay down beside her.

Mam didn't make it downstairs all day. Dad took her up some tomato soup and sat in bed with her. The rest of us spent the day watching *Lord of the Rings*. In times of extreme grief, you need a good blockbuster. And tomato soup. You always know what you're getting with Peter Jackson and tomato soup.

Later that night we sat in the garden, sharing cigarettes and wine, laughing over Gramps' recent fall-outs with the neighbours. Do you know when, in films, the characters all go back to someone's house after the service, and stay up sharing stories over a few drinks? I used to think how odd that was. How could anyone be in any fit state to have a normal conversation, let alone laugh, after a day like that? But there we all were, together in our grief, trying to find some joy before we said goodbye.

I stayed up long after everyone went to bed. I was dazed and confused and moving on autopilot. The alcohol didn't seem to be having any effect on me, so I eventually gave up, crept into Mam and Dad's room with my duvet, and fell asleep on the floor beside their bed.

I woke in the early afternoon the following day, back in my own bed, not remembering how I got there. I went downstairs to find Mam sitting in the kitchen, staring out into the garden.

'I'm sorry for yesterday,' she said.

'Don't be silly,' I said, stroking her hair.

'I couldn't . . .'

'If you want to stay in bed all day, you can.'

'Thank you, darling.'

I went over to give her a *cwtch*; she buried her face into my neck and let out a quiet sob.

'We've started making arrangements, for next Monday,' she said.

'Is there anything I can do?'

'No. I'm just glad you're here.'

'Me too.'

'Your grandfather worshipped you, Ivy.'

'He was the best.'

'He really was, wasn't he?'

She moved slowly that day. She didn't listen when you spoke to her, she didn't quite manage to make eye contact and her speech was quiet, as if it pained her to talk. Mark and Anna went for a walk along the beach and Dad suggested we join them for some fresh air. It was a lovely summer's day and the cycle path was rammed with people making the most of their weekend. We walked down to the beach gripping each other's hand. Dad said that Owen and his wife wanted to pop round later to see us all. Seeing Owen would be like seeing Gramps again.

We walked down to the pier and sat on the rocks waiting for Mark and Anna. When they found us, Anna said it was time for a Joe's.

We talked about the time Gramps came to London and took me and Anna out shopping. He waited patiently in the Topshop changing rooms for three hours while we tried on everything in sight. He made comments on every outfit we showed him, though none of them were very constructive. We talked about the time he and Dad went swimming in the sea at 7am after they'd stayed up all night watching the Ashes; and the time he took Anna to the park and she cried because she wasn't allowed to take a duck home. Gramps bought her a big toy one for the bath and, despite initially hating it and throwing it in his face, Anna soon wouldn't go anywhere without it.

We walked all the way home and when we got back to the house, Mam said, 'I fancy fish and chips tonight.'

Fish and chips and a Knickerbocker Glory. Gramps would've loved that.

Chapter 34

A happy heart

Liz and Henry offered us their pub for the memorial service. It was the perfect venue because it overlooked the Gower, Gramps' favourite spot. There would be no time for faff in the morning, so we got ourselves ready the night before. We moved like zombies around the house as we ironed our clothes and packed our handbags with tissues and chewing gum. I don't know why, but we chewed a lot of gum that week. Afterwards, we sat in silence in the kitchen as we moved pilau rice and chicken tikka masala around our plates. I remember Radio 4 was on in the background. When Nat King Cole's 'When I Fall in Love' came on, Mam got out of her seat and walked upstairs. We gave up eating after that. Anna went upstairs to have a bath. I hadn't showered since Friday, when we'd come back from another walk on the beach. I remember it because *Have I Got News for You* was on, and all I could think was how damp I smelt.

I drove Anna to Gramps' house so we could pick out some records for the memorial: Frank, Nat, Ella and Billy. There was a half-eaten banana on the arm of the sofa and he'd been looking at photos of gran. There were albums scattered across the floor of their holidays in Germany, Milan and the Canary Islands. Anna took one look at the living room and walked back to the car.

I packed the photos up, putting them all back in their boxes and to one side, ready to take back to Mam and Dad's. I put the ironing board away, did the dishes and put all the fresh food from the fridge into the bin. As I was emptying the bins around the back, I saw Jean, the only neighbour Gramps ever liked. She waved at me and mouthed, 'I'm sorry.' I nodded and went back indoors.

As I walked back into the house, I looked out into the front where the car was parked; I couldn't see Anna. I went into the front garden, thinking she might have taken a walk down the street, but when I got to the gate I saw her lying in a foetal position across the back seat of the car. She was holding her face in her hands and crying. Her whole body was shaking. I turned back inside to finish up.

When everyone went to bed that night, I put *Sleepless in Seattle* in the DVD player and poured myself some whisky. I found an old stash of Diazepam from when Mam had her fear of flying phase and took a few for later. If I wanted to sleep, I could at least try. When the film was over, I rewound the DVD and started watching it again from the start. By the time I'd finished watching it the second time round, it was 5am. I took a tablet and went to bed. Anna woke me up at 8am.

'I didn't hear you come up,' she said, as she opened the curtains and put a mug of tea down beside me.

'I wasn't far behind you,' I lied.

'Can I run you a bath?'

'I don't want a bath.'

'Have a bath, Ivy.'

'Is Mam up?'

'Yeah.'

She grabbed my hand.

'We can do this,' she said.

'Can we?'

'Yes, we can.'

I didn't realise how long I'd been in the bath until Anna came in and told me to hurry up. I remained sitting in the cold water, staring at the wall, my body turning into a prune. She came in a second time and raised her voice at me. We were going to be late. I got out and found Mam sitting on the floor outside the bathroom. She was in her dressing gown, staring at the wall ahead. I sat down beside her.

'Have you eaten?' I asked.

'I can't remember, darling.'

'Let's go downstairs and make some toast.'

'OK.'

She cupped my face in her hands, the tears welling up in her eyes.

'It's important we're together today.'

'We will be. I'm right here.'

'Good. Good.'

After eating our toast in silence, Mam went out to the garden for a cigarette. I went back upstairs to the bathroom, sat in the bath and stared at the wall. Anna knocked on the door and asked if I was nearly ready. I shouted that I needed a minute. When I finally got out, she was waiting outside the door for me.

'Your face . . . ' she said.

'What?' I asked.

She took me back into the bathroom to see. There were bloodstains all around my eyes. I looked down at my hands, fingers red raw and bleeding from where I'd torn the skin around my nails.

'You can't keep doing that to yourself,' she said, taking my hands and running cold water on them. She wiped my eyes before wrapping my hands in a towel. She placed her hands on top of mine and we stood there in silence, heads bowed together, holding onto each other for dear life.

'Let's go,' I said.

'I guess we should,' she replied, but she didn't move. It took us a while to move.

The crematorium wasn't far from the house, but that car journey will always be the longest of my life. Dad, Owen, Mark and three friends from the bowls team served as pallbearers. They walked ahead of us while Mam, Anna and I hung back for a minute longer. When we started walking, 'Calon Lân' began to play out from the speakers.

Owen was first to say a few words. He spoke of Gramps' loyalty as a friend and his undying commitment to the bowls team. He talked about his love of the Tories, how strange it was considering he'd lived his whole life in a mining town where most of the population wanted to throttle the living daylights out of them all. He called Mam the second favourite Margaret, to which everyone laughed. He talked about how much he loved to wind people up, no matter who they were. He talked about what a good man he was, how he loved his family more than life itself. He'd married the woman of his dreams, and even through her long and painful battle with bowel cancer, he was a pillar of strength, for her and for everyone around her. His unfailing positivity and love made those final few months bearable. He refused to let up on date nights to the old cinema; they still went to Joe's for ice cream once a week and, on the weekend, if she was up to it, he'd drive her to Rhossili Beach, their favourite spot, and they'd have a picnic by the sea. He was the most selfless and generous man, even though in the past year he was more likely to be called senile, or rude, perhaps even a little mentally unstable. That got a laugh. Owen told everyone how much he loved him. How much he'd miss his best friend from school, the boy who always shared his milk and spam sandwiches with him.

When it was Mam's turn to get up, I saw Dad whisper in her ear. She walked towards the lectern, took the notes out of her bag and placed them in front of her. She looked up again, and Dad gave her a nod. She went to speak but, before the words came out, she stopped herself. She fiddled with her papers, folded them up and put them into her pocket. Then, she started speaking.

'Thank you all for coming today, it's lovely to see so many of you here. Thank you, Owen, for those lovely words. Ivan Thomas was my father and he meant the world to me. There's nothing more he loved in life than his family. His family and, as Owen said, Margaret Thatcher. I'm joking ... I think. You all knew my mother. My God how he loved her. I could never have imagined a day when they wouldn't be here, but they're together now, and if they're together, then they're happy. I'd like to think that, at this very moment, they're dancing away to Nat King Cole, sharing a bottle of champagne. That's the way it should be. I miss him. I miss him so much. I feel I should apologise to everyone he's sworn and shouted at over the past year, but I've written far too many apology letters to keep track of now and, to be honest, you lot probably deserved it anyway. I'd written something else, but there we go. Anyway. The beginning of "Calon Lân" goes like this: "I don't ask for a life of luxury, the world's gold or its fine pearls. I ask for a happy heart, an honest heart, a pure heart". That's why we're here, isn't it? To love openly and fiercely and cherish those who make our hearts soar. He made my heart soar. He made my children's hearts soar. I love him more now than ever. Dad, give Mam a *cwtch* from me and be nice to your new neighbours.'

Then, it was my turn. I'd tried to write a few words earlier that week, but nothing made sense to me. Nothing came close to what I wanted to say. I didn't know what was going to come out when I got up to the lectern.

Everyone was looking at me, expecting me to cry, to break down.

I looked to Anna and took a deep breath.

'Good morning, everyone. I'm Ivy.'

I cleared my throat.

'You already know I'm Ivy, sorry.'

I looked to Mam.

'Go on,' she mouthed.

I continued.

'I want to talk about how much I loved him. How much I do love him. He said everything how it was, you know? It's where Mam gets it from and as much as I hate to admit it, we all need a bit of that in our lives. I don't know what my day looks like when I can't pick up the phone to ring him. I want to be able to run over to his house and have him greet me with the biggest *cwtch*. He was ... he is ... my best friend.'

I stopped and looked out to the audience. I couldn't cry, because if I started to cry, I would never stop. I took another deep breath.

'When I was trying to write something down for this, I kept thinking about his boat shoes. I used to make fun of his clothes so much. He was obsessed with ironing everything, even his socks. Who does that? Do you know he bought me an iron for my twenty-fifth birthday? I think it's still in its box.'

I looked down at my shaking hands and tried to steady myself.

'People just want to be loved, and all he did was love us, every single day. He would have done anything for every single person in this room. That's just the sort of man he was.

We should all be grateful that he came into our lives and loved us as much as he did.'

I cleared my throat again.

'You are the best man I know, Gramps. I love you, always will.'

Chapter 35

How hard can it be?

While we could only fit eighty people into the crematorium, we had close to two hundred in the Anchor. There were cheese and pickle sandwiches and kidney pies on every table, Gramps' favourite. Cold jugs of bitter were passed through the crowds alongside bottles of whisky. People were sitting in the front garden, sharing cigars and stories. Laughter and swearing reverberated through the room. It was exactly what he would've wanted.

Liz clocked me walking to the toilets. She knocked on the door of the cubicle and I let her in.

'How are you, *cariad*?' she asked, crouching down in front of me and putting her hand to my cheek.

'I want to hit something.'

'Don't hit me,' she joked.

'I'll try not to.'

She stroked my legs. Her hands were warm and comforting.

'You're freezing, Ives.'

'Am I?'

She took her cardigan off and wrapped it around my shoulders.

'When did everything become so fucking hard?'

I dropped my head so it was resting on her chest as she held me.

My phone beeped. I thought it would be Mia.

> Ivy, I bumped into Noah.
>> I didn't know, I'm sorry.
>> I'm so sorry.
>> Are you OK?
>> xxx

I showed Liz the phone.

'Jamie?' she asked.

'Yeah, Jamie.'

What happens when you have a person, and then that person goes away, and you're left with nothing, and then another person goes away, and when you thought it couldn't get any worse, there you are, feeling so awful that you could dig yourself into a hole and never come back out again? What do you do then?

I asked Liz to give me some space. I ran cold water from the tap, splashing it onto my face. Bits of mascara had congealed in the tips of my eyelashes, while the rest had run down my cheeks. It was my own fault; who wears mascara to a funeral? My eyes were bloodshot and my pores were wide open and greasy, making my face look like it was littered with little black holes. I drank some tap water, swirling the putrid mix of spirits, wine and tobacco around my mouth. I looked at myself in the mirror. Then, I went to find Anna.

I saw Mark first; he was having a cigar with Owen's grandson, Gareth, and laughing over his recent trip to Tenerife. He took one look at me, excused himself and walked in my direction. He took my arm in his and we walked down to the edge of the cliff to get away from the crowd.

'Oh, Christ,' he said, reading the message.

'What do I do?'

'What do you want to do?'

'I don't have a fucking clue.'

'I'm so shit at this, Ives. I don't know what to say.'

'Well, what would you do?'

'I don't know.'

'You do know. If your fiancé splits up with you five minutes after you'd had sex, then falls off the face of the planet, and then you see him with another woman and he lies to you about it and carries on acting like you don't exist, then he messages you on the day of your grandfather's funeral, what would you do?'

'Ivy, I don't know.'

'No, I don't know either. Nobody fucking knows. I just want somebody to tell me what to fucking do.'

'Ivy, come here.'

'No, Mark, fuck off. Fuck you. Tell me what to do, tell me right now what do I do?'

He grabbed my arm, but I flung it away and whacked him across the chest. He just stood there, not saying anything, so I carried on hitting him. Hitting him, stamping my feet and screaming. I don't know how long I was doing it for, but Anna came up behind me and pulled me off him. I collapsed into a heap on the ground and she huddled over me. I cried into her until there was nothing left. When I got up, I realised that one side of my dress was tucked into my knickers and the whole of the Anchor could see my right bum cheek. As if things couldn't get any worse.

I showed Anna the message from Jamie. She said it was selfish of him to get in touch that day. I don't know if I agreed with that; it's not like he could have won either way. I'd be

226

lying if I said I hadn't thought about him during the funeral. Of course, I wanted him to be there; it was still baffling to me that he wasn't. I didn't think he would message though, only because of her. When his face came into my mind, all I could see was her and seeing her was a million times worse than seeing him. Anna told me not to message him, but she also said that she knew I would, and that would be OK. So, I did the inevitable and I messaged him back.

'I can't believe you're not here.'

A minute later he replied.

'When are you back in London?'

'Sunday,' I said.

'Can I see you?'

'I don't think so, no.'

'Ivy, please. I need to explain.'

I went to reply but stopped myself. This was just an excuse to unburden the guilt, to make himself feel better. I didn't want to give him the opportunity. He didn't deserve it.

'I don't need your explanation. I don't know why I messaged back.'

'I need to know you're OK, Ivy.'

'Are you for real? No, I am not OK. It's Gramps' funeral. Fuck, Jamie. What happened to you?'

'Ivy, I care about you. You know I do.'

'Go fuck yourself.'

He didn't reply; I went to find Mam.

I found her at the bar, her dirty laugh reverberating through the room. She was perched on a barstool, and as she clocked me walking over, her face lit up. I grabbed her face and kissed her cheeks. As I squeezed in beside her, I told myself it was time to start being there for her. I would be there for her because she needed me, and I knew all too well what it felt like to want somebody to need you.

We had a lock-in that night. The moon was full, and, in the early hours of the morning, we took some whisky bottles and torches and walked out of the pub, down a dark path and onto the beach. There were about twenty of us left at that point: friends, cousins, wives, and a random man called Duncan who nobody seemed to know but had excellent chat and an unlimited supply of cigarettes. When we hit the sand, we took off our shoes and ran down to the shore. Dad picked Mam up and carried her into the ocean, Anna got on Mark's back and I got on Gareth's, and we raced each other down to the sea.

After splashing around the ice-cold water long enough for my feet to start aching, I walked back onto the beach, sat down on the sand and lit a cigarette. I could hear Mam shouting, 'Wait for me!' as she ran towards me.

'Give me one of those now, you naughty little girl.'

'Mam, you don't smoke, remember?'

'Oh, sod off. I need one.'

I put my arms around her and she got the bottle of whisky out of the sand, took a big gulp, then passed it to me.

'Look at the size of the moon,' I said.

'You know your grandfather had a real thing for astrology?'

'Gramps? Come off it.'

'Honest to God. Your grandmother was an Aries and he wouldn't go anywhere near her during a full moon. He'd say, "Mags love, stay away from Mammy. You know what she gets like."'

'What, all because she was an Aries?'

'Yes, Ives. She was ruled by Mars – conflict ran deep inside her. When the full moon was out – well, it was best to stay away.'

'That's ridiculous.'

'It's totally ridiculous. But Gramps loved that sort of stuff.

He had a point; she was a feisty little Welsh woman and any little thing set her off.'

'Kind of like you?'

'Don't be a cheeky shit, darling.'

We both laughed.

'Always looking at compatibility, he was. When I met your father, he said we'd have a stressful sex life.'

'Are you being serious?' I laughed.

'Yeah, Cancer and Aquarius. Honest.'

'I wish I'd known all this.'

'He'd have loved that today was on a full moon and that we're here, by the ocean.'

'I hope so.'

'I know so, darling.'

I put out my cigarette in the sand.

'Come for a dip in the sea with me?' I asked.

'Yes, why not.'

A happy heart. How hard can it be?

Chapter 36

Sympathy sex

Gramps' death was a bonus when it came to my professional life. Suddenly it was OK to come into work with unwashed hair, greasy pores and clothes that smelt like a brewery. I was desperate for the August bank holiday to come; I needed three days without having to look at Jane. John, our chief executive, said we could leave early on the Friday to make the most of the long weekend. He kindly put some money behind the bar for the whole office, but of course Jane went and put in a meeting for us at 4pm. How can you rationalise with someone who puts in a meeting at 4pm on a Bank Holiday Friday?

I knocked on Jane's door and waited to be called in. I pictured her sitting there googling how many calories tomatoes have, or something as equally depressing. When she finally let me in, she made a point of re-tidying her desk just so she could keep me there longer.

'Ivy, thank you for coming today,' she said. 'I wanted to start by saying how sorry I am about your grandfather. I know you two were very close.'

'Thank you.'

What I wanted to say was that her faux-sympathy meant nothing to me, but I bit my tongue.

'I know this year hasn't been easy for you.'

Look at me; I'm having a whale of a time.

'And I don't mean to add to your stress.'

Yes, you do. That's all you mean to do.

'But I think we need to have a serious conversation.'

Fuck. Off.

'What do you mean?' I slumped back in my chair and folded my arms like a petulant child.

'I know we were meant to review your action plan this month, but I'm going to put it on hold until you're a bit more settled.'

'Thank you.' I said it more like a question, and she gave me a confused look.

'Your attitude, your personal appearance ... It would be great if you could try to make more of an effort. I think that would be a step in the right direction, for you and for us.'

'Well, I'll try to make more of an effort.'

'OK, good. Ivy, I like you and I want to see you do well, not just here but, in life, generally.'

I was confused by the change in tone, the look on her face – like she cared about me.

I shuffled my feet and looked up at the ceiling.

'If there's anything I can do, anything at all, please let me know. I'd like to help, Ivy.'

'OK.'

I got up from the seat and walked out the door, just as she was bidding me a nice long weekend.

Obviously, Jane had a point – to say I wasn't looking my best would be an understatement. It had been just under two weeks since the funeral and everything about me sagged. All my energy was going into work because I knew that if I put a foot out of place, I'd be sacked, but I still couldn't get that right. There was only so long I could dine out on heartache.

I arranged to meet Rob that night after work. I thought an orgasm would help cheer me up, kick-start the weekend and all that. I wanted to be held, and, despite the awful kissing, the sex was better than good, and he's kind. If I had to put up with a little bit of pretentious behaviour before I got an orgasm, so be it. We can't have it all.

On my way home, I stopped off at the supermarket to buy a few miniature bottles of wine for the weekend. This was my new thing, well, since the funeral. If I bought whole bottles, I would drink them all, then seeing them empty the next morning would make me feel even worse about myself. If I drank several mini bottles, it didn't count. Like at Christmas when you eat a whole box of Quality Street; they're only little.

When I got home, I threw everything onto the bedroom floor and ran into the shower, but I clipped my knee on the bed and had to hobble around the flat for ages until the pain subsided. I needed to shave my legs; the razor blade was rusty, but I didn't have anything else and I couldn't be bothered to go out to the shops. I got what was left of the shampoo and ran it over my legs to try to get a lather going. When I went to shave my knee, I nipped the skin and blood started streaming down my leg. I didn't have any plasters, so I hopped to the kitchen and found some masking tape, which I taped to some cotton wool around my knee. I didn't have any dresses that went below the knee, so I put on a pair of old jeans and a scrunched-up T-shirt I found on the floor. As date outfits go, it wasn't my finest.

I ran through the doors of the Quiet Lady, congratulating myself that I was only half an hour late, and scanned the room to find him. The first thing that caught my eye were the ugly pendants hanging around his neck; he was twirling them around his fingers in one hand whilst holding a tattered copy of *How Should a Person Be?* in the other. I let out a little sigh and walked towards him.

'Babe, come here,' he said, as he stood up from his seat and wrapped his arms around me. As ever, he smelt a bit off, but, as usual, I found it sexy. Also, when did he start saying 'babe'?

He took my hand in his.

'How are you? Such a relentless year for you.'

'Yeah, not ideal.'

We stood for a moment as he put his hand to my shoulder and gave me the sympathetic head tilt I'd become so accustomed to.

'Anyway, can I get you a drink?' I asked.

'No, don't be silly. You sit down, babe. Take it easy.'

How was it possible that he'd become more annoying?

I picked up the book he was reading and read the back cover. It was about sex, femininity and artistic ambition. Obviously, this was a major contributing factor.

He came back and put a pint of cider down in front of me.

'Have you read it?' he said, as I moved the book away.

'God, no.'

'Ivy, you should. What was it that Lena Dunham said? "It's where metafiction meets nonfiction."'

'I'm not really into this stuff.'

'What stuff? It's about being authentic and original and artistic.'

'Right.'

'It's about being true to ourselves, listening to our voice.'

'OK.'

'It's about not doing what society tells us we should be doing.'

'I don't do what society tells me to,' I said, getting more annoyed at him by the second.

'But that's it, we all do.'

I downed half my pint.

He started tapping his fingers on the table and humming an infuriating tune.

Suddenly, his eyes lit up, as if he'd had some bright idea. He went into his pocket and got out a small bag of cocaine.

'Do you want some?' he asked.

'No,' I said.

'OK. No need to be like that.'

'You just got here, Rob.'

'What does that mean?'

'Nothing. I'm fine with my pint, thanks.'

'Suit yourself.'

He got up from his seat and I saw him go into the disabled toilets. I don't know what I was thinking, but I downed the rest of the pint and followed him into the bathroom. I pushed through the queue as the girl in front gave me a face of thunder. I told her to piss off as I knocked on the door. He let me in and, as he did, I grabbed the neck of his T-shirt, pinned him up against the wall and started kissing him.

'I want you, Rob,' I said.

'Woah! Slow down a sec.'

'I want you now.'

'Let me do this line, then we can go back to mine.'

'No. Now.'

I pulled his T-shirt over his head and pressed my lips against his torso as he fumbled to find a condom in his wallet. His skin tasted salty and as I moved my face to his groin he pushed my head into his crotch. My hands fumbled to open the zip of his jeans. He grabbed the back of my head and tugged at my hair while I tried not to get my teeth attached to his foreskin. His hands kept pulling my hair harder and faster and I had to grip the wall with one hand to steady myself. I knew he was

234

going to come because his legs were shaking so I stood up, put the condom on him, and steadied myself against the wall as he hoisted me up onto his waist and entered me. It was quick, and when it was over, he held me and kissed my neck ever so gently.

'I can't work you out, Miss Edwards.'

I shrugged my shoulders and walked out the door.

We stayed in the pub for another few hours. In all honesty, despite his many infuriating characteristics, he made me laugh, and I was thankful for that. When they called last orders, I asked Rob if he wanted to come home with me. At least at mine there was no risk of having to listen to Jeff Buckley.

We got back to my flat and poured ourselves more booze. It was late, and all I wanted was for him to put his lips all over me. I was glad when his hands touched my face and he started kissing my neck again. He took my top off and unclipped my bra. I asked him if we could move to the bedroom, being a little anxious that the sofa was going to topple over now that it was being held up with books. On the bed, he went to take his shirt off, and that's when the horrible wave of grief came colliding into me. As he took my jeans off, I closed my eyes and tried to push the feeling away.

'What's on your leg?' he asked, as he stared down at the bloody cotton wool pad tied onto my knee.

'Shit, sorry,' I said, trying to hide it.

'Your leg's all bruised.'

'I fell into the bed.'

'Fuck, Ivy. That looks painful.'

'It's fine,' I said, grabbing his face and pulling it into mine. I kissed him, and he put his fingers on the lining of my pants. He pulled them off, being careful not to touch the cotton wool. He opened my legs and put his tongue on my clitoris.

At first, everything was fine, but after a couple of minutes, I started to cry.

'Hey, hey slow down. What's the matter?'

'Nothing,' I said as I wiped the tears away and tried to move his head back down to my crotch.

'Ivy, stop. You're upset.'

'I'm fine.'

'No, you're not.'

'Oh, so it's OK for me to suck you off in the toilet but now you won't go down on me?'

'Ivy, you know I want to, but not like—'

'Like what?'

'You're all over the place.'

'Leave then.'

'What?'

'Leave. If that's what you want, then go.'

'Don't be like that, come on.'

'Don't tell me to come on. Please, go.'

'Ivy, please—'

'No, just go. Please, go.'

I was crying even more now; humongous, uncontrollable sobs.

He looked at me with his big brown eyes and mouthed, 'OK.' Then he got his clothes, walked into the hallway and out the front door.

Chapter 37

The blind leading the blind

Shortly after Rob left, I got dressed and walked out the door. I couldn't be inside the flat on my own. It was a horrible night; the rain was relentless and I felt like the wind could topple me over at any minute. I buttoned up my flimsy jacket as best I could, cursing myself for grabbing the first thing I saw, and walked towards the marshes.

There was barely anyone out, just me and a few homeless men with their dogs. Everyone did their best to ignore me, to move out of my way. I didn't look well; stone-cold expression, clothes soaking through and hair matted all over my face. I tried to light cigarette after cigarette, but the rain kept soaking them through, so I gave up and carried on walking alone in the dark. I walked for a couple of hours before I came off the canal and made my way into a park, where I found a bench to sit on.

When the rain finally stopped, I got up and started walking again. I was sobering up, and it was getting clearer by the minute that I shouldn't be walking alone, in the middle of the night, in a desolate park. I moved onto a residential street and saw a woman sitting on the doorstep of a beautiful Victorian townhouse. There was an enormous tree outside, with yellow flowers hanging from its branches. I stood there and stared at it, unmoving.

'It's nice, innit?' the woman said.

'It's a Golden Rain,' I said, walking over to her.

'How'd you know that?'

'My grandfather likes . . . he liked trees.'

She looked me up and down.

'Where you been tonight?' she asked.

'For a walk.'

'Bit wet, innit?'

'Yeah, it's wet.' I leant against the wall and stared up at the Golden Rain.

'Do you wanna sit with me?' she asked.

I looked at her face; sores everywhere, a mouth filled with gaps and broken yellow teeth. I sat down beside her.

'Want some?' she asked, as she held up a can of Skol Super. 'I've got some ket too.'

'No, thank you.'

'You sure? Can give you a hit for a fiver?'

'I'm fine.'

'Whatever.'

She took off her necklace, which had a little vial of white powder and a tiny spoon attached to it. She opened the vial and dabbed some of the powder onto the spoon. She held the powder up to her nose and inhaled. She started coughing, then downed the last of her can. She lay back on the steps and closed her eyes. I watched her in silence for a minute or so, fascinated by how a woman like that could end up here, like this.

'Do you live here?' I asked.

'Do I fuck!'

'Sorry, stupid question. I should go.'

'There's a bus stop around the corner.'

'I need to walk,' I said.

'OK.'

I got six pounds out of my pocket and gave it to her.

'Here, it's all I have.'

'Thanks – appreciate it.'

She eyed me up and down again.

'You really can't spare a tenner?'

'That's all I have, promise.'

'Well, better than nothing.'

I patted her on the shoulder and told her to take care.

It was light by the time I got home.

I woke with a jolt. I had the drowning dream again. I died and nobody came to my funeral. I grabbed my phone to check the time: 2.53pm. I was going to see Maude, and I was late.

I splashed my face with water, brushed my hair and called an Uber, arriving at the reception at 3.26pm – a miracle, really. I rang the buzzer repeatedly, but nobody was answering the door. I could see the party banners and balloons inside as I banged against the window. After a few minutes, one of the nurses came to the door.

'I'm so sorry I'm late,' I said.

'It's fine. Don't get yourself into a state.'

'Sorry, sorry. Have we done the cake yet?'

'Not yet.'

I ran into the sitting room, and there was Maude. You could spot her from a mile off: tiara on her head and a big pink sash across her body with 'happy birthday' written in gold block letters. She was sat by the window; her curls bouncier than ever and a smile that lit up the whole room.

Befitting for a woman who loved the seaside, the birthday party was themed 'a day at the beach'. There were blue drinks with cocktail straws, buckets and spades filled with mountains of colourful sweets and fake sandcastles. There were inflated palm trees and beach balls at every turn, and everyone was wearing Hawaiian lei. Someone had made biscuits in the shape of flip-flops and cupcakes with starfish on top. Never in my entire life have I had such a party thrown for me. Then again, I'm no Maude.

I hugged her and apologised for my poor timekeeping.

'You young people today are always up to no good,' she said.

She said it affectionately, but her eyes couldn't hide her disappointment. She looked at me for a little longer than I was comfortable with.

'Why don't you have a glass of water?' she said. She took my hand in hers and I looked at the floor to avoid eye contact. Old people have a way of seeing right through you.

'That's a good idea,' I said, clearing the lump in my throat. 'I'll get some water.'

As soon as I sat back down, the mood had turned, and she asked me if I'd met anyone.

'No, Maude. Don't be silly.'

'Ivy, get yourself out there. You're going to end up an old spinster,' she joked.

'I don't think I'd be a very good girlfriend to anyone right now, I—'

I was interrupted by one of the care workers looking for Bill.

'He's having a nap,' Maude told her.

'He's only just got up!' the woman said.

Maude turned back to face me.

'We'll get the karaoke started as soon as Bill is up.'

'Karaoke?'

'Oh yes, dear. We've been looking forward to it for weeks.'

Maude pointed to a pink machine in the corner of the room, with two bright pink microphones on top. Maude said Bill was going to sing Tom Jones, just for me. The lady next to her was overcome with excitement, smiling away at me with no teeth.

Elvis Presley belted out from the speakers. Maude was clapping away to every song, making sure we all joined in on the chorus. When Bill came down, everyone cheered, and he bowed. He was wearing a three-piece pinstriped suit, with a pocket square, bow tie and gold pocket watch. On his head was a Homburg hat and he had a plastic cigar in his mouth.

He didn't remember me but I wanted to tell him how excited I was to hear him sing. He sat down beside us and started singing to himself.

'You look like a younger, more handsome Churchill today, Bill.'

'Who's Churchill? What on earth are you on about, dear?'

'It doesn't matter,' I said. 'Maude said you're going to sing a bit of Tom Jones for us?'

'Oh yes, I love Tom Jones.'

'Me too, though I guess I have to. I am Welsh.'

'Are you Welsh? My goodness, child.'

He looked like I'd just told him I was his birth daughter.

'Yes, of course I am. Maude said that's why you're ... Oh, never mind.'

He ignored this and went back to puffing on his fake cigar.

'You know, I was a very successful singer in my day,' he said.

'Really? Where did you sing?'

'All over. Manchester, Bristol, Sheffield, Bath.'

'You must have been very good.'

'I was one of the best, they said. One of the very best.'

'Well, I can't wait to hear you sing.'

He got up from his seat and went over to the karaoke machine. The song was already loaded up for him; all he had to do was get the crowd's attention and press play. He surveyed the room and did another bow. We all clapped, and I caught him giving Maude a cheeky wink.

One of the care workers pressed play on the machine.

It's not unusual to be loved by anyone
It's not unusual to have fun with anyone
But when I see you hanging about with anyone
It's not unusual to see me cry, I wanna die ...

It was the worst rendition I'd ever heard, but Bill thought he was up there with Cliff playing to a crowd of thousands, and that's all that mattered. When it was over, he dropped the microphone to the floor and did a final bow. Those that were able to got out of their seats and started chanting his name. Despite Bill being tone-deaf and having zero stage presence, it really was quite the show.

I rolled Maude's wheelchair out into the garden with me as I had a cigarette.

'Oh, that hasn't half tired me out!' she said.

'I hope you're having a great birthday?'

'The best, my dear.'

'That's the main thing.'

'Now then, we're alone. How are you doing?'

I tried my best to smile.

'I'm doing fine, Maude. I promise.'

'You don't look so well, if I'm being honest.'

I wasn't going to say anything, but the words fell out of me.

'My grandfather died earlier this month.'

'Oh, my love. I am sorry.'

'And ... I was engaged, but, a few months ago, he left me. I wasn't expecting it. I don't really know what happened ... I don't know why he left ... '

I was struggling to speak.

'To be honest, it's all been a bit of a mess, Maude.'

'Oh, dear. I am sorry.'

I leant into her and she put her arm around me. I rested my head on her shoulder as she stroked my hair. She smelt of Imperial Leather and ginger snap biscuits.

'I didn't think it was possible to miss someone this much,' I said.

'Oh, pet. I know that feeling all too well. It gets better, I promise you. It really does.'

She got a handkerchief out of her pocket and passed it to me.

'Grief is nothing like we expect it to be. You can't run from it, Ivy. You mustn't try to fight it. It comes for us, wherever we are and whatever we're doing, whether we like it or not.'

I nodded.

'Grief is the price we pay for love. And you loved him tremendously. It's very special, what you had.'

'My heart hurts, Maude.'

She pulled my face into hers and kissed my cheeks.

'You need to look after yourself, petal,' she said. 'Stop the smoking for one.'

'You sound like Gramps.'

I looked at her and couldn't help but smile.

'Do you want to talk about what happened with your fiancé?'

'No, thank you. Not today, at least.'

We sat in silence for a while, staring out into the garden. The sun was shining down on the resident cat, who was washing herself beside the flower beds.

'I'm really glad I came to see you today,' I told Maude.

'Me too, my darling.'

'And we're not going to talk about death anymore.'

'Well, at least nobody's talking about my death.'

We moved back into the common room to join everyone for a game of Uno. After an hour or so, I said my goodbyes.

'Happy birthday, Maude,' I said, kissing her forehead.

'Thank you for coming, darling. Please come again soon? I love our chats.'

'I promise. Thank you for today, for what you said.'

'You don't need to thank me, my love.'

I was walking out the door when one of the care workers tapped me on the shoulder.

'Ivy? It is Ivy, isn't it?' she said.

'Yes?'

'I'm Karen, hi.'

'Hi, is everything OK?'

'Yes, I'm sorry to have to say this but, some of my colleagues mentioned that you might have been drinking before your visit?'

'What?'

'I'm sorry, but we can't allow you to come into the home if you've been drinking.'

'I haven't. I was drinking last night but—'

'Look, I know Maude loves seeing you, and I don't want to see your friendship jeopardised.'

'Right, OK. I'm sorry.'

I walked out of the nursing home, full of shame, and picked up the phone to rant at Dan.

'Look, don't get hung up by what some bored care worker says to you,' he said.

'I feel so stupid.'

'Don't! You'll have forgotten about it by tonight.'

'I'm not sure about that.'

'It's all OK, Ivy!' he shouted. I could barely hear him through the music in the background.

'Where are you?' I asked.

'At a rave in Elephant and Castle.'

'It's six pm, Dan. It's a bit early, isn't it?'

'It started at two pm. We'll be finished by ten.'

'Big day all around then.'

'Oh, shush. Are you coming to meet us later?'

'Yeah, might as well.'

'It's going to be fine, babe!' he screamed, before hanging up.

It was far from fine.

Chapter 38

Birthday balloons

'Emilia Clarke is so beautiful. She looks just like me when I was her age.'

I moved my phone away for a split second so that Mam couldn't see me eye rolling on FaceTime.

'Are you still there?' she asked.

'Yeah, Mam. I'm still here,' I said.

I was sitting in Anna's garden; she was on her hands and knees crouched beside me, attending to the vegetable patch. Mam rang in tears, pretending to be upset over the fact that Khaleesi had fallen in love with her nephew, Jon Snow.

'Mam, turn it off. If you want to cry, just cry.'

'I'm not upset, Ivy. I'm empathetic.'

'Meaning you understand what it's like to have sexual feelings for your nephew?'

'You are impossible today, Ivy. Impossible.'

I laughed, and she smirked.

'Where's Dad?' Anna asked. She was holding shears and wearing an old bowls T-shirt and a frayed straw hat — all Gramps'.

'He's gone to town to buy a shirt for tonight.'

'What's tonight?'

'He's taking me out. It's a surprise.'

'And you made him buy a new shirt?'

'All the man's got are golf shirts! Zero class.'

'What are you wearing?'

'I don't know.' She sighed. 'Something that hides my flat bum.'

'You don't have a flat bum.'

'I very much do, Ivy. Not only did I lose your grandfather, but I also lost an arse cheek.'

'You look great, Mam.'

'Well, thank God it didn't go the other way. Some people get so fat with grief.'

Anna started to snigger, and I kicked her to be quiet. We were trying our very best to be nicer to Mam, to not rise to her comments. She wasn't making it very easy.

'Are you having a nice birthday, my darling?' Mam asked.

'I told you, we're not celebrating.'

'Fine. Look, I've got to go. Olga's friend is coming over to give me a manicure.'

Everyone was under strict instructions not to mention my birthday, but obviously Mam had already mentioned it five times that day. I told her I was going to Mia's for her annual end-of-summer party that night, so she sent me £50 to spend on something nice for myself. I was hoping to find an outfit that would hide the despair and shame I constantly carried around with me, but I knew I would do the inevitable and spend it on vodka instead. Mam threatened to come up to London for the weekend, but we all knew she wouldn't. She'd barely left the house since the funeral. She'd not been to the golf club or to any charity events, and she hadn't been to town to gossip with the girls in the nail salon. Dad said that we shouldn't worry; six weeks was nothing in the grand scheme of grief.

I looked over at Anna, crouched down by the soil. The garden was her new project, and it was thriving.

'Do you have time to watch *Line of Duty* with me before you go out?' she asked.

'Where are you up to?'

'Season one, episode five.'

'Ah, no. I've almost finished season three.'

'But you were only on season two yesterday?'

'I'm single, Anna. Adrian Dunbar is all I have.'

'It's weird how much you fancy him.'

'He'd be a great suitor,' I said, mocking Mam.

'You seem happy today, Ives.'

'I'm OK.'

'OK is OK, you know?'

'I'm going to have a nice time tonight, then tomorrow I'm going to reassess my life choices.'

Anna laughed.

'I'm being serious!'

'Ivy, I love you, but now's not the time to be making life affirmations. Just take each day as it comes.'

'I should be saying the same to you.'

'Yes, but I'm older, wiser and a lot smarter than you.'

'Fair play.'

'You're sad, and it's OK to be sad. Just don't be a dick about it.'

'Sage advice as always.'

'As I said, older, wiser—'

'Oh, get over yourself.'

'So, is Rob going to be at Mia's party tonight?'

I let out a loud moan and put my head in my hands.

'You tried to make him have sex with you, and then forced him to flee your flat. It's fine!' Anna said.

'Your tone suggests otherwise.'

248

I'd sent a message to Rob a few days after our ill-fated date, trying to explain myself, but all I could pull together was, 'Sorry for being a total nightmare.' His reply was short and sweet, 'It's OK, look after number one.' Mia said I shouldn't feel embarrassed about my behaviour. I said I wasn't embarrassed; I was learning to accept the person I was becoming, even if I really didn't like that person.

Anna was making black bean chilli for dinner and insisted I have some before the party. On Monday she'd be starting her injections again and her new obsession, as well as gardening, was plant-based protein. I had no idea how this was going to help her get pregnant, but I knew better than to ask. I did point out that eating a kilo of lentils and beans before going to a party with my recently-ex lover wasn't the best plan. But, Anna was less than sympathetic, and told me to eat up.

I rang Mia to tell her I'd be at the party for about 10pm. She was listening to the soundtrack from the *Cats* musical, something she does to psyche herself up before a big night. She was in a foul mood because Clara's play was being transferred to Broadway while she'd been rejected for an advert about vaginal thrush. We were all having a low week, month, year. I told Anna I would take it easy that night, and I wanted to believe myself, but I felt like I was on a treadmill, and if I got off at the speed I was going, I would fall flat on my face and hurt myself. I wasn't ready to get off.

When I arrived at Mia's, I found her pouring vodka into a massive bowl of pink punch. She was wearing black biker boots, skinny black jeans and a cropped, ruffled gingham top that exposed her delicate waist. Her hair was messily plaited to one side and she was surrounded by a host of attractive men, all vying for her attention.

She saw me smiling at her and rushed over to greet me.

'I know you don't want to acknowledge it, but happy birth-day,' she whispered in my ear.

I kissed her, then pushed her off me and demanded a drink.

'What do you think of my look?' she asked.

'Yeah, it's fine.'

'Fine isn't the vibe I was going for, Ivy.'

'Right, sorry. You look amazing.'

She rolled her eyes at me.

'What! I mean it!'

'I'm trying to instil a bit of Alexa Chung in me.'

'OK.'

'I was scrolling through my Instagram last night and I fear my look's a bit too Pre-Raphaelite, you know?'

I didn't know, and at times like these it's best not to say anything, so I went to pour myself a glass of punch.

'Oh! The apothecary is here!' she squealed, as she pointed towards a man walking through the hallway.

'Who's the apothecary?' I asked.

'I don't know his actual name. But wait until you see his treasure chest.'

I rolled my eyes and took a sip of the punch. It was three-parts vodka, one-part juice – otherwise known as rocket fuel.

The usual suspects were all in attendance. Theatre actors, a couple of agents, authors and artists from Noah's art class. There was a group of older men milling about by the piano wearing the same uniform: shirt, silk scarf around their neck, waistcoat and blazer. So many people dressing for a part and there I was in muddy trainers and a crumpled dress I'd found at the back of Anna's wardrobe.

After a couple of rounds of punch, I was introduced to the apothecary. His actual name was Nico, but of course nobody called him that. It doesn't have the same ring to it. Nico sat in the corner of the room, and, just as Mia said, he had a small box on his lap that looked exactly like a treasure chest.

'This is my best friend, Ivy,' Mia said, introducing me.

'Hi Ivy. How's it going?'

'She's never done a balloon,' Mia said.

Nico went inside his treasure chest and brought out two small canisters and a few balloons.

'You're such a gem,' Mia said, kissing him on the cheek.

I followed her upstairs to the bathroom, nudging people out of the way. It seemed as if everyone had gone from zero to blind drunk very quickly; there were bodies scattered everywhere, cutting up lines on hardbacks, dabbing MDMA onto their sticky fingers and sniffing whatnot from rolled-up notes. Who were these people?

We sat down on the cold bathroom floor with our vodka punch and canisters. Mia told me to watch her carefully, so I did as I was told. She opened the canister and filled the balloon with nitrous oxide, breathing in and out slowly for a couple of breaths. Then she put her hand over the nib of the balloon and closed her eyes. Her shoulders relaxed, and she leant her head back so I couldn't see her eyes. A moment later, she was upright again.

'Christ, that's good.'

'Is that your come face?'

'Pretty much, yeah.' She lay down on the floor and I joined her.

'Who were those people on the stairs?' I asked.

'God knows. I don't even think Noah knows.'

'Did you ever read about the party Freddie Mercury hosted in New Orleans?'

'The one with the dwarves carrying trays of cocaine on their heads?'

'Yeah! This reminds of that.'

'They're just trying to escape boredom, Ivy.'

'I know the feeling.'

'Don't do that face, that's your sad face. Do a balloon with me!'

'You're the worst, Mia.'

'Yeah, but I'm great fun though, aren't I?'

I did exactly as she did and as soon as I inhaled the gas from the balloon, my head went dizzy and ringing started in my ears. I closed my eyes and let the feeling ride over me as I breathed in and out the balloon. When I opened my eyes again, Mia was out of focus. I reached my hand out to her and rolled over on the floor in hysterics.

'Fucking hell!' I cried.

'I know, right?'

Just like that, the black curtain was lifted, if only for a second.

Chapter 39

Moments of gold

I clocked him as soon as he arrived at the party. He walked through to the kitchen carrying a load of beers, and, as he put them down on the table, I watched the veins in his forearms pulsate. I must have been staring, because Noah told me to get a grip of myself and stop being, 'So fucking obvious.' He was over six foot and when he smiled in my direction, his teeth glistened, and I felt my face go hot.

I messaged Anna to tell her that a young Idris Elba was at the party. She replied telling me I should be myself, but not so much my current self, which was harsh but fair. I went to find Mia to berate her for not telling me that such a man was going to be at the party. I would have at least ironed my dress, or put on some lipstick, or washed my hair. A heads up would have been appreciated.

I found her in the master bedroom; she had changed into Noah's dressing gown – a thick navy towelling robe – and was sitting on the floor, legs splayed out in front of her, leaning against the bed with her arms out like Jesus on the cross. Sitting on the bed, with her legs over Mia, was a young woman giving Mia a head massage. She had a man at each hand, also giving her massages, and a very contented cat sitting in her lap. Another man was by her feet, massaging her ankles. Joni Mitchell was playing on the record player and lavender incense was filling the room. There was a woman sitting on the window ledge smoking a joint, and when she turned towards me, I saw that one side of her face was entirely covered in gold glitter. She nodded my way sullenly then turned to face outside again.

I sat down beside Mia and whispered her name into her ear. She jumped.

'Don't do that to me, Ivy.'

'Who's Noah's friend who looks like Idris Elba?'

'Ah, yes. Young Keith.'

'His name is not Keith.'

'It's Keith.'

'How can a man like that have a name like Keith?'

'It was the name bestowed to him upon birth.'

'Why did you not tell me about him?'

'What's there to tell? Oh, you mean like, to shag? I didn't think about it.'

'Well, thanks very much.'

'I think you need more time by yourself to figure out what you want.'

'You are so annoying.'

'It's true.'

'OK, fine. But I also need to have sex.'

'So, talk to him.'

'No, I'm too nervous. I'll have shit chat.'

'You have great chat.'

'Is he single?'

'Ask Noah.'

'Is he gay?'

'He identifies as a heterosexual.'

'Why can't you ever answer a question in a straightforward manner?'

'Piss off, you're ruining my zen.'

I kissed her on the forehead and got up to leave. As I was by the door I turned back around.

'Mia, this, what you've got going on here, is ridiculous . . . even for you.'

She smiled and closed her eyes.

Back downstairs I found Noah, who had changed into one of Mia's lavish velvet kimonos and was playing the piano while someone sang a horrendous version of 'Defying Gravity'. I went into the kitchen to get myself a drink and saw Keith by the punch.

'Would you mind pouring me some?' I asked, as I nudged in beside him.

'Yeah, sure. I have to warn you, it's not very nice.'

'Well, Mia has no concept of measurements.'

He laughed; I was overjoyed.

'Where is she? I've not seen her yet.'

'She's upstairs getting a full body massage.'

Another laugh. I was on fire.

'Genuinely, that's what she's doing,' I said.

'I won't ask.'

'I'm Ivy, by the way.'

'Keith,' he said. 'How do you know Mia?'

'I went to university with her. But these other guys, I have no clue.' I pulled a face so that he knew I was not to be associated with the other guests.

He smiled and held my gaze.

'I think I saw you at a party last year? You were with your fiancé?'

'Um, no. That wasn't me.'

'Sorry, I could've sworn that was you.'

'No, not me,' I lied.

We both held eye contact as we sipped our drinks and my vagina did a little somersault.

'Do you smoke? I was heading to the garden to have a cigarette,' I said.

'I shouldn't; I have a rugby game tomorrow morning.'

That explains the arms, I thought. I tried to think of something funny but all I could think of was the time I rang Gramps to tell him about Jamie. I said that although he was English, he was a good rugby player and respected the Welsh team.

'Don't be fooled,' Gramps said. 'He's lulling you into a false sense of security. The English are all the same, sneaky little buggers.'

The thought of Gramps put a lump in my throat. I don't have the best poker face, so when Keith asked me if everything was all right, I just started walking towards the garden, leaving him standing there alone.

I joined a group sitting on the grass and chain-smoked, pretending to go along with their conversation until someone started playing the banjo, and then I had to leave. I draw the line at musical instruments at parties.

I walked back into the living room to find Mia sitting next to Noah on the piano, midway through a sensational rendition of 'It's All Coming Back to Me'. I was standing by the doorway watching them when Keith caught my eye. I held my hand up to say hello then quickly regretted it, choosing to fiddle with my fingers in embarrassment instead. When they finished singing Celine Dion, they both got up and bowed. As Mia turned to walk away, Noah grabbed her and started kissing her all over her face. I looked at Keith and wished he'd snog my face off like that too.

Blondie came on and bodies started making their way into the middle of the room, moving furniture out of the way for the dance floor. I was about to join in when someone tapped me on the shoulder. He was about eight inches shorter than me and sweating like mad, probably because of the three-piece tweed suit he was wearing.

'I'm Cam, how do you do?' he said, as he took my hand.

His palms were clammy and his smile revealed a mass amount of food wedged in one tooth.

'Hi, I'm Ivy.'

'Pleasure, Ivy. I'm a friend of Noah's second cousin, Charles.'

'OK.'

'What do you do?'

'In life?'

'Yes, for paid employment?'

'I'm a PA.'

'Good stuff. I work with Peter Wetherell Frics.'

'Sorry, I don't know who that is.'

'It's an estate agent in Marylebone.'

'Right.'

'Do you live around here?'

'No, I live in Hackney.'

'Hackney? Gosh.'

'Yup.'

'And do you rent?'

'I do rent, it's actually my brother-in-law's—'

'I don't blame you. The market's so chaotic now.'

'Excuse me, I'm going to get a drink.'

'Good stuff, I'll come with you.'

I gritted my teeth as I walked into the kitchen. I could feel his beady little eyes on me as I opened the fridge. Someone called my name and when I turned around, there was Keith.

'I wanted to say goodbye. I have to go, bloody rugby.'

I saw him look at Cam and then back at me, as if to say 'really?'

257

'Oh, this isn't ... Sorry, this is Cam, Noah's cousin's ... We've just met.'

Cam held his hand out for Keith.

'Gosh, you are tall,' Cam said.

'Um, thanks. Ivy, good to meet you. See you next time?'

'Yes,' I said, a little too enthusiastically. 'See you next time, and good luck for tomorrow.'

He flashed me that killer smile again and walked out the kitchen.

'What are you doing tomorrow?' Cam asked when Keith was out of sight.

'I'm seeing my sister.'

'I was going to suggest a spot of lunch.'

'Thank you, but no.'

'Another time?'

'Look, I've just lost my grandfather. I don't want to go for lunch.'

'Oh, gosh. I'm terribly sorry.'

'Yeah, well, so am I,' I said, grabbing a drink and walking out into the garden.

I immediately regretted it. All I wanted was to snog someone like it was the end of the fucking world. Well, someone other than Cam.

I went into the garden to find Mia. I lay my head in her lap, and closed my eyes.

Chapter 40

Curveball

'Why are you wearing that tracksuit?' Mia asked.

We were in the pub the next day; I hadn't been able to sleep and told her I'd buy her lunch if she kept me company.

'It was clean,' I said. 'What's with the coat?'

'What's wrong with it?'

'It's a bit ... "Joseph any dream will do".'

'What?'

'Never mind.'

'Don't you like it?'

'I like it. It's just a bit ... dramatic.'

'Ives, you can't comment.' She laughed. 'You look like you haven't slept for three days.'

'Try six months.'

'I hate this place. Their sauvignon blanc tastes like piss.'

'Well, drink something else.'

She slouched back in the seat and frowned as she surveyed the pub.

'Do you think ulcers are a sign of cancer?'

'What are you on about, Mia?'

'Nothing. Where's Anna?'

'At yoga; she'll meet us at the cinema.'

'Fine.'

'Are you all right?'

'I'm just tired and fed-up of being hungover.'

'Yeah, I know the feeling.'

'Do "Sober October" with me and Noah?'

'No.'

'Come on, it'll do you the world of good.'

She looked me dead in the eye as she said it and put her hand on my arm.

'What?' I asked, moving her away. 'Why are you doing that?'

'Nothing. I'm not doing anything.'

'Why did you say it like that?'

'I didn't say it like anything, Ivy.'

'You're judging.'

'I'm not judging. I'm suggesting.'

'Why are you allowed to be hungover but I'm not?'

'Ivy, that's not what I meant.'

'Yes, it is.'

'I'm trying to look out for you.'

'Hang on. You drank all night too, why's it different for you?'

'It's not! You know I didn't mean—'

'What?'

'Well, I stopped drinking hours before you did.'

'I saw you smoke a joint, Mia.'

'I had like, one toke.'

'Oh, so now this is a numbers game?'

'Ivy, stop being so defensive. I'm trying to have a conversation with you.'

'No, you're not. You're being unfair.'

As I said this, I got out of my seat and went to grab my stuff. She got up too, and tried to get me to sit down, but

I was starting to cry and didn't want to make a scene. I shrugged her off and told her I was going home and that I'd prefer it if she didn't follow me. I walked out of the pub as quickly as I could, but not quick enough so that it looked like I was storming out of an argument. There's nothing worse than a public row.

I knew she was right. Mia and Noah were the King and Queens of hosting because they knew when to stop. I remember her telling me about something she'd read in a novel, *The Deception Glass*, a trick she employed whenever they threw parties. In Georgian times, the host of a party would use a deception glass, which had thickened glass to the sides or base to reduce the capacity. So, whenever the glass was topped up, the host would always be drinking less than everyone else, and nobody would suspect a thing. That's the thing about Mia — blind drunk or stone-cold sober, she's fun on a stick. It's one of the many reasons why I love her.

I should have stayed in the pub, told her I was losing my mind and asked for help. I don't know why I didn't say anything. I convinced myself it was because she had her own stuff to deal with and didn't need mine too, which was of course complete bollocks.

I arranged to meet Anna to watch the new Ryan Gosling film. Seeing him shirtless and sweaty for two and half hours was my birthday present to myself. Also, the only films I was prepared to see were ones with bland narratives, so that one fitted the bill perfectly. I still couldn't bring myself to watch anything remotely romantic. Well, there was *Four Weddings and a Funeral*, but that was in Dorset and all the vegan food had gone to my head, so it didn't count. *Titanic* didn't count either; it's got Billy Zane in it.

Jamie's parents had a cinema room in their house in

Hambleton. We'd get loads of snacks and spend all day watching the classics – *Casablanca, Citizen Kane, The Godfather*. A couple of weeks before we broke up, we spent the weekend at his parents'. Jamie was on edge; he and his father had argued again, and I could tell that this time it had really got to him. Sometimes, Will's words would fly right over his head, but other times, they lingered for days, weeks even. I never spoke to Cressida about it; I wouldn't have a clue where to start. I know she disagreed with her husband; she was kind and warm and Will Langdon was the sort of person who'd put you down in front of everyone just for a cheap laugh – even if he was the only one laughing. I could hear them shouting at each other as I waited in the cinema room. I was so uncomfortable that, by the time Jamie came into the room, I'd polished off a bottle of red wine and eaten four Creme Eggs. I knew it was a mistake – I ran six miles that afternoon and not had any dinner.

When he came into the room, I had the opening credits of *Jaws* paused on the TV and was shoving yet another Creme Egg into my mouth at lightning speed.

'You look very cute and very naughty, Ivy,' he said, walking towards me.

'You don't look happy.'

'Dad's being an arse.'

'What happened?'

'I don't want to talk about.'

'OK. Whatever you want.'

He sat down on the sofa beside me and took my hand in his.

'I love you so much, Ivy.'

'I love you too, you know I do.'

'Why is your dad so normal and mine's such a cunt.'

'Jamie, you can't call your dad a cunt.'

'I can.'

'You really don't want to talk about it?'

'I really don't.'

He leant into me and we kissed for ages. His hands were around my waist, gripping me tight – like he was holding on for dear life. We watched *Jaws* then put on our wellies, took a bottle of wine from the cellar and went into the garden – well, it's not so much a garden as a golf course. We sat in our pyjamas on the wet grass, drinking wine from the bottle and talking about our upcoming trip to Thailand. All that, just two weeks before he walked out the door.

Anna was waiting outside the cinema for me.

'You don't look happy,' she said, as she hugged me.

'I'm hungover and Mia's annoyed me. You?'

'I'm fed up and I'm about to lose it with these fucking doctors.'

'Well, this is great, isn't it?'

'What's up with Mia?'

'I don't want to talk about it.'

'Fine. If I don't see a glimpse of Ryan Gosling's crotch in this film, I'm going to lose my shit.'

After the film, we made our way to the local Thai. Anna was acting off; a bit erratic and vacant. She was about to start another punishing cycle of treatment on Monday and had already told me she was on the verge of tears, so I didn't press her. But, halfway through the meal, I got tired of her long, audible sighs, and asked her to talk to me, properly.

'OK, OK. I'm sorry. I don't know how to put this ...'

'There's nothing left to go wrong, Anna. So, whatever you say, it'll be fine.'

'Hmmm ...'

'Don't "hmmm" me, Anna. What is it?'

'OK. Do you want the good news, or the "news news"?'

'What's "news news"?'

'It's neither good nor bad.'

'Start with that.'

'Jamie has been in touch with Mark.'

'Right.'

'Mark wants to speak to you about it.'

'Anna, I can't.'

'I know, but—'

'But, what?'

'I don't know, Ivy. I want you to have some closure.'

'He left. That's closure.'

'Ivy, I love you, so please don't take this the wrong way—'

'Here we go . . . '

'You're barely existing.'

I crossed my arms against my chest.

'Stop it,' she said, pointing at my chest. 'Stop being so defensive.'

I didn't say anything; I couldn't look her in the eye.

'I'm saying it because I love you,' she said.

'You sound like Mia.'

'We're both worried about you.'

'You've been talking about me behind my back?'

'This isn't sixth form, Ivy. We're concerned, that's all.'

'You told me yesterday that it's OK to be sad!'

'Yeah, but it's not OK to be a dick so—'

'Just hurry up and tell me the second piece of news.'

'Gramps left us both twenty-two thousand pounds in his will.'

I had no words. I assumed I might be left a couple of thousand, nothing more. I was banking on it – I'd racked up quite a hefty credit card bill over the past few months. I never, ever expected anything more than that.

'Ivy, say something,' Anna said, touching my arm across the table.

'Fucking hell.'

'Yeah, I know.'

'What am I meant to do with twenty-two thousand pounds?'

'Oh yeah, I forget you pay like, twenty pounds rent.'

'Don't be jealous, Anna. It's unbecoming.'

She smiled and we sat in silence for a few moments, holding hands across the table.

'What are you going to do?' I asked her.

'Buy another IVF package. Hurrah!'

'You might not need it.'

'I'll throw all the money I've got at the situation until we get that bloody baby.'

'That's the spirit.'

'It's big though, isn't it?'

'I don't know what to say.'

'Sleep on it, have a think. But, I think this is a really good thing.'

'Yeah.'

'It opens up a lot of opportunities.'

'Yeah.'

'So, in a nutshell, Jamie wants to see you, and you've inherited a substantial amount of money.'

'Yeah . . .what a Sunday.'

'Look, take your time. Jamie can wait. I want you to be happy, Ives. That's all.'

'Yeah.'

'Mia and I say these things because we love you, and only because we love you.'

'Yeah.'

'And if what Jamie says can help you move forward, then that can only be a good thing.'

'Yeah.'

'Stop saying "yeah"!'

As I walked home I got my phone out to message Mia, but she'd already beaten me to it.

> I was being a smug wanker and I'm sorry.
> I love you to the moon and back, always will.
> From one hot mess to another xxxxxxx

It was quite a lot to take in for a Sunday.

Chapter 41

Sobering up with sausage rolls

The next day, I met Mark in the pub after work.

'Do you want to know what I think? What I actually think?'

'Yes, of course I do,' I said.

'He's not been doing so good.'

'How can you say that? He's got a girlfriend!'

'You said I could be honest.'

'Fine, be honest then.'

'He's been in therapy.'

'What?'

'And he's not seeing that girl anymore.'

'I don't even care.'

'Yes, you do, Ivy.'

'Fine, I do.'

'She was a mistake.'

'It didn't look like a mistake.'

'He was holding on to a lot of anger.'

'Oh, come off it, Mark. Now you sound like the therapist.'

'He knows he messed up, Ivy, and he's trying to work out why.'

'I know why. Because he's a cunt.'

'He did a cuntish thing, yes.'

'Is there a difference?'

'I think you can do a cuntish thing and not necessarily be a cunt.'

'I don't know about that.'

'Do you still love him?'

'Yes, of course.'

'Look, I know he's sorry, I know he hates himself for what he did, and I know that if he could undo everything, he would.'

'Did he say that?'

'Not in so many words, but yes.'

'So how do you know for sure?'

'Because I know. He's desperate to see you, desperate for you to hear him out.'

'Isn't that only to make himself feel better, though?'

'I don't think it is. I really don't.'

'What am I meant to do with this?'

'You know I could kill him for what he did to you, but seeing you, and him, and how miserable you both are, I think you need to talk to him.'

'What does Anna think?'

'You know what Anna thinks; she hates him.'

'Good.'

'And I'm not excusing what he did.'

'I know.'

'So . . . what are you going to do?'

I didn't do anything that night; I didn't do anything for another three weeks, in fact. In that time, Jamie messaged to ask if we could meet up. I couldn't think of anything else but what he was doing and what it was that he wanted to say to me. But despite this, I couldn't bring myself to reply. For all the noise in my head, when it came down to it, I had no idea

268

what to say to him, so I didn't say anything at all. Whatever Jamie had to tell me wouldn't change the fact that I was still alone or make me forget the look on his face when I saw him kiss that other woman. Nothing.

Jane replaced the snack machine in work with a fruit basket and everyone was raging, so Ethan organised a pub crawl for Friday night. We needed something to boost morale.

As Friday after-work drinks always go, it got to 8pm and everyone was off their face, having drunk for three hours straight on an empty stomach. Ethan was trying to get me to come to a rave with him in Epping Forest the next day.

'What is with everyone and day raves?' I asked.

'Oh, yeah, I forgot. You like to go to Hyde Park and watch Robbie Williams.'

'He was in Take That!' I cried.

'He's well shit, Ives.'

He put his hand on my arm, his fingers lightly stroking me. I moved back a little to make more space between us.

'Come tomorrow, it'll be fun. I bought six Blue Supermans,' he said.

'I don't know what that is?'

'The pills! Come on ... Take a little E, dance to some Farveblind—'

'What is Farveblind?'

'Ives! Come on! If you weren't so lame I'd have tried to shag you.'

'Well, that's lucky then, isn't it?' I said.

I walked over to the bar, bought a sausage roll and went to the bathroom to sober up. I put the toilet seat down, scoffed the roll in seconds, and rang Mia.

'Ives, I can't talk now. What's up?'

'What are you doing?' I asked.

'Watching this Hebrew programme.'

'Is it actually in Hebrew?'

'Yeah.'

'Sobriety has changed you.'

'I know. I'm like, actually highbrow now.'

I laughed at her, almost choking on some pastry.

'What's that noise?' she asked.

'The flush. I'm in the bathroom, trying to escape from Ethan.'

'Classic.'

'Tell me what to do about Jamie.'

'You know what I think.'

'Tell me again.'

'I think you need to message him back. It's the only way, Ivy.'

'OK.'

'You need closure.'

'Why does everyone keep saying that?'

'Because it's true.'

Closure is a funny thing, isn't it? Closure is great when you want to move on but what would I be moving on to exactly? And what was I meant to do with £22,000? Well, £19,200 after the credit card bill.

Mam thinks it's tasteless to discuss finances, so nobody spoke about the money and I had no idea when I was going to see it. Anna, Mark and I were going down to Wales in a few weeks to scatter Gramps' ashes, so I hoped we'd talk about it then. You know when someone asks you what you'd do if you won the lottery, and you want to look good so say you'd donate it to charity? Well, that's rubbish. I wasn't donating anything to charity. Anna suggested a yoga retreat, but I couldn't think of anything worse than spending a week with a bunch of lonely vegans. She'd even suggested it to Mam and now it was all they talked about. Well, that and the upcoming trip to Loch Lomond. The only walking Mam will ever do is towards Liz and Henry's pub, so I couldn't quite get my head around how she was going to cope with the daily eight- to ten-mile hikes. When I asked her this, she accused me of being 'deliberately hostile'. Similarly, she'd never done a yoga class or gone a week booze-free before, but a wellness retreat with three hours of yoga every day coupled with an alcohol ban seemed like a great idea.

Having spent the best part of an hour sitting on the toilet trying to sober up with mediocre puff pastry, I decided to call it a night. I was seeing Maude the next day, and I wanted to show her that I was doing OK. I'd gone to see her a couple of times since her birthday, though the last time was on the back of an all-nighter in Halo with Dan – my strongly worded letter worked wonders – and I didn't like the way she looked at me when she saw me. It was the way Gramps' would've looked at me.

I was on time for once. I found her in the communal sitting room; she had big green curlers in her hair and was watching *Pointless*. There was always either *Pointless* on the TV or Alexander Armstrong on the CD player. There were no alternative entertainment options.

I gave her a hug and sat down beside her.

'You look tense, my dear.'

'I'm always tense, Maude.'

There was that look, of disappointment, annoyance even. Here I was again, hungover and anxious. I was meant to be keeping her company, not making her worry sick for my well-being.

'Ivy, I wasn't born yesterday.'

'I'm sorry, Maude.' I sighed.

'Let's start from the beginning. Tell me the matter and we'll sort through it together.'

'Right, well—'

'Hang on,' she said, as she turned around in her chair and called over to Irene.

Irene put down her cards and looked over at us.

'You know that tea your daughter brought in? The Whittard's one?'

'Best cuppa we've had in all our lives, Maude!' Irene said, beaming.

'You wouldn't mind if me and Ivy took a tea bag, would you. We're having a little heart to heart, see.'

Irene put her cards down immediately.

'Why didn't you say, for goodness' sake. I'll go fetch them from my cupboard.'

She got up from her seat and steadied herself on her stroller.

Before she was out the kitchen door, she turned back towards us.

'How about I trade you two Whittard's tea bags for a couple of those Fortnum & Mason biscuits you have? The ones the Queen likes.'

Maude looked over at me to check whether this was an acceptable request.

I nodded.

'Right you are, Irene. Two rich tea biscuits coming your way.'

'Ah, you're so good to me, Maude.'

Maude told her not to be silly, and Irene pottered off to get the fancy tea bags.

'Now you can start, my love.'

Where do you start? I had a fiancé, but he broke up with me five minutes after we had sex. I still love him, even though I hate him. I'm convinced he was unfaithful to me, so our whole relationship feels like one big lie. The closest person to me in the world just died, and I've inherited a small sum of money that I've no clue what to do with.

272

Maude listened intently, offering me wisdom – and more biscuits – for over an hour.

'Sit on the money for a while. As Anna said, there's no rush.'

'You're right.'

'You do need closure, petal.'

'Everyone keeps saying that.'

'Everyone is right, Ivy.'

'I know.'

'There are three important questions you need to ask yourself.'

'You sound like Gramps,' I said. 'Yes, he has property and earns good money.'

'Nonsense, none of that matters.'

'Right, go on then.'

'Does he make you laugh? Is he kind?' She stopped herself, leant in towards me and lowered her voice to a whisper, 'And does he bring you to climax?'

'Maude!'

'My dear, I have seen it all.'

'Well, clearly.'

'I kissed my friend Sylvie once.'

I burst out laughing.

'But that's for another day, Ivy.'

I got the impression that Maude's husband Martin was a little bit naughty, just like her. I told her about Gramps, how naughty he was, and we agreed that they would have got along like a house on fire. Maude said that Martin had the kindest face in all of London, and when he smiled she felt like the whole world was on her side. She'd known him all her life, but they didn't get married until she was thirty-six years old. She couldn't have children, so she kept telling him he should marry someone else, but he kept refusing, and one day, she caved. She thinks about his face every minute of every day, and the way he used to look at her, as if she were the only person in the room. They went dancing twice a week and they loved walking. She told me about the old railway line that runs from Finsbury Park all the way up to Highgate; they'd follow it through to Highgate village, then onto Hampstead Lane. Before they got to the Spaniards Inn for a sherry and pint of bitter for Martin, they'd take a detour onto The Bishops Avenue to have a gander at all the fancy mansions. Maude would make up stories for each house; who was having the affairs, who'd fathered the illegitimate love child, who ruined their fortune on gambling debts. I told her that I loved going to cemeteries and making up stories about the deceased. It's not something I go around telling people; nobody thinks its romantic, they just think I'm odd, but Maude beamed when I told her.

'We are one and the same, you and me, dear,' she said.

We talked more about Martin and watched more *Pointless*, with my hands cupped in hers the whole time.

'Will you promise me you'll take better care of yourself?'

'I will, Maude.'

'No more of this gallivanting around London at four in the morning.'

'OK.'

'Does it ever make you feel any better?'

'No, not really.'

'Well, exactly.'

I left the care home that afternoon with a lighter heart and a clearer head. I knew she would make everything better; old people are good like that.

I messaged Jamie as soon as I was outside.

I'm sorry I've not replied. I will meet you.

I got a response back within a minute

> Thank you, Ivy. I'm away with work for a couple
> of weeks. What about Saturday 29th? Name a
> time and a place and I'll be there. x

It was going to be a long couple of weeks.

Chapter 42

It's all kicking off

It took a long time for Saturday 29th October to come. I created so many distractions, but nothing worked. I even slept with Rob again; I liked the fact that we had sex just days before I was to meet Jamie. It gave me an odd sense of power.

D-Day came. I woke before sunrise and cleaned the flat, rearranged the furniture in my bedroom and cleared out three bags of old clothes. Keith had invited me to his Halloween party that same night and the timing had done nothing for my anxiety. All I wanted was for Jamie to beg for me back, and for Keith to beg me to have sex with him. Unfortunately, the universe had other ideas and I was forced to spend a large portion of the morning dealing with an ingrown hair on my vagina.

I told Mam and Dad that I was seeing Jamie. Dad wasn't so keen on the idea, but Mam actually gave me some sound advice. I was to be quiet and let him do all the talking. Then, I should leave. Nothing more, nothing less. I wanted to ring Gramps so much that afternoon that I began rearranging all the kitchen cupboards in a bid to stop me from having a total meltdown. It worked for all of fifteen minutes.

We met on the Southbank; I wanted a neutral location. This

way, he could tell me he'd fathered a love child or whatever it was that he wanted to tell me, and I could run off crying and nobody would mind because the place would be filled with tourists and not a single soul would notice me.

I clocked him as soon as I walked into the pub. He was sat in the corner, looking out the window towards the Thames. He had a beautiful cream cable knit jumper on under his Barbour jacket, which brought out his tan. As soon as I saw him, I was overcome with sadness: sadness for the past eight months, sadness for everything we'd lost. I'm not going to lie and pretend that I didn't think about his hands on my breasts. I did that too.

I walked towards him and when his face turned to meet mine, he smiled and got up from his seat.

'Hi Welshie.'

'Hi Jamie.'

Neither of us broke eye contact. He had faint tan lines around his eyes where his glasses had been. He looked so handsome.

'I ordered you a wine,' he said, sitting down.

'Thank you.'

'How are you?'

'I'm . . . OK.'

'I'm so sorry about Gramps.'

'Yeah, me too.'

I turned to stare out the window, overcome by how useless and vulnerable I suddenly felt.

'I don't know what I'm doing here, Jamie. I . . . '

I had no idea what to say to him.

'No, please. Let me explain, Ivy.'

I was about to launch into a tirade of abuse, when I thought of Mam, and her advice. I took a large gulp of wine, a deep breath and told him to continue.

'I never cheated on you. Never,' he said.

I took another gulp of wine.

'Cat is Niall's sister,' he said.

'Niall from work?'

'Yes. It's over.'

Another gulp of wine.

'I was in a state after we ended.'

'Oh, you were in a state, were you?'

'Ivy—'

'It must have been really difficult for you, I am sorry.'

'You have every reason to be mad.'

'Thank you for permitting me to be angry at you. That's incredibly considerate, Jamie.'

'I only saw her for a month or so. I don't know what I was doing, I was—'

'Wanting sex, probably?'

'I'll take that.'

I bit my tongue and tried to compose myself.

'Apparently you've been seeing a therapist?' I said.

'I have, yes. It's helped a lot.'

'Right.'

'You know I'm not good at that sort of thing. But I'm trying.'

'Right.'

'It was never anything to do with you, Ivy. I realise that now.'

'It has everything to do with me. I was your fiancée.'

'I was depressed, Ivy.'

'It's not like I've been having the time of my life, is it?'

'You don't owe me anything, I appreciate that, but if I can just try to explain.'

I grabbed one the cushions beside us and held it against my chest.

'OK. Please, explain.'

'Do you remember the last time you came to Hambleton? The argument I had with my dad?'

'Yeah, of course I do.'

'Everything spiralled from there.'

'But what did I do? I only ever tried to help.'

'I know you did. Sorry, I'm not doing a very good job of explaining this.'

'Keep trying.'

'It's years of being told I'm not good enough. Years of being told I need to work harder, be better, that if I'm going to get anywhere in life I need to be a bit more like him. I don't want to be like my dad, Ivy. He doesn't give a shit about anything or anyone except himself. I've never wanted that. I wanted to be a better man for you, not for him. But I lost it, and I ran, and you didn't fight.'

'Hang on, what?'

'You didn't fight. You let me go.'

'What was I meant to do? I spent the first few weeks in total shock and then when I thought I was getting a grip on things, I saw you kissing that girl.'

'I'm not blaming you, I'm not. But when you didn't fight I thought, well, maybe Dad's right, maybe I'm not good enough and maybe we shouldn't be together. I couldn't see a future with you . . . with anyone.'

'So, you just ran away?'

'I lost it. It was like everything he'd ever said to me was true and I didn't know what to do.'

'And now you have some clarity?'

'Ivy, I don't want to run anymore.'

He inched a little closer to me and took hold of my hand. I shrugged him away and placed my hands under my bum, so he couldn't reach them.

'Ivy, I'm sorry.'

'You've said that already.'

'I love you, Ivy. With everything.'

When he said it, I was looking down at my feet and think-ing that my right shoe needed to be re-heeled. I didn't hear him properly. I looked up at him, not saying anything.

'I can't lose you again, Ivy. I love you.'

There was no wine left. I started to tremble; he moved towards me and I didn't stop him. He looked me right in the eye and said it again, 'I love you, Ivy. Please ...'

He kissed me, so softly that I could barely feel his lips. But he kissed me, and without even knowing it, my lips parted to greet his. He moved in closer; his hand went to the small of my back and I felt my whole body relax in submission. His hand moved up into my hair while mine stayed firmly under my bum. He said my name again. He said how much he'd missed me. He said too much. It was all too much.

'I can't,' I said, pushing him away from me.

'Please, Ivy. I know you still love me.'

'Jamie, I can't.'

I grabbed my stuff and walked out of the pub.

Suddenly, the ingrown hair on my vagina was the least of my worries.

I rang Mia, but she didn't answer. It was still October, which meant she was still sober and probably engaged in a ceramic painting class or some other ridiculous creative pursuit she'd taken up to replace going out.

I walked away from the pub as fast as I could, turning corners in case he was behind me. He kept calling my phone.

I stopped on the pavement and stared down at the phone for a few minutes before I messaged him.

I can't deal with this right now, Jamie.

He said he loved me. I didn't respond. I walked all the way to Anna's, picking up a bottle of wine on the way. Considering the day I was having, I assumed she'd save her lectures and give me a free pass.

'Ivy, you don't need that. Come sit down, darling.'

'Please don't tell me what I need right now, Anna,' I said, pouring myself a large glass.

I went to sit down on the floor by her feet, rested my head on her knees and told her everything he said, word for word.

'What does your gut say?' she asked. 'You always trust your gut.'

'It's not saying anything right now.'

'Well, that's unhelpful timing, isn't it?'

'He said he'd do anything.'

'I believe him, he's stubborn like that.'

'What do I do?'

'Ives, you've got to follow your heart.'

'Don't say shit like that to me.'

'I mean it; you always know what to do.'

'I never know what to do.'

I got up and poured myself another drink.

'Ivy, cool it.'

'Please don't tell me to cool it, Anna.'

'Why don't you stay in with me tonight? Mark's out, it'll be just us two.'

'No, I want to try to have sex with Keith.'

'Who's Keith?'

'Idris Elba.'

'Oh, yes. I don't think shagging Keith is the answer, darling.'

'Thank you for that, Anna.'

'Don't be like that.'

'I'm sorry. I can't . . . '

'I know, Ives. I know.'

I finished the rest of my drink, then I left to get ready for Keith's party. Anna told me to look after myself and made me promise to be at hers – sober – for Sunday lunch the next day. In the meantime, I was going to do whatever I could to help me forget what had just happened. I didn't want to think about the fact that my ex-fiancé told me he was still in love with me. I didn't want to think about the fact that my body was crying out for help, and I certainly didn't want to think about the fact that Gramps was gone. I didn't want to think about anything at all.

Chapter 43

Socially acceptable Halloween attire

There were no costume instructions for the party, so I decided to go as Cher from *Clueless*. I needed something that highlighted my boobs. Weight loss had made them perkier, and I wasn't going to let them go unnoticed.

After hearing what had happened earlier in the day, Noah and Mia were breaking 'Sober October' for one night only to keep me company at Keith's. Mia made a massive deal out of it but it was basically the end of the month anyway, so I told her to stop being such a martyr and get over herself. Mia said she wanted to be home by 1am but I said I would stay for as long as it took to see Keith naked. Or at least get a flash of his forearms again. I was in no position to be picky.

Jamie messaged me just as I was leaving the flat.

> I will do anything to make it up to you. Whatever
> it takes, Ivy.

I turned my phone off and threw it on the sofa before walking out the door.

Keith's house was done out in spectacular fashion for

the party. There were tombstones, severed heads and fake machetes all over the place. In the kitchen, they'd left enormous fake knives on the cooker alongside pots and pans filled with makeshift bloody limbs. There was a smoke machine and illustrations of ghouls and spider webs all over the walls, pumpkins filled with bottles of green booze and biscuits shaped as witches. What sort of person has the time to make all this?

I was standing by the bobbin apples when I saw Dan come through the gate. He was wearing a white sheet and as he got closer I realised that his face was completely black. I ran up to him, grabbed his arm and took him round the side of the building.

'Dan, what's happened to your face?'

'What?' he said, touching his cheeks.

'Why are you blacked-up?'

'I'm not blacked-up.'

'Your whole face is black.'

'Oh shit, the make-up must have run. I was going for "a bit dirty".'

'It's more than a bit dirty; you're completely black.'

'Oh shit, is it bad?'

'Dan, under no circumstances can you come into Keith's house dressed as a blacked-up ghost.'

'Shit. It was a mistake, Ives.'

I shook my head at him in bemusement.

'Don't look at me like that!'

'Dan, wash it off now.'

'Fine, I'll go to the bathroom. One of these prats is bound to have some micellar water.'

We went into the bathroom together and, as he washed the make-up off his face, I went to check on the ingrown hair situation. As luck would have it, it had filled with puss and doubled in size. I got some concealer out of my bag and started dabbing it onto the area.

'What the hell are you doing?' Dan asked.

'I'm having an ingrown hair mare.'

'Why are you putting make-up on it?'

'Because I want to have sex with Keith.'

'Oh,' he said, inching his head towards my crotch to take a good look at it. 'Christ, he won't be going anywhere near that.'

'Oh, fuck off,' I said.

When we got out of the bathroom, I saw Keith standing in the hallway chatting to a friend. He caught my eye and called me over.

'Really glad you came, Ivy,' he said, kissing me on the cheek.

'Amazing house,' I said.

'Can I give you a tour?'

'Sure, I'd love that.'

He grabbed my hand and led me up the stairs. I looked behind me and Dan was standing there, giving me two thumbs up.

Keith showed me around and I tried to look interested in what he was saying, but all I could think about was Jamie's words, 'I'll do anything'. The only way to distract myself was to neck the vodka mix, so that's what I did.

We got to his bedroom and he showed me inside, closing the door behind him. The walls were covered with beautiful black and white photographs – people playing rugby, on cricket tours, Brooklyn Bridge, a safari trip in Zimbabwe, Rio Carnival.

'I have a bit of a photography habit,' he said, as he watched me looking around the room wide-eyed.

'You took all these?'

'Yeah.'

'You're really good.'

'Thanks, Ivy.'

'I know nothing about photography but yeah, you're really good.'

He laughed and moved towards me.

'Cher?' he asked, looking me up and down.

'Yes! I'm surprised you guessed it.'

'I have a younger sister.'

'Ah, that would be it.'

We sat on his bed and talked about his photographs, the places he'd travelled to, the places I want to travel to. He showed me a photograph he took of the Botataung Pagoda, when he was in Myanmar, the most spectacular place he'd visited. He asked me about Wales and about my family. He moved so close to me that I could almost feel his breath on my skin as he spoke.

'I've been thinking about you ever since the party,' he said.

'Keith . . . ' I said, moving away from him.

'Are you OK?'

'I'm sorry. I can't do this.'

'OK, we don't have to do anything.'

'I'm sorry, I want to but . . . '

'Don't apologise, you don't need to be sorry for anything.'

I let out a big sigh as I put my head between my hands.

'This is not how I wanted tonight to go,' I said.

'Do you want to talk about it?'

'It's been a bit of a shitty day, on top of a shitty month and a very shitty year.'

'Noah did mention things haven't been great.'

'Yeah.'

'I knew I remembered you from the party.'

'I'm sorry. I was embarrassed . . . '

He took my hand in his.

'Look, I like you. I think you're funny and your smile is . . . it's incredible.'

'Keith—'

'But if you're not ready, or you can't do this, then that's cool.'

I looked up at his perfect face.

'We'll just head back out into the party and I'll pretend that you didn't just totally humiliate me.'

We both laughed.

'I'm not in the right place ... for this. For anything, really. Not now. I'm sorry.'

'It's OK,' he said.

'I want to. I want you to know that I really want to. But my head's all over the place.'

I got off the bed. He got up with me and wrapped his arms around me. I kissed his cheek and walked out.

I debated going back inside to snog the face off him. He was one of the most beautiful human beings I'd ever laid eyes on. But I couldn't even bring myself to kiss more than a small portion of his left cheek. Somehow, it felt like a betrayal to Jamie.

I got so drunk that night that Dan had to take me home. Mia and Noah had long gone, and I, apparently, had lost the ability to stand. I woke the next morning fully clothed on my sofa with a blanket wrapped over me. There was a note on the table.

Babe, hope you are OK. Not seen you like that before. Love you, take it easy today. xxxxx

I went into the bathroom and looked in the mirror. There were dark circles under my eyes and my skin was red and patchy. I had a gash across my forehead and big purple bruises on my legs. There was nothing I could do about it, so I got in the shower and hoped Anna would be lenient with me.

I walked to her house, hoping the cold air would help sober

me up. I picked up a bottle of wine on the way and some of her favourite red velvet cupcakes from the bakery, hoping this would appease her.

Mark opened the door and shook his head at me.

'You look like shit, Ives.'

'Yeah, I know.'

I got myself a glass and a bottle opener and went to sit on the sofa with the wine.

Anna came to sit beside me and started stroking my hair.

'Darling, are you OK?'

'Can you stop being so patronising, please?'

'I'm only asking.'

'I'm fine.'

'What's that cut on your forehead?'

'It's nothing.'

She shook her head and walked into the kitchen. She kept popping her head around the door to check on me. I couldn't bear it any longer, so I got up from the sofa and went into the garden.

Mark followed me.

'Ivy, you've got to talk to her.'

'I am talking to her.'

'Are you?'

'I don't want a lecture, Mark.'

'This is getting old, Ivy.'

'Can we not go over this again?'

'No, we need to. You're a mess—'

'That's not very—'

'Everyone is treading on eggshells around you and we're sick of it.'

'That's unfair—'

'We've all got our shit. It's not just you in this, you know?'

'I'm sorry my problems are too much for you, Mark.'

'Fuck me, you're selfish. Can you stop for just a second and consider what else is going on around you?'

'I am! I do.'

'Do you? What about your sister, who's desperate for some good news, or your mum, who's lost the only parent she had left. What about them?'

Anna came up behind me and put her hands on my shoulder.

I shrugged her off me and walked back into the living room. She followed me inside.

'I've had enough,' she said.

'Fine,' I shouted, walking into the bathroom and slamming the door behind me.

She opened the door right away.

'Ivy, you have got to stop this.'

'Stop what?' I seethed.

She paused and looked me dead in the eye.

'Stop feeling like everyone is against you.'

'Everyone is fucking against me!'

'No, Ivy. You're against you ... You and only you.'

I leant against the door and tried to stop myself from screaming.

'You've got to pull yourself together.'

'I'm trying.'

'Try harder.'

'I'm sorry, OK? I'm fucking sorry.'

'Stop being sorry and get a grip. I'm over this pity act, it's done my fucking head in.'

We stood there in silence, staring at each other.

'I'm going to make us some tea, and we're going to sit in the living room and we're going to talk, about everything.'

'I don't want to talk.'

'I don't care what you want. This wallowing has got to stop. Now.'

She moved towards me and pulled me into her chest. I hugged her tight as I breathed deeply into her.

Mark knocked on the door.

'I'm going to leave you guys to it, OK?' he said.

'Yes, thanks darling,' Anna said.

'Mark?' I said, as he was about to leave.

'Yes, Ivy?'

'I'm sorry,' I said.

'I know, Ives. Just ... this needs to stop, OK?'

I nodded. He gave me a half-smile and walked out the door.

Chapter 44

The observation deck

I sat under the clock at Paddington Station, with Mia talking nonsense down the phone.

'I'm going to book myself in for a colonic irrigation,' she said.

I mumbled something inaudible under my breath.

'Ivy, are you even listening?'

'What? Sorry, I thought I saw Lisa from work and was about to make a swift exit.'

'Well, listen, this colon thing—'

'But, why?'

'All the celebs do it before awards season.'

'You're not a celeb and you're not going to any awards.'

'I might be.'

'When?'

'Well, who knows, but in the future, perhaps.'

'I can't discuss this with you right now, Mia.'

'You better perk up before Anna and Mark get there. A four-hour train journey with that attitude won't get you anywhere.'

'You're the worst.'

'Come on now. Any more news?'

'He wrote me a letter.'

'Oh, give me a break. Who has the time to write letters these days?'

'He's trying, Mia.'

'I bet he is.'

'Don't say it like that.'

'I'm not saying anything.'

'Anyway, I better try find them. Good luck for tomorrow.'

'I'm breaking out into a sweat just thinking about it.'

'You'll be great.'

'No big deal ... only a workshop at the Royal Court, the greatest theatre in the history of theatres.'

'Try putting less pressure on yourself.'

'That's impossible, Ivy. I can't undo thirty-two years of negative self-talk, can I?'

'Well, no. But, I think you're amazing, for what it's worth.'

'You're amazing, Ivy.'

'Oh, go away.'

'I'm being serious. I'm so proud of you.'

'Stop it.'

'Fine. You're a fucking mess.'

'Call me after the audition, yes?'

'I will. Good luck in Wales, I'll be thinking of you.'

I scanned the station for Mark and Anna. I hadn't seen them since Sunday, when Anna told me in no uncertain terms that I had to pull myself together. She knew how to get to me, and finally, she got to me.

Jamie had been pulling out the stops all week. There'd been lengthy phones calls, where I heard about his therapy sessions, the final showdown with his dad, how he quit his job and how supportive his mother had been. He said he would do anything to go back to how things were. The problem with that was, I'd forgotten what that looked like.

I kept the letter on me all week. I must have read it a hundred times.

My Ivy,

You know how much I love you. I can't imagine how hard these past few months have been on you, but please try to understand, they've been hard on me too. I'm not asking for your pity, or sympathy, but forgiveness.

I should have got help years ago. I don't know why I didn't. I'm sorry for making you feel like it was your fault. All you ever did was try to help, to listen to me. It should have been me listening to you.

I've been able to see a lot more clearly since I started seeing my counsellor. I never wanted to admit how angry I was that I never had a proper father, that he never spoke to me like a son. I never spoke to Mum about how hurt I've been all these years, how unloved I felt and how mad I was at her for never doing anything about it. We've been able to have some good talks recently, and whilst I can't see Dad changing anytime soon, I know I've got Mum's support. I knew I had to get out of that job and find something on my own, something that wasn't tied up in all our family bullshit. All of this just made me realise how much I've missed your family. You're so lucky to have each other.

I'm not saying I'm fixed; I'm not. But I'm getting there, slowly. I understand how much I have hurt you, and I will do whatever it takes to make it up to you. You're the best thing that ever happened to me, and I'll never forgive myself for what I did — to you, and us.

I want to spend the rest of my life with you. I love you, Welshie xxx

I saw Anna before she saw me, and when her eyes finally met mine, she picked up her pace and ran towards me. She started sobbing as she hugged me, and when I told her to stop embarrassing me, she kissed me all over my face. She told me that she loved me very much, even though I was a total nightmare. She passed me a bag of Percy Pigs and said that she'd downloaded three new episodes of *Line of Duty*, so she wouldn't be speaking to me throughout the duration of the train journey. Mark walked up behind me, put his arms around me and said, 'I've downloaded *Absolutely Fabulous* for us and I've bought a multipack of Quavers, so we're sorted.'

'What did I do to deserve you?' I said.

'I don't know, but you better be grateful.'

'I am, Mark. I really, really am.'

'Let's have a great weekend, OK?' he said.

That, I was up for.

When we arrived home in Wales, Mam greeted us at the front door with a tray of sushi and champagne.

'What's this?' Anna asked, laughing.

'My new course; your father got it for me.'

'She was driving me mad being in all day,' Dad said over her shoulder.

'Look at those perfectly formed hand rolls. Ivy! Ivy, look at them.'

'This one's a bit off,' I said.

'Stop it, come here!' Mam said and pulled me in close to her.

Despite looking like a child's attempt at play dough, Mam's creations were, overall, surprisingly good. As I shoved a prawn tempura in my mouth, Dad whispered in my ear, 'They're undercooked and soggy, but smile and tell her they're amazing,' so that's what I did.

We were standing in the corridor, funnelling raw fish into our mouths, when I realised Anna was still over by the door, watching us all in silence.

'Come and tuck in,' I said.

'I can't eat raw fish.'

'You love raw fish.'

'I'm pregnant.'

Everyone turned to face her.

'You're pregnant?' Dad asked.

'I've only just taken the test ... there's a long way to go,' Anna said.

I looked at Mam; her lower lip began to quiver, and her eyes welled up. Anna walked over and held her.

'I know it sounds stupid but, it feels different this time. I feel pregnant.' As she said this, Mam let out a cry and downed a glass full of fizz.

'I'm chuffed to bits for you both,' Dad said.

'It's going to be a long few months,' Anna said, 'but I'm hopeful.'

'Hopeful is good,' I said.

'You're allowed to be hopeful, my darling,' Mam said.

'Yes, and for once I am.'

We went into the kitchen and Mam started getting out various bottles of champagne from the fridge.

'This is the perfect opportunity to do the taste test for Christmas Day,' she said.

'Oh Christ, Margaret. Not now.'

'Tony, stop it, please. Girls, Mark, I have bought a variety of champagne from different supermarkets and I want your honest opinion on all of them.'

'How many have you bought?' I asked.

'A few.'

'Mags, tell them the number,' Dad said.

'Oh, for goodness' sake. Fine, I bought fourteen bottles.'

'I can't even name fourteen supermarkets,' I said.

'Well, I bought the big house names too, to mix it up a bit.'

'I don't even like champagne, and Anna can't drink, can she?' Dad said.

'Tony, everyone likes champagne. Stop being so antagonistic and start drinking.'

We needed some good news, and here it was, the best news we could have imagined. Gramps would've been over the moon. He'd have read the baby old Tory manifestos and would've refused to stop swearing – the rows would have been monumental.

After more cheers, I went to take my bag upstairs, with Dad following behind me. As we sat down on the bed, he put his arm around me. I closed my eyes and lay my head on his shoulder.

'I want someone to tell me exactly what to do.'

'That's not going to happen, Ives.'

We sat in silence for a little while.

'I'm so glad she's pregnant,' I said.

'Me too.'

'Being an adult is hard.'

'It gets easier, I promise.'

'That's rubbish and you know it.'

'Yeah.' Dad laughed. 'It is.'

When Dad went back downstairs I got my phone out to message Jamie and thanked him again for his beautiful letter. He replied to say that he was thinking of me and hoped I would be able to get some sleep. He said he missed me. I said I missed him too, because I did. I really did.

I didn't sleep much that night. At about 5am, I admitted defeat and got up to go for a run. I was in a punishing sort of mood.

I went downstairs to find Mam sat in the living room, watching *Sleepless in Seattle*.

'Why are you up?' I asked.

'Can't sleep. How come you're up?'

'Can't sleep.'

I sat down beside her; there were wet tissues all around her lap.

'How many times did you and Gramps watch this together?' she asked.

'Hundreds.'

'He really loved you, Ives.'

'I loved him too.'

'You and me both, darling. You and me both.'

We sat and finished the film. By the time Sam and Jonah were at the top of the Empire State Building, looking at Annie and her stuffed bear, we were both sobbing. When the scene ended, and the credits rolled, we turned to each other and burst out laughing.

'What a right pair we are,' Mam said.

Dad came in wearing Mam's dressing gown, carrying a pot of tea and breakfast on a tray.

'I've not made this for nothing, Mags. Get yourself back up to bed now.'

'Urgh, Dad. Don't say it like that.'

'Like what?' He laughed, giving Mam a wink.

'You're disgusting,' I said. 'I'm going out.'

Chapter 45

My way

That next day, we walked along the Rhossili Coastal Trail carrying Gramps' ashes. When we got to the highest point of the Gower, we put out the picnic blanket, champagne and fish and chips we'd picked up on the way. They were cold and soggy from the excess vinegar, just as Gramps would've liked. When we finished eating, I got out my phone and put on Frank Sinatra's 'My Way'. As the song began to play, Mam opened the urn.

'I don't know if I can do this, you know,' she said.

Dad got up from the picnic blanket and put his arm around her.

'Do you want us to do it together?' he asked.

'No, I just need a minute.'

Dad sat back down with us and we waited in silence.

She walked a little closer to the edge and started talking.

'You're the best father I could've ever hoped for, you know that, don't you?' she said, speaking to the urn.

'I want you to give Mammy a kiss from me, a big one. Get your dancing shoes on and show her what she's been missing.'

She took another minute to compose herself. She lifted her head to the sky and shook her head in disbelief.

'How on earth did we get here?' she asked.

'Mam,' I said, 'we can help.'

We all got up and stood beside her. She kissed the tip of the urn and tipped it so that the ashes fell along the cliff edge, onto Rhossili Beach, Gramps' favourite place in the world – where he'd proposed to Gran and where he and Mam had spread her ashes, all those years ago. They were together now.

When all the ashes were scattered, we huddled together and looked out towards the ocean. I thought I wouldn't be able to do it, but Gramps was right, just go by the sea, and everything will be better. I stood there thinking about all our days out on that beach. The fights between me and Anna over who got to sit under the nice umbrella, the one with the pink flowers on it, Gran's favourite. The countless paddles in the sea, even when it was below zero and we felt like our toes were going to fall off. All the many times Gramps and I walked hand in hand together in the sand. All the times he listened to my worries, about boys, about university and moving to London. The time we sat in the pouring rain eating fish and chips, waiting for a taxi because Gramps had lost his car keys in the sea. It was all there. It would always be there.

We stopped at Henry and Liz's on the way back home, and much to everyone's confusion, I didn't drink. I couldn't remember the last time I hadn't been blind drunk on a Saturday afternoon. When I asked for a packet of crisps and a pint of Coke, Liz asked me if I was OK. She tried to get me to open up about Jamie, but I didn't have the energy. This wasn't about him. It was about Gramps, and Mam, and Anna. For once, it had nothing to do with him.

I slept for fourteen hours that night. No drowning dreams, no late-night cigarettes or tumblers of whisky. Everyone was up and out of the house when I woke, aside from Mam, who was reorganising her wardrobe.

'Precious baby lamb, you're up!'

I gave her a look of, 'Please stop calling me that.'

'Not like you to sleep so long, darling.'

'I know,' I said. 'Must be the sea.'

I started rooting through the pile of handbags on the bed. I picked up her gold clutch and let out a little laugh.

'What?' she said.

'This bag, I wore it to the Ritz. Remember that surprise date with Jamie?'

'The one with all the sandwiches?'

'Yeah.'

'Do you want to talk about it?'

'Not really.'

'Well, OK then, we won't.'

She came over and cupped my face between her hands.

'All I want is for you to be happy.'

'Me too, Mam.'

We talked about the money and what I wanted to do with it. It was in a high interest savings account, ready for me to use whenever I was ready. I had no idea when I'd be ready though, and I certainly didn't have a clue what to spend it on. I wanted Gramps to be proud of me, for him to know I wasn't going to piss it all down the drain. Mam was still very keen on the idea of a yoga retreat, and I was still very much of the opinion that it was the world's worst idea.

I've always wanted to go scuba diving, and then there was Rio Carnival – Keith's recommendation. I'd been thinking about Keith a lot. I couldn't remember much of what happened after we talked at his party. As I said, I got paralytic drunk and blacked out. He messaged a few days later to say he hoped he wasn't too forward, but he liked me and, when I was ready, he'd be there. The man wanted to take me out on a date. That's all.

Mam was staring at me from across the room, shouting my name.

'Sorry. What?' I said.

'Christmas chocolates, Ivy.'

'What?'

'Should we go with Hotel Chocolat or the new luxury M&S selection?'

'Mam, nobody cares.'

'I care. I'm tense just thinking about it.'

We always spent Christmas at home in Wales; Mam would cook because Gramps didn't like going out with what he called 'riff-raff'. He'd come over for 10am, presents in tow; we'd have Bucks Fizz, open our gifts, then Dad would make everyone bacon sandwiches. I'd help Mam cook, while everyone else sat in the living room watching *It's a Wonderful Life*. Gramps would come into the kitchen after the film was through and berate us for getting too tipsy before dinner. Owen and his wife would come over for a drink and by the time they left, everyone would be well on their way. Well, everyone aside from Gramps. Anna and I would put our pyjamas on right after dinner, which always riled Gramps up. He never quite understood the beauty of loungewear, let alone matching onesies. One year, we put them on before dinner and he went berserk, refusing to eat until we'd changed back into our Christmas best.

I was hoping that this year we could do something different, start a new tradition. I always wanted to go somewhere hot for Christmas, but Mam said that hot weather in December was the 'absolute opposite of festive'. Maybe this year would be different.

As I ran along the cycle path that morning, Jamie called and asked if he could see me when I got back to London. There was a new restaurant in King's Cross that he wanted to take me to, somewhere he knew I would love.

'Can I let you know? I don't know what time I'm getting back on Thursday.'

'It's hard to get a reservation there, so the sooner the better.'

'Jamie, please don't push me. I'm doing my best here.'

'I'm sorry. I don't want to push you. We'll find another time to go.'

'I need a bit of time, that's all.'

I ran past the Anchor; Liz was in the front garden taking the bins out. She shouted at me from across the lawn and asked if I was coming in.

'No, I'm going to keep on running,' I shouted back at her.

'You're acting very strange, young lady,' she said, laughing.

I blew her a kiss and ran out to the beach.

Chapter 46

Modern Britain

After almost a week in Wales, it was time to go back to London. I was doing my best to replace bottles of wine and pints of Tia Maria with excessively long runs and trips to Joe's for Knickerbocker Glories. But despite visible, marked improvements, everyone continued to fuss and faff around me and I was about to lose it. As expected, Mam was at peak annoying.

On our last night in Wales, we sat around the table for dinner. I tried to eat, but I kept getting distracted by Mam, who'd been staring at me for a solid ten minutes

'Can you stop looking at me like that?' I finally said to her.

'I'm allowed to look at my precious baby lamb.'

Mark laughed, and I kicked him under the table.

'Can I be excused?' I asked.

'Ives, if you want to go upstairs, go upstairs. You don't need to ask,' Dad said.

I got up, gave him a kiss on the cheek then went up to my room. I'd packed and unpacked my bag so many times. There was nothing left for me to do, but somehow it felt like there was everything left for me to do.

Anna knocked on the door.

'You OK?' she asked.

'I'm stuck, Anna.'

'How do you mean?'

'I'm sick of hanging around waiting for the next disaster to strike.'

'Gramps always said that fear was a good thing; it meant you had something to lose.'

'Yeah, but he also said things like, "she's all fur coat no knickers," which makes no sense whatsoever.'

'Yeah, you've got a point. Ignore everything I said.'

'I want to do the right thing.'

'You will.'

'But mainly I want a holiday.'

'Then book a holiday.'

'I've wasted so much money this year, with nothing to show for it.'

'Don't be so dramatic. So, you went out too much; get over it.'

'I like it when you're mean.'

'It's my new tactic.'

I smiled. 'I can tell.'

'I love you, Ives.'

'I love you too. And I promise, I'm going to be the best auntie in the whole world.'

'I don't doubt that for a second.'

'Can I take them on their first trip to the pub?'

'Don't push it, Ives.'

'Sorry.' I laughed. 'You're going to be the most amazing mam.'

'Second best to our mam, obvs.'

'Second best to our mam but much less annoying.'

We walked back downstairs to find Mam waiting by the door, angrily.

'Bloody Linda's late again,' she said.

'What's tonight?'

'Fundraiser for Foreign Accent Syndrome.'

'Why did I even ask?'

We got the train back to London on Thursday night. Jane emailed to say she wanted to take me out for lunch the following day. I was terrified – where would we go that would allow her to bring her own tea bags, tiny cherry tomatoes and bite-size avocado? Also, what in the world would we talk about? I thought of calling in sick, but then I thought about Mam and her unwavering faith in my ability to do the right thing. I'd spent the past eight months in a perpetual state of avoidance and it had done me no favours. I would have to be an adult and go into work.

I decided not to see Jamie that night. Instead, we arranged to have dinner the next day, back at his flat in Bermondsey. We talked at length that night. He asked me all the right questions about Wales, my family, how it felt to be back on Rhossili Beach without Gramps. I couldn't help it; I was so excited to see him.

The next day, I went for a run before work, stopping in the corner shop on the way home. Instead of my usual breakfast of half a pack of cigarettes, I bought a grapefruit and a bag of granola, one of those very posh, overpriced ones that comes with a load of dried fruit nobody's ever heard of. Buying posh food makes me feel like I can achieve anything in life, and that was the sort of feeling I was going for that morning.

I powerwalked to work listening to Helen Mirren's *Desert Island Discs*. I needed a soothing voice to calm my nerves and Helen delivered. I got into work half an hour early and Jane was already in her office. I waved at her through the glass and she gestured at me to come inside.

'How was Wales, Ivy?'

'It was good, thanks. As good as it could've been.'

'I hope you got some rest.'

'I did, thank you.'

'Are we still OK for lunch?'

'We are, yes.'

'I'm looking forward to it,' she said, smiling at me in a way I didn't recognise. I wondered if this was a manipulation tactic – butter me up before sacking me. Or, perhaps she was genuinely looking forward to lunch. It was too confusing to think about.

At 10am, Gerald came in holding a McDonald's. It stank, and I told him so.

'You've changed your tune,' he said.

'Gerald, I am trying my very best.'

'Good for you, love.'

'Thanks, I appreciate your support.'

Jane booked a table at Blossom Veg, the new vegetarian restaurant near our office. This really riled me up. There were normal restaurants that had veggie options. Why did we have to go to a restaurant that only served vegetables? I shouldn't be forced to eat spinach leaves just because she's punishing herself with a celery stick.

I browsed the menu online before we left the office, which was the worst thing I could have done as it only made me more irate. I messaged Jamie, knowing he would find it funny. All posh people hate vegetarians; it doesn't blend in with their whole 'let's go shoot some guinea fowl' aesthetic.

Jane and I made uncomfortable small talk all the way to the restaurant. It was the longest eleven minutes of my life. When we got there, people were queuing outside the door waiting for tables. Restaurants with a no-reservation policy are exactly what's wrong with modern Britain.

We finally sat down, and Jane took out a zip lock bag from her purse that housed a collection of tea bags. I tried to ignore this, but I don't have the best poker face.

'I think it's important to know precisely where our food and drink come from,' she said.

'OK.'

'It's only a tea bag, but I know that the tea leaves are organic and fair trade.'

'OK.'

'When I ask waiters about the origin of their produce, they tend to look at me like I'm some sort of freak.'

I thought it best not to respond to this, so I went to look at the menu again.

I ordered myself a peculiar-looking green juice and some sort of hummus falafel thing. Jane ordered a raw vegetable salad. My mood was plummeting at a rapid rate. Nobody should ever be forced to pay £15 for a plate of chickpeas. All I could do was hope she'd pick up the bill.

'So, Ivy,' she said, 'I wanted to get some time out of the office to discuss how things are going with you.'

'OK.'

'I want to be honest.'

'OK.'

'I think you're spiralling.'

I smiled.

'What?' she said.

'You're not the only one.'

I could see her shoulders relax, just a little.

'Who else?'

'My mother, for one.'

'Mothers always know best.'

'Unfortunately, you're right.'

'It may not look like it, but I am on your side, Ivy.'

She looked at me with genuine concern and, for the first time in our relationship, I understood the part I'd played in all of this. I'd been a terrible employee: late starts; shitty attitude; and a permanent smell of booze hanging over me. She hadn't even been particularly hard on me. Yes, the incessant micromanaging was annoying, but, she had her reasons – I was hungover half the time and angry the rest. It was a miracle I was still in gainful employment.

Chapter 47

Talking about feelings

Over organic, fair trade tea, Jane and I spent the best part of three hours engrossed in conversation. I told her all about the money, about Jamie and how all I wanted was to feel real joy again.

'I'm sorry,' I said. 'I've been such a shit.'

'Let's not dwell, Ivy.'

'OK, but I mean it; I'm ashamed at how reckless I've been.'

She nodded her head.

'We have to figure these things out for ourselves, Ivy. Sometimes it takes a lot longer than we want it to.'

I didn't say anything in response and she went back to playing with the baby gem lettuce on her plate.

'Did you know that I'm in therapy?'

I didn't.

'My boyfriend . . .' Her voice trailed off and her eyes started welling up with tears.

'You don't have to tell me if you don't want to.'

'No, I want to.'

I nodded my head and let her speak.

'My boyfriend, Simon . . . he passed away. We were together sixteen years. He was complaining of chest pains and after four months of antibiotics and multiple appointments, we were told it was cancer. By that point, it had spread all over his body. He was put into a hospice about four weeks after the diagnosis, and he died three weeks later.'

I took her hand from across the table.

'Jane, I had no idea.'

'It's not something I like to talk about.'

'When did this happen?'

'Four years ago. When something like that happens, it changes you. It changes you forever.'

'I'm sorry.'

'I wasn't always like this. I was much more fun.'

'You don't have to explain yourself.'

'I'm trying to be better at talking about my feelings.'

'You and me both.'

'I buried everything so deeply ... I became a different person. I'm only starting to see now how damaging that was.'

'Yes ...'

'It's so isolating living like that.'

I had no idea what to say to her, so I just listened as she spoke.

'The most important thing I've learnt is that the only person who can give you everything is you,' she said.

I nodded.

'I know this job isn't right for you, Ivy.'

'It's not that, it's ... '

'If you want, and only if you want, we can sit down together next week and look at opportunities elsewhere.'

'Are you sacking me?'

'No, I want you to work somewhere where you thrive.'

'I'd like to work at somewhere like Netflix,' I mused.

'Ivy, I don't think that's realistic; technology isn't your strongest point.'

I laughed. For once, I loved her honesty.

'I saw the drawing you did for Lisa's nephew; you're very good.'

'Oh, thank you,' I said, a little embarrassed. 'I used to paint all the time. Gramps' house was filled with my watercolours. I can't remember when or why I stopped.'

'It's important that we take time for ourselves to be creative. It's good for the soul.'

'I know, you're right. I've been thinking about doing an art course.'

'That's a great idea, it'll help you get back into it.'

'Yeah, and it'll keep me out of the pub.'

'Well, exactly,' she said, laughing.

By the time we got back to the office, most people had packed up, so Jane told me to go home. I went into her office to say goodbye, thanking her again for such a lovely lunch. We had a very awkward hug where I told her that she was a good person and gave great advice, and that I was sorry for being such an awful employee. I meant every word of it.

I left the office, walked down to Waterloo Bridge and along the Southbank. Jamie and I used to take this route a lot. We'd start at his flat in Bermondsey, then make our way all the way down to Battersea, before crossing the bridge into Chelsea. I don't understand Chelsea; all the women have Mulberry hand-bags and all the men are in Barbour jackets. So many clones. It's like that 90s Michael Keaton film, *Multiplicity*, only worse. Despite my objections, Jamie and I always went to the same restaurant on the King's Road. The last time we were there, he said their mac and cheese was better than mine and we had a massive row. If I had £3,000 to spend on rare French truffles, perhaps mine would taste like that too.

I made my way along the river to the Tate Modern. I used to love walking around museums, but I couldn't remember the last time I went to an exhibition. Going to exhibitions makes me feel a lot more refined than I am. I like to spend my time mulling over the individual pieces, nodding my head in contemplation and making all the necessary noises to give off the impression that I know what I'm talking about. I should know what I'm talking about, considering my degree, but like most graduates, I spent more time in the students' union bar than in the lecture theatre.

I once took Gramps to the Tate Modern; we were in the queue in the cafe, and he went into a rant about how expensive everything in London is. He was talking too loud, swearing too much, and a woman behind us asked him to keep his voice down When we turned around, she was holding her hands over her child's ears. Gramps gave her one look and said, 'If you don't like it, you can sod off.' We had an absolute ball that day.

I went to browse the gift shop. There was a woman with her two daughters; one no older than ten and the other a teenager. The elder sibling had her headphones in, and Stormzy was blasting out of them. She was chewing gum loudly and picking the polish off her nails. The younger one was running between everyone's legs, shrieking with delight.

'Olive, stop it!' her mother cried, grabbing her younger daughter's arm and pulling her in close. Her sister pulled a headphone out of her ear and said, 'Olive, you are such a child.'

'I am a child,' Olive replied.

Her mother looked at me and mouthed, 'Sorry,' but I told her not to worry about it. I said hello to Olive and she beamed back at me before taking off again, screaming and bumping into everyone. I watched her as she picked up a postcard. I moved in closer to see it, it was a black and white photograph of four elderly men standing outside a betting shop in

Hammersmith. She went over to her sister and pulled her headphones out of her ears.

'The fat one looks like Daddy!' she cried.

Her sister burst out laughing and beckoned their mother to come over. They all stood together, in stitches, staring at the postcard.

I got my phone out and dialled home.

'Precious baby lamb!' Mam said.

'What are you up to?' I asked.

'Olga's over, she's helping me with the nursery.'

'She's your cleaner, Mam, not your assistant.'

'Ivy, she's so much more than that.'

'OK.'

'And I want the nursery completely redone.'

'It's not even been used yet.'

'So?'

'So, why can't you leave it as it is?'

'Ivy, please don't question my creativity.'

'OK.'

'Where are you? Why can I hear children?'

'I'm in the Tate Modern.'

'Oh, how very cultured of you, darling. That's my Ivy.'

'I've only been people watching in the shop.'

'Still, people will think you're cultured just being there.'

'That's exactly what I thought, Mam.'

'Darling, sorry, I'm terribly busy. Can I ring you back?'

'Hang on, I was thinking . . . We should go on holiday. You, me and Anna.'

'The yoga retreat!'

'Mam, Anna can't even do yoga right now.'

'But I just bought some gorgeous wet-look leggings from Sweaty Betty.'

'You don't do yoga.'

'Yes, but we will on the retreat.'

'We're not going on a retreat.'

'Fine, let's do what you want to do.'

'I thought perhaps some winter sun, some spa treatments—'

'You hate the spa.'

'Nobody hates the spa, Mam. I didn't like it that one time the woman practically sat on my back.'

'She was terribly overweight. You don't see that in masseurs these days.'

'I'll speak to Anna and we'll look at some options this weekend.'

'Well, this is exciting. Your father will be thrilled to see the back of us.'

I didn't know what I was letting myself in for.

Chapter 48

Family portraiture

I picked up a classy £12 bottle of wine on route to Jamie's – anything more is a waste of money. I'd conjured up so many scenarios of this moment in my head; what I would say, how I would say it. But it wasn't at all like I thought it would be. No matter how much this notion of being back with him had consumed my every thought for the past eight months, the reality was that I was totally unprepared.

He opened the door in an apron, with a tea towel thrown across his shoulder. He was so impossibly good-looking, even in his red trousers.

'Hello, Welshie,' he said.

'Hello.'

He came towards me, kissed me on the cheek and my heart stirred. When he pulled away, our eyes met, he smiled, and his lips moved to my mouth. I dropped my bag and pulled him in closer. I dropped my bags. My hands went into his hair; I could smell his shampoo, his aftershave. He tasted the same as he always tasted. He tasted like home.

I was the one who finally pulled away. He took my bags and told me to relax on the sofa.

He started talking about how things were with his dad. They were on speaking terms again; Cressida had facilitated the initial conversation, and for the first time he could remember, his dad was trying.

'I'm thinking of going back to work with him.'

I was surprised by this. This certainly wasn't the impression he gave off when we met in the pub, or in his letter, or when we'd talked for hours on the phone.

'What does your therapist say?' I asked.

'She says I need to separate our professional and personal relationship.'

'I don't see how you can ever do that, though, if you work with him. I mean, there's too much history.'

'I know, but things are getting better, and I love the team. I miss them.'

'Have you started to look at other options?'

'Not really. You know job hunting is such a slog.'

'Yes, but—'

'Anyway, I'm only going to do a few more sessions with her.'

'Oh, really?'

'She's been great, but I think I'm good now.'

He came over and gave me a kiss on the forehead. I didn't tell him that I thought stopping therapy was a terrible idea. I didn't tell him that jumping right back into a job he hated so much was too.

I changed the subject and asked him what he was cooking. He said spaghetti Bolognese, my favourite. I was about to tell him that it was no longer my favourite, but I didn't want to ruin the moment. He carried on talking, talking and stirring the Bolognese. Cressida would be in London next week, he said; she wanted to take me to her private members' club in Mayfair for drinks on Thursday. He'd forgotten that I hated it there; it was a pompous club for wealthy old white men and their silent wives, and there was no way I was going to spend my Thursday night there. Jamie said it would mean a lot to her; he'd already told her I'd be looking forward to it.

I hadn't said much at this point. He kept talking, and I kept looking around the room, half listening. The same frames adorned the walls: photos of his gap year with the boys, skiing in Verbier, family Boxing Day shoots, oil-on-canvas paintings of his beloved horses and a portrait of his great-grandfather, sporting a thousand medals, with a very fat beagle beside him. The fancy wine fridge was still making the world's most annoying hum; matching Le Creuset pans decked the kitchen shelves and I recognised an electric wine cork that always managed to make it harder to open a bottle. There were copies of the *Financial Times* littered across the coffee table. I found the mark on the carpet from the time I got blind drunk and knocked a bottle of £190 claret onto the floor. I didn't know it was £190, but he was certainly reminded of it for weeks afterwards.

He asked me to come over and taste the sauce. I tasted a little off the spoon and told him it was delicious. It reminded me of our old Sunday night ritual. Jamie would pour me a glass of wine and run me a bath as he made dinner. We'd eat at the table then finish off the bottle on the sofa with a film, something classic with Marlon Brando or Elizabeth Taylor. I'd missed our Sundays so much.

I went to get some water when he put his hand on my arm and pulled me back towards him. He was leaning against the counter as I stood in front of him. His hands went to my waist as he nuzzled pulled me towards him so that I could feel his erection against me. My hands moved under his T-shirt and he rubbed my crotch through the fabric of my jeans. He picked me up, sat me on the counter and took off my T-shirt. His lips were around my nipples, kissing, biting, squeezing. My hands went to take off his shirt and, as I did, the beagle caught my eye. I couldn't stop looking at it. Jamie was all over me, and all I could do was look at that ugly, overweight beagle.

'Stop,' I said, suddenly feeling claustrophobic and overwhelmed. 'Please, stop.'

'What? What is it?'

I got off the counter, put my T-shirt back on and went over to the window.

'Ivy? Are you OK?'

I looked around the room. Everything was the exact same.

'I'm sorry. I can't do this.'

'What do you mean?' he asked.

'I can't do this, Jamie. I can't.'

His face changed as he registered what I was saying.

'You left me, Jamie.'

'Ivy, you know I—'

'You left me for the best part of a year.'

'I would never do that to you again, ever.'

'You want everything to go back to how it was, and it can't.'

'Ivy, it can. We can get through this.'

'I've been trying really hard to get through this, really fucking hard, in fact.'

'I know you have.'

If I'd let him carry on kissing me on that counter, everything would be the same as it was before. It wasn't good enough.

'I don't want to go back to how things were. I'm not the same person, Jamie.'

'Ivy, please.'

'I'm really glad you've been to therapy and you're sorting stuff out with your dad. I am, but—'

'Ivy—'

'You can't pretend it's all better now. You can't just quit therapy.'

'Things are different now ... I'm different.'

'You can't be all that different, Jamie.'

'Ivy, listen to me. All that matters is that we're together.'

'But, you left, and now you're back and I . . .'

'What are you saying?'

'I'm saying I want more.'

'But, I love you. And you love me.'

'It's not enough.'

'Ivy—'

'This year has gone so spectacularly badly that it's laughable—'

'I know—'

'Let me finish. I'm finally getting my shit together, I'm learning to be happy, on my own, and now you want to go right back to before. It's not good enough.'

'I can make you happy.'

'I want something better. I want joy, Jamie.'

He walked towards me.

'I can give you that,' he said, as he put his hand on my cheek. 'I can take care of you.'

I moved his hand away from my face.

'I don't want you to take care of me.'

'Are you leaving me?'

'Yes.'

'But—'

'It may not look like it, but I want the best for you.'

'You're the best for me.'

'Listen to me. I'm not, and you're not for me, and that's OK.'

We looked at each other, both knowing that this was the last time we'd ever look at each other like that.

'I don't know what to say,' he said.

'I don't think there's anything more to say.'

I told him I needed to go. This was the right decision, I said. I knew it in my bones.

I left his flat and walked down Bermondsey High Street, through to Tower Bridge. I sat in Potters Fields Park and watched the people go by: couples out on date nights; gaggles of girls going out on the town; rebellious teenagers drinking from cans.

I knew it in my bones; this was right.

That night, I dreamt I was on a sailing boat. The water was calm, azure-blue and I could see white coastal cliffs in front of me. I was sitting on deck, laughing, with the sun radiating on my back. I don't know who was on the boat with me, or where we were, but I knew what I felt, and it was joy.

Chapter 49

Airport money doesn't count

'I can't believe it, Ives,' Mia said.

'I'm so proud of you.'

'I've totally smashed it.'

'You really have.'

'Do you know how fucking good this is?'

'I do. Even I know Vicky Featherstone is a big deal.'

'It's fucking massive!'

'Stop swearing, Mia. People will think you're unhinged.'

'I'll be a working actress, Ivy!'

'Well, it's about time.'

'Fuck off.'

'I love you and I'm very, very proud.'

'Clara called me to say congratulations. She's started liking all my content.'

'What content?'

'My social media content. It's killer at the moment.'

'You're an idiot, Mia.'

'Oh, Ivy. I miss you already.'

'You saw me this morning.'

'Yeah, but I won't see you for a while.'

'Two weeks, Mia.'

'That's ages!'

'You'll be busy with rehearsals anyway.'

'Yeah, I will be!'

'I need to go find Mam. She's probably being conned into buying some overpriced face cream.'

'Classic Mags. What time is the flight?'

'Not for another hour or so.'

'Have the most amazing time.'

'I'll try to.'

'I'm so proud of you, Ivy.'

'I've not done anything.'

'You've done everything.'

I love being in an airport, plugging my headphones in as I watch all the people go by. I like sitting near couples and waiting for them to get into an argument, which they inevitably do. Airports can be such fraught places.

I found Mam sipping champagne at the bar, surrounded by duty-free bags.

'Darling, where have you been? I've been so bored.'

'Not that bored, clearly.'

'With the discount on this stuff, it would be silly not to.'

'What did you buy?'

'Just a few bits and pieces. You know airport money doesn't count.'

I ordered a glass of Coke and took my book out from my bag.

'Don't go spending the entire holiday reading, Ivy. I need some conversation.'

'I've literally just opened page one, Mam.'

'I'm just saying. Where's Anna?'

'Getting her last few minutes of peace?'

'You're impossible, darling.'

She ordered more champagne for herself and rang Dad,

who sounded chirpier than ever. He had big things planned for when Mam was away: he was going to reorganise the garage and throw away some old shirts. The man was having the time of his life.

Anna arrived at the bar.

'Did you buy the cream?' Mam asked her.

'Yes. God knows why I let you talk me into a fifty-eight pounds neck cream.'

'You're thirty-six, Anna. You should have started wearing it years ago.'

Anna ignored this and got out yet another pregnancy book.

'In no time at all, I'll be carrying an actual watermelon.'

'Horrible fruits,' Mam said.

'It's not about the fruit.'

'I know, I'm just saying. I don't like watermelons.'

Anna rolled her eyes and went back to her book. Our gate was called. Mam had successfully polished off a bottle of champagne on her own and was now talking very loudly.

'I don't know why we even asked Linda to come with us; she hates walking,' Mam said, as we walked hand in hand to the gate.

'Why did you invite her to Loch Lomond with you on a walking holiday then?' Anna asked.

'Anna, maybe it's because you and your husband – and your bloody sister – refused to holiday with us.'

'And we stand by that decision.'

Anna got her phone out to ring Mark and Mam grabbed it off her and changed the audio call to FaceTime. Mark was also thrilled to be having some time out from the Edwards women, especially after Mam said his face looked a bit bloated.

We boarded the plane. Anna sat down by the aisle so she could stretch her feet out, Mam was in the middle – she insists on sitting between us whenever we travel – and I sat by the window.

Mam got out her iPad to watch the final episode of *Game of Thrones*.

'I should've never left it this long, Ivy. I can't tell you how tense I've been.'

'I don't know why you've not watched it sooner, to be honest,' I said.

'Ivy! As if I had any choice in the matter. I don't get a minute's peace around here. Your father can't do anything for himself and Anna is acting like she's the only person in the world who's ever been pregnant. It's non-stop.'

At that moment, the loudspeaker came on and we were told to fasten our seatbelts for take-off. I gave Mam a kiss on the cheek and looked over at Anna, who was already drifting off to sleep. I sank deep into my seat and plugged my headphones in.

You know that feeling where you feel like you should be doing better and then one day you realise that maybe you're exactly where you should be, and that's OK? That's exactly how I felt, as I sat on that plane with the two greatest loves of my life. I thought about Mia, how ecstatic she was. I thought about Jane, her kind parting words to me, and of Dan and how perhaps I should've taken my spare keys off him while I was out of the country. I thought about Maude and her little cardigans, and I thought of Jamie and how I knew deep down in the pit of my stomach that what I did was right, not just for me, but for the both of us. And then I thought about Gramps, and how proud he'd have been. Now I just had to get through two whole weeks with Mam.

Acknowledgements

Thank you to my wonderful friends and family for all your love and support.

To my agent, Hayley Steed, for championing and believing in me. You are a great mentor and guiding hand. To everyone at The Madeleine Milburn Agency for their energy, enthusiasm and ambition for Ivy Edwards. It has been a dream of mine to work with you, thank you for living up to all my expectations.

To Emma Beswetherick, for being the best editor a girl could wish for. I knew from our first meeting that I would love working with you – you are a powerhouse and I owe so much to you. To your fabulous team at Little, Brown. A massive shout out to Sarah Murphy for such brilliant, astute feedback. And to Beth Wright for always being there to calm my nerves. I couldn't have hoped for a better bunch to work with.

To the Faber Academy class of June 2018. To our Captain, Richard, for forcing me out of my comfort zone and making me write from the stomach, not the heart. To my first readers, Vanessa and Freya, for being so honest with your comments, and for suggesting we move our catch-ups to Paris. To Lissa, for your wisdom, and to Nasri, for the title – you got it in one!

To Wales, for inspiring me with your beaches and hills and

magical people who don't realise they're the most dramatic, funniest people in the world.

To Dads, for being the kindest grandfather there is.

To Sarah, Mam and Dad. Sarah, you are the best sister and friend – thank you for everything. Mam, you are a constant source of joy and inspiration; we'd all be lost without you. Dad, thank you for always reminding me that worrying gets me nowhere. I love you all so much.

Most of all, thank you to Philip, for making my heart soar. You are the dream. I couldn't love you more if I tried.

10 Break-Up Survival Tips
by Ivy Edwards

1. **Drink wine.** It's not like it's going to run out. If you drink champagne, drink it fast, before the bubbles die. You want the fizz to go straight to your head – deal with the consequences later. Treat yourself to Waitrose-branded prosecco. You deserve it. When drinking wine, go for something a bit higher-end than Echo Falls, you'll feel much better for it in the morning. Don't mix colours, you know how that ends up.

2. **Block them**. You'll go on Instagram thinking that it's fine to check their feed and see all the fun things they've been up to since they ripped your heart out of your chest. But without even knowing it, you'll be two years deep and you'll accidentally 'like' one of their photos. What will you do then? You'll crawl into a deep, dark hole of shame. A Shame Hole, if you will, one that you'll spend the next forty-eight hours trying to scramble out of. Don't do this to yourself - block them.

3. **Get rid of everything**. You'll be tempted to keep that ridiculous, overpriced cartoon drawing you got of the two of you sitting in that square in Florence, on your last holiday together. You'll have forgotten that you screamed, 'Why do we always have to go where you want to go!?!' at them because they made you spend yet another two hours in a sports bar just to watch their favourite, mediocre, regional rugby team. No, all you remember

is that moment when the little Italian woman handed you your drawing, and you both laughed and commented on how cute you looked. You didn't look cute, you looked stupid. So throw everything away. Tear it up into hundreds of tiny pieces. Then go to a forest or nearby park that doesn't have strict fire rules and burn everything. Then, go for a wine.

4. **Have sex**. Getting under – or over, whatever your preference – someone is integral to the healing process. Ideally, this person would be someone removed from your friendship group, so that you don't have to endure any awkward social encounters further down the line. Also, they would be a good kisser, but I appreciate that it's hard to find that information out about a person until you've kissed them. Remember that even though you're desperate and drunk, you can still make positive choices. So, don't rebound with your friend's brother, or mother, or co-worker, don't convince yourself they're the one and above all, don't forget to use protection.

5. **Go 'out out'**. Grab a few select friends and go get bladdered. Go somewhere where they play 'All I Want for Christmas Is You' all year round, and the last song of the night is always Take That's 'Never Forget.' Buy cheap tequila shots, partake in some awful dancing, and make a new friend in the bathroom. Tell this new friend your life story, share a few tears, swap numbers. Never, ever use said number.

6. **Write hate mail.** Write down every little shitty thing they have ever done. Maybe mention that it's annoying that they don't know how to use a washing machine, or that they're approaching their thirties and still call their mother Mummy. Maybe that they think it's acceptable for men under the age of sixty to wear red trousers, or that they hardly ever go home to see your parents with you, but make you feel obligated to go see theirs all the time (it isn't your fault Mummy is unhappy, is it?) Maybe you'd have preferred them to go down on your more? (Of course, you'd have preferred this.) Write it all down and then send it – to yourself. Do **not** send it to them.

7. **Blockbusters are your friend**. You know who isn't your friend? Richard Curtis. You'll be sitting there enjoying all the posh accents and romance; Hugh Grant will be lulling you into a false sense of security, and then, without even knowing it, you're sobbing your guts out, snot streaming down your nose, wondering if you'll ever meet anyone ever again. Ditto, any track by Adele, and be wary of YouTube – there's too many small animals. Stick to blockbusters. Terminator is an excellent shout. Linda Hamilton's acting will make you feel much, much better about your own failures.

8. **Channel J Lo**. Your confidence is at rock bottom, and whilst the odd night out is going to help get some juice back in you, all that neat liquor won't be good for you in the long term. If you want to channel J Lo, you need to do the boring stuff like eat well, read and exercise. Do this for you, not your ex. They don't give a shit.

9. **Don't overthink**. You'll be coming home from a night out, kebab in hand, thinking about all the things you could've done differently. Maybe you could've shown more interest in their work, or that dog they lost when they were eight but still bring up every other week. Maybe you could've been sexier, funnier, smarter, had less hair around your nipples, not let them see you wee, not worn underwear with holes in them. But that's not the point. You did everything you could, and they still didn't love you. That's on them, not you.

10. **Stop being a dick to yourself**. You'll wake up feeling like the world has ended, that you'll die alone. You'll check your phone – no, they haven't called. You'll get mad at yourself for checking your phone. You'll tell yourself that today will be different, that you won't spend every minute looking down at the screen, waiting to see if they've contacted you. They won't be contacting you. You'll cry, and then you'll get mad at yourself for not being able to last a minute of the day without crying. STOP THIS. You're doing the best you can and that's much better than you think.

A Quick Q & A with Hannah Tovey

What's your all-time favourite book?
It would have to be *The Secret History* by Donna Tartt. I have read it so many times, and it keeps getting better. I dislike almost all the characters, but they fascinate me. Also, anything by JoJo Moyes, Jessie Burton and David Nicholls will always take priority on my book shelf.

What are your top three tips for aspiring writers?

- Try to write every day
- Adverbs are not your friend
- Wine does not make you funnier

In *The Education of Ivy Edwards*, Dorset provides Ivy with the perfect escape from London. Where is your ideal getaway location?

I'm happiest when I'm by the ocean and often daydream about packing it all in and moving to the Amalfi Coast. And then there's the Gower, in South Wales. I might be biased but, there's nothing quite like it.